WHAT THEY SAW

BOOKS BY M.M. CHOUINARD

DETECTIVE JO FOURNIER NOVELS

The Dancing Girls

Taken to the Grave

Her Daughter's Cry

The Other Mothers

The Vacation

WHAT THEY SAW

M.M. CHOUINARD

bookouture

Published by Bookouture in 2022

An imprint of Storyfire Ltd.
Carmelite House
50 Victoria Embankment
London EC4Y 0DZ

www.bookouture.com

ISBN: 978-1-80314-719-2
eBook ISBN: 978-1-80314-718-5

This book is dedicated to:
Five hundred twenty-five thousand six hundred
coffees

DAY ONE

CHAPTER ONE

Sandra Ashville yawned as she pulled the door closed behind her and peered out toward the slowly illuminating sky over Lake Pocomtuk. She sipped her steaming Lady Grey tea and smiled—gone were the pink-and-blue cotton-candy stripes of the summer sunrises; now the sun reflected a rich saffron yellow from the changing fall foliage, a stunning contrast with the gentle lavender of the lake. Her sister wheedled her on a weekly basis to move to Arizona now that she was retiring, and there'd be moments during the New England winter when she'd be sorely tempted. But this—she'd never be able to leave this behind. The way the seasons shifted, the world always new, with fresh sights and smells to soak in.

Fortified by another warming sip of tea, she trotted down the wooden stairs and out across to the dock. With a practiced flick of her wrist, she unfurled her yoga mat out over the planks, then lowered herself down. She placed the tea far enough away that she wouldn't knock it over, then put in her earbuds and pulled up her playlist on her phone. The right music enhanced the beauty of the lake while smoothing over the disruptive aspects.

As if on cue, a red fox screamed in the distance, startling her with his last bit of business before bedtime. She shook her head and smiled.

How could she move away now, just when she finally had the time to slow down and appreciate it all? For years she had been out of the house before the sun rose and not back until well after it set, including the longer summer days. Even her weekends at home were filled with court prep.

She sighed as she moved through her initial stretches. Everything had turned out so differently than she'd envisioned as an idealistic law-school graduate who'd truly thought she was on the path to make the world a better place. But then, that was the beauty of youth, wasn't it? If you had any clue how things really worked, you'd never have the courage, let alone the energy, to try to make a difference. And unlike some of the young ones who came through, she'd never deluded herself that being a district attorney was going to be easy. But the things she'd dealt with—it caved in your soul. Especially when it came from all sides, from the criminals *and* from above *and* from those you were trying to protect. Yes, a part of her rebelled against early retirement, screamed that it was somehow a failure, but if she didn't—well, if she didn't, a breakdown was inevitable. Or something very bad would happen. The yoga was helping, but it wasn't enough.

As she shifted into downward-facing dog, a bird flew by, dropping and skimming just above the surface of the lake. She craned her neck to follow it, wondering what kind of bird it was. She'd buy a book about them—she'd have time now every day to watch birds and do sunrise yoga and read books, far away from the ugliness that forced her to make impossible choices and hamstrung her from making things right.

She smiled peacefully as she eased into her next position.

———

Hunkered down amid the elm trees, I checked my watch.

Just a few more minutes.

A creak pulled my attention back to the house. She appeared through the door, sipping from her steaming mug, then crossed to the dock. She went through the newly formed ritual—mat, earbuds, phone. It was a good omen—some days she didn't listen to anything, preferring the serenity of the lake, but today her music would be my cover.

As she navigated her app, a red fox cried out in the distance. Sandra jumped—but then laughed and eased into her first downward-facing dog.

Her face in these moments was my focus—so different from who she was the rest of the day. Unguarded, vulnerable, her deeper layers washing over her face. Struggle. Self-doubt.

It proved she knew better.

The relaxed contentment settled over her face far too easily; at the sight of it my hands reflexively clenched into fists, causing the bark of the tree I'd been leaning against to bite into my skin. I flinched, then took a hurried step to keep from falling. Startled by my quick movement, a bird burst from the tree—I ducked out of sight, adrenaline bursting through me. But she hadn't heard, and she didn't see the bird until it dropped and flew past her.

I chastised myself. I couldn't afford another mistake.

Breathing deeply to restore my focus, I calculated the timing of her positions. She eased herself into warrior two. For the next three minutes she'd be facing the lake, her back fully toward me.

I slipped out from between the shrubbery as she slid one arm down her front leg into triangle pose. I couldn't see it any longer, but I continued to picture the expression on her face—the lines on her forehead smoothed, the tension gone from her jaw—and let the anger wash over me.

Reverse warrior. I shifted closer.

Part of me hoped she'd lean far enough back to glimpse me. It was too late for her to get away now, and the fear as she struggled from her pretzeled posture would be gratifying. But no, this way was better.

As she eased back into warrior two, I crept up behind her and raised the gun.

"Hello, Sandra," I said, loudly enough to be heard over her app.

She jerked around, dropping to one knee as she awkwardly flailed to see who was behind her.

"Stay down." Gun mere inches from her forehead, I drank in the confusion and fear as she tried to figure out what was going on.

"I don't understand—" she started.

"No, I'm sure you don't," I cut her off.

Then I explained, watching as realization and horror bloomed across her face. She opened her mouth to respond, to beg for her life and make meaningless promises she was obtuse enough to think I'd actually believe. I drank in her fear, let it wash over me like a soothing salve, cherishing the tremor in her voice and the desperation on her face.

She stopped when I didn't respond, recalculated, and opened her mouth to try another tack.

I'll never know what it was. Because I pulled the trigger, sending a bullet deep into her brain.

CHAPTER TWO

Josette Fournier tugged at her messy brown ponytail and stared down at the pile of boxes and furniture growing steadily in her garage.

Bedroom. Office. Kitchen. Living room.

Cleopatra, the Sphynx cat she'd adopted after the cat's owner had been carted off to jail, hopped up onto the topmost box, flicked her tail around her back legs, and yowled at Jo in indignant protest.

"I know how you feel," she grumbled.

Jo inhaled deeply, turned on her heel, and strode into the kitchen. Still trying to keep her breath even, she grabbed a bottle of water out of the refrigerator, wrenched off the cap, and downed half of the contents.

This is a good thing, she reminded herself. *You wanted this. You still want this. You love Matt.*

And all that was true. But some PTSD-damaged portion of her brain railed against every box and chair and tchotchke, sending fight-or-flight alerts coursing through her body.

She closed her eyes and took another gulp as she tried to

talk herself down. What was this really about? Where was the fear coming from?

Their discussions about it all had gone well. She'd offered her guest bedroom up as an office for him, but he suggested they keep a room available for visitors and use the office jointly. It was big enough, and neither of them really worked from home all that much since he had a full office in a medical complex for his neurology practice, so the compromise had seemed a good one. In terms of furniture, he'd decided to rent out his house fully furnished to his nephew Roderigo, which meant they'd stick mostly with her furniture, except for a few pieces that had special meaning for him. She'd never been a clotheshorse, so dividing closet and drawer space would be relatively painless. And, it was only right that he have personal touches in what would now be his home, too.

Each and every bit of it made sense when she examined it.

But when they'd shifted her treadmill so his desk could slip into the office, her abdomen had flipped and flopped like she'd eaten roadside sushi. When she restacked her pots and pans to create space for his gourmet cooking gear, her chest clenched like a boa constrictor had squeezed it. And when she shifted the perfectly symmetrical layout of her mantle to make room for the picture of his siblings and his parents, she'd broken out into a cold sweat.

As the overhead garage door rattled and clanged down into place, she hurried to erase the panic from her expression and replace it with pleasant optimism.

The interior garage door swung open into the kitchen and Matt appeared, a wide smile across his tired face. "That's the last of it."

Jo held out the water bottle to him and returned his smile. "Fast and easy, just like you promised."

He took the bottle, drained it, then pulled her into his arms. "Looks like you're officially stuck with me."

She gazed up into his warm, brown eyes and shifted her attention to the feel of his hands on her hips. In his mid-forties, Matt had the physique of a man a decade younger, and only the smallest sprinkle of salt peppered his black hair. His square-jawed, laugh-line-creased good looks always set off a flutter in her chest and a wave of warm electricity to liquify her legs. She lifted her head up to his and kissed him, allowing herself to sink into those feelings.

"Mmm," he said when she finally pulled away. "That's what I call a welcome."

Jo smiled up at him, then glanced at the clock on the wall. "I'm starving. How about some Saturday-morning brunch? You've been doing most of the heavy lifting, so the least I can do is whip up some *pain perdu* for you with that leftover brioche in there."

"That sounds amazing." He gave her a quick squeeze, then reached for the Moka pot on the counter. "Tell you what. You start that, and I'll make us a couple of mochas."

As she juggled the bread, eggs, and milk out of the refrigerator, he packed coffee and water into the pot. She mentally noted the well-orchestrated ballet they danced around each other, Cleopatra weaving in and out, and tried to take comfort from it. They'd found a way to share this space together, and they'd find a way to work out the rest.

"So. Roderigo called me. He decided he's going to move in with his girlfriend in Boston after all," Matt said.

Jo dropped a piece of batter-coated bread into the sizzling pan and shook her head. Matt's nephew had been the perfect solution to their two-house situation, someone he trusted enough to rent his furnished house to. "Wow, nothing like waiting until the last minute to let you know you need to find another renter. I don't suppose you have any other family waiting in the wings?"

He shot her a wary look as he screwed the Moka pot closed. "Depends on what you mean by family."

A low-level alarm bell rang in Jo's head. "That doesn't sound good."

He didn't meet her eyes as he wiped up a water spill. "David told me if the arrangement fell through, he'd like to rent it."

Jo poked at the French toast with her spatula before responding. David, Jo's brother-in-law, had recently been discovered cheating on Sophie, Jo's sister. Not only cheating—he'd gotten his mistress pregnant. David claimed to have ended the affair, but Sophie wasn't sure whether she could forgive him and had asked David to move out of their shared house while she decided for or against a divorce. "And you want to rent it to him," Jo stated.

Matt looked up at her as the pot gurgled, his expression sheepish. "I know it's not ideal, and I never would have offered it to him. He's the one who brought it up."

Jo half-smiled. "Effectively placing you in an extremely awkward situation. If you say no, you're turning your back on someone you've formed a fledgling friendship with. If you say yes, you're pissing off Sophie, and making my life difficult."

His brows bounced once as he split the coffee into two waiting mugs. "That's about the size of it."

Jo scowled as she flipped the French toast, and tried to buy herself a moment. "What are your thoughts on the subject?"

Matt sprinkled chocolate powder on the drinks. "I don't like what he did, but I don't see how refusing to rent to him would help anything."

Intellectually, Jo agreed. No matter what happened, David had paternal rights to Isabelle and Emily, his and Sophie's daughters, and would always be part of their lives. Embracing that made sense. But on a personal level, Jo was so angry with him she could barely stand the sight of him, and the thought of having any legal tie to him made her cringe. Plus, since Sophie hadn't yet made up her mind about how to proceed, this was a craggy stretch of shoreline to walk—Jo and Sophie's complicated relationship was fraught with hidden land mines. If Jo refused and Sophie reconciled with David, Jo would be the hard-ass sister-in-law who'd been a jerk. But if Sophie permanently kicked him to the curb while he was living in Matt's house, Sophie would want David kicked out, and that could create problems for Matt.

Jo sighed. "Probably the best thing for me to do is call Sophie."

Matt managed to infuse his nod with apology and sympathy, and slid one of the mochas over toward her.

She grabbed her phone, opened Duo, and tapped through a video call—she wanted to be able to read Sophie's expressions. Sophie picked up on the second ring.

"We have a situation," Jo said after initial greetings. "David asked if he can rent Matt's house."

"Of course he did." Sophie's green eyes, identical to Jo's own, narrowed in suspicion, and her hand raked through her perfect brown bob.

Jo looked up at Matt as she answered. "We'll do whatever you want us to do."

She blew out a puff of air. "I don't know what to do. I suppose it doesn't really matter. He has to live somewhere."

"If that's what you think is best, that's what we'll do," Jo said cautiously.

Sophie's eyes flicked off into the distance. "*She* called me yesterday."

A frozen lump dropped into Jo's stomach. *She* was David's pregnant mistress, a twenty-eight-year-old blonde with a Ph.D in English Lit and a wealthy, influential family.

"You're kidding."

"Nope. Luckily, I never answer the phone unless I recognize the number. But she left a message."

Jo rubbed the bridge of her nose. "Oh God."

"Yeah." Sophie gave a single, dry laugh. "Hearing her voice made me want to leap through the phone and scratch her eyes out."

"What did she want?"

"To convince me she'd also been duped by David."

"What, he told her he was single?" Jo asked.

"Oh, no, he wasn't that stupid. He told her our marriage was *troubled*. That I was an unreasonable harpy that didn't understand him."

Jo slapped the French toast onto the waiting plates with her free hand. "That you hadn't had sex in months, and he was just waiting for the right moment to ask for a divorce?"

Sophie repeated the dry laugh. "I *so* love being caught inside a living cliché."

"No other reason?"

One of Sophie's manicured nails tapped in the background. "To assure me he's all mine."

Jo nearly choked. "How generous of her."

"And that she's keeping the baby. So she hopes we can be *friends*, since we're both victims of David's *bad judgment*, and because our children will be siblings."

Jo's wry laugh was an unconscious twin of Sophie's. "Ah, the delusional audacity of youth. She better buckle up, she's got a wild ride coming."

Sophie surprised her with a sigh. "I suppose I'll eventually have to find a way to be civil. She's right, Isabelle and Emily are going to have a little brother—it's a boy, by the way—and they have a right to know him. But right now, I'll be damned if I can even imagine what that's going to look like."

Jo reached for her coffee. "How are the girls handling it?"

"We haven't told them yet. So far they just think Daddy's

on an extended business trip. I've been delaying as long as possible because I'm terrified of how Emily is going to respond."

Jo winced. The previous spring, Emily had been kidnapped, and witnessed Jo shoot her captor in order to recover her. Despite some struggles dealing with the trauma, she'd been recovering steadily, but Jo knew well that psychological progress could be all too easily derailed by new stressors. "If there's anything I can do to help, I'm just a phone call away."

"I know." Sophie's voice softened as she said it, then hardened again. "For now, go ahead and tell David he can move in. I'll figure out what to do from there."

"Will do," Jo said. "Take care of yourself, please."

Once they'd hung up, she grabbed the plates and set them on the kitchen table. "Well. That's easy then, at least for now."

Matt slid their coffees next to their plates, then rubbed her shoulder. "Don't worry. She'll figure it all out."

Jo sawed off a bite of her French toast. "I know she will. But it's—" A text notification cut her off. She snatched up the phone, hoping Sophie hadn't changed her mind.

But it wasn't Sophie. "Oh God."

Matt's eyes snapped up from his food, and his posture stiffened at her tone. "What's wrong?"

Jo jumped up and snatched her jacket from the back of the chair. "One of our assistant district attorneys has been murdered."

CHAPTER THREE

When Jo picked up Bob Arnett, her partner, he slid into the car silently. The lines creasing his late-fifties forehead and webbing his eyes were deeper than normal, and his pupils so widened they turned his brown eyes nearly black. His hands couldn't find a place to settle; between desperate gulps from his travel mug, his hands alternated between rubbing the back of his salt-and-pepper hair and the Saturday-afternoon shadow on his chin.

"Two months from retirement," he finally said.

Jo took a moment to control her voice before she spoke. "I didn't realize she was so close. Isn't she young for that?"

He stared out the windshield, thumbs rubbing the texturized plastic of his travel mug. "Early retirement. She was hired just slightly before I made detective."

In over twenty years, she'd never seen Arnett this quiet before, and it magnified her own alarm. She gripped the steering wheel to steady her shaking hands. Yes, she'd seen more than a few officers and detectives killed during her time on the force, it was a part of the job. But never an ADA—and never a cold-blooded murder outside the line of duty. It was a violation that struck at not just the safety of every law enforcement officer, but the rule of law itself.

Steering into a turn, she shifted into compartmentalizing her emotions, for the sake of both her objectivity and sanity, and oriented herself firmly into the investigatory logic of the case. All she had at this point was victimology, what she knew about Sandra. She'd worked with Sandra any number of times, and had tremendous professional respect for her. Justice for the victims Sandra served was of primary importance to her, and she worked hard to get it for them, far beyond even the twelve-plus-hour days most prosecutors worked. In the course of that dedication, she was averse to BS, demanded respect, and demanded excellence from herself and others, but also was always ready with a smile or a joke or a positive word when someone was having a bad day.

But as Jo searched her memory, she couldn't come up with much about Sandra's personal life. "She was married, right? But no kids?"

"Divorced not long ago." He continued to stare out of the window.

Jo sucked in breath through her teeth. "Divorce, then early retirement. That's a lot of life change all at once."

Arnett nodded.

Jo made the final turn toward the crime scene in Cheltam, off the stem of a T-shaped dirt road up the right prong. After running a few hundred yards along the shore of the lake, it dead-ended between Sandra Ashville's house nestled into an elm-covered hillside on the right, and a dock jutting into the lake on the left. Crime-scene tape ran across the road, conveniently preventing access to the house, the dock, and the woods beyond. As Jo parked next to it, she spotted Janet Marzillo, head of the Oakhurst County State Police Detective Unit's CSI team, and Hakeem Peterson, a relatively new hire who'd quickly become indispensable, squatting carefully around a supine figure on the dock. Two other CSIs she didn't recognize searched the woods near the house. All of them worked in an unusual silence.

As she and Arnett made their way toward the tall, white, blond officer standing stock-still over the tape, they scanned the area.

"Hard-packed dusty road and hard-packed dusty shore. Won't get much in terms of tire marks or footprints," Arnett said.

"Racinsky," Jo read off the officer's nameplate as they reached the tape and identified themselves. "You're the responding officer?"

"Yes, ma'am." He noted their names on the log. "Multiple residents from around the lake called in a potential gunshot just before seven this morning. Forty-five minutes later, we received another call from the southern neighbors Marianne and Jeff Nelson. As they set out to do some morning fishing, they noticed Ashville on her pier, but when they called out to her, she didn't respond. As they neared, they realized she was deceased."

Arnett's brow shot up. "Forty-five minutes later? A small, low-crime area like this and it took you forty-five minutes to respond to a gunshot?"

"No, sir." Racinsky's jaw flexed. "My partner and I were patrolling the area, attempting to locate the source."

Jo glanced at the still water; her mind flew to morning sunrises over the bayou where her father's family lived in Cajun country. "When it's quiet, sound carries and echoes. Almost impossible to zero in on."

Racinsky nodded at her. "Sometimes you can hear a conversation half a mile away that sounds like it's at your neighbor's house."

"Which likely gave our killer plenty of time to get away, and if they're from this area, they probably realized that." She gazed back down the road. "Any reports of suspicious people or vehicles in the area, anything like that?"

"Nothing yet. We're in the process of canvassing."

Jo and Arnett reached for their PPE. "Great. Where are the neighbors that found her?" Jo said.

He pointed to the south. "Waiting at home to talk with you."

"Got it. Thanks," Jo said. When she and Arnett finished suiting up, Racinsky waved them under the tape.

Jo pulled out her phone and hit record. "Very secluded thanks to the dead-end road and all the foliage. The hill behind the house creates a perfect natural barrier from the outside road and the surrounding houses. I can see glimpses of other houses, but no real direct line of sight except over the lake. Great for privacy, but plenty of places for our perp to hide, especially in the dark before dawn."

Arnett followed her line of sight. "Even in broad daylight, an entire battalion could hide out in those trees."

Jo shifted her attention to the pier. Next to a bobbing Ski Nautique, Sandra Ashville, clad in black yoga clothes, sprawled over a cobalt-blue yoga mat, arms extended and legs crumpled under her as though she was twisting and struggling to right herself. Jo's stomach roiled, and a vague memory pulled at her. As they neared, it came to her in a rush: *Pompeii*. The oddly twisted pose reminded her of the victims found at the ancient archaeological site who'd been frozen forever as struggling to escape the heat, gases, and ash of the sudden eruption. The posture was discordant with the serenity of the lake surrounding her, the comfort of the tea next to her, the careful, deliberate postures of yoga—why had it all been stripped from her without warning?

Marzillo stood and approached to greet them as they neared. "Jo. Bob," she said abruptly and with a scowl in her voice.

Jo resonated with Marzillo's mood. "Never a good day to lose one of our own."

Marzillo gave a sharp nod. "Add to that an underwater scene."

Jo grimaced. Marzillo preferred a hands-on approach to all aspects of her investigation, but underwater scenes required specially trained divers. "What do we know?"

"Not much yet, I'm still orienting myself." She motioned them forward and squatted down near where Peterson waited.

Jo followed, and stared down at the now-visible head and face. Sandra had been a small woman who had managed to project more height and presence than she actually had; she dressed and coiffed flawlessly, and carried herself with dignity and power. But the woman in front of her looked almost like a child, helpless and chaotic, her light-brown hair matted with blood that dripped over the edge of the yoga mat and between the wooden planks beneath it. And nearly half of her face, including her eyes, was covered with a swath of blood-streaked white cloth. "Strange—usually when a killer blindfolds a victim and shoots them execution style, they also use restraints."

Marzillo swapped out her gloves. "It's worse than that." She gently shifted down the top of the blindfold, revealing a bullet hole underneath.

Ice pricked at Jo's spine. "There's no hole in the blindfold. The killer must have blindfolded her *after* shooting her."

"What's the point of blindfolding someone who's dead?" Arnett asked.

"Exactly—it makes no sense," Jo said. "And the entry wound is stippled, but not burned. So the gun was close, but not in direct contact."

"Up to about thirty inches away," Peterson said.

"Point-blank range. Rules out a sniper," Arnett said.

Jo crouched and examined Sandra's position. "She placed the yoga mat right up at the tip of the pier, which suggests she wanted to face the water. But the way she's laying, she was facing back toward the house when she was shot." She pointed to the earbuds lying next to Sandra's right hand. "Someone snuck up behind her, and she didn't hear them until they were close. But why bother to get that close to her? Were there signs of a struggle?"

"None that I can see so far." Marzillo's voice was cautious.

"And there's plenty of cover here." Jo stood and looked back toward the house. "Our killer didn't need to do this face to face, they chose to. This was personal."

Arnett squatted and peered at Sandra's head. "Couldn't have been easy, tying on a blindfold to a bleeding head wound without transfer?"

"That depends." Marzillo carefully shifted Sandra's head. "No exit wound, so penetrating, not perforating. Considerably less messy. And the knot is simple, so it wouldn't take much."

"They could have pre-tied it," Peterson said. "Even easier to get on."

Jo swiveled her head. "If she'd been facing the front of the pier, she'd have seen someone coming up the road in her periphery. She must have been facing that way." She pointed northeast, diagonally away from the positioning of the yoga mat.

Arnett rubbed his chin. "The few times I did yoga, I don't remember being in any one position very long. Our killer would have had to be extremely lucky to drive up unnoticed."

Both Jo and Marzillo turned to stare at him.

"Laura," he grumbled.

Jo hid a half-smile. Arnett and his wife Laura had almost divorced, and part of their reconciliation involved Arnett making 'an effort' by engaging in leisure activities with her. They'd cycled through several possibilities, from painting classes to ballroom dancing. And, apparently, yoga.

Jo straightened and glanced around the lake again. "It depends on the type of yoga you're doing. Or maybe she was meditating at the beginning or end, with her eyes closed. Or, it was someone she was expecting, who pulled out a gun at the last minute."

She turned back to Marzillo. "Anything else you can tell us so far?"

Marzillo gestured around Sandra. "I can't be sure yet, but based on what I'm seeing with the tight workout clothes, my guess is she wasn't sexually assaulted. It would be too difficult to get the clothes back on and restore her to this state. No other obvious injuries, but there may be something under her clothes and there may be bruises still developing. My guess until the ME confirms, is the gunshot wound was the cause of death. And my guess, based on the size of the entrance wound, is a twenty-two caliber. Other than that, not much until the divers do their bit and we process the boat, the house, and the woods."

"Sounds good, thank you. We'll take a look around ourselves and then go talk to the neighbors—" Jo stopped short as she caught a flash of movement out of the corner of her eye. Two vehicles pulled up to the crime-scene tape, a dark blue Chevy Camaro she wasn't familiar with, and a silver Lexus she knew all too well.

She jutted her chin toward it.

Arnett turned to follow her gaze. "Shit."

CHAPTER FOUR

Lieutenant Lindsay Hayes emerged from the Lexus and strode toward the Camaro, one hand smoothing her tight blonde bun while the other smoothed the skirt of her blue suit. ADA Reid Hanson, one of the most senior prosecutors in the DA's office, stepped out of the Camaro clutching a folder and rounded the vehicle toward Racinsky, eyes flashing around the property. Angry red patches covered his pale cheeks and balding pate, and he shook his head curtly when Racinsky indicated the PPE. Instead, he waved to Jo and Arnett, indicating they should come to the tape. As she caught up to him, Hayes imitated the gesture.

Jo kept her face professionally blank. Lieutenant Hayes was the newest solution to the Oakhurst County State Police Detective Unit's ongoing difficulty filling the lieutenant spot that Jo herself had occupied briefly. Hayes had transferred in from upstate New York, and from the day she arrived had set her sights on 'revamping' the SPDU. She'd also set her sights on taking Jo down a peg, a new experience for Jo, who was generally well liked by both her colleagues and superiors. She'd found it hard to understand at first, until Hayes let slip several hints about the origin of her acrimony: she was threatened by Jo's previous tenure in the position.

Jo overheard a snippet of conversation as they neared. "There wasn't any reason for you to come out here," Hayes said to Hanson. "My team has this under control."

"Barbieri asked me to come." Hanson turned toward Jo and Arnett.

Hayes flushed. Why? She had to know the district attorney would want to be hands-on when one of his prosecutors had been killed?

Hayes met Jo's eyes. "What have you got?" she barked.

As Jo and Arnett stripped off and bagged their PPE, Jo gave them an overview, monitoring Hanson's face as she did. Police were used to the daily risk associated with their jobs, but an ADA's job description didn't generally include the same specter of death hanging over them.

Hanson's jaw tightened. "Shot in the head. That sounds like an execution."

Hayes threw up a hand. "Let's not get ahead of ourselves. Shot in the head could just be a hunting accident so close to these woods. They have deer everywhere out here, and I'm sure they even get a bear now and then. Could be some random serial killer. Time will tell."

Jo started to respond, but Arnett spoke over her. "Someone put a blindfold on her, *over* the wound, not under it, and there's stippling around the entry wound."

"And the way she was killed was far too personal for it to have been a random killing," Jo said.

"Has the ME been here yet?" Hayes glared at Arnett, then Jo.

Jo knew Hayes was aware there hadn't been time for the medical examiner to arrive. "No."

"Then, like I said, let's not get ahead of ourselves. That's how rumors start, and we don't want people overreacting."

Hayes pulled her phone from inside her suit pocket. "But we need to get to work, because Barbieri called me on my way over here, and he wants answers PDQ."

"Got it," Jo said.

Hayes looked up from whatever text she was sending and narrowed her eyes at Jo, sniffing out disrespect. "I sure as hell hope so, Fournier. Because I'm already on the fence about letting you handle this after that stunt you pulled. Not only is the DA leaning on me, but the press is gonna make my life a living nightmare. Screw this up and it'll be my pleasure to bust you down to traffic cop. Got *that*?"

Jo pushed down a flash of anger. The 'stunt' she'd pulled was putting a previously undetected serial killer who'd been murdering men for a decade behind bars. It had taken years of tenacity on her part and creative teamwork to accomplish it, especially from Christine Lopez, their tech expert. In fact, Jo, Arnett, and Lopez had all received commendations for it. But she'd done it without Hayes' permission, and Hayes couldn't forgive that.

Jo kept her expression steady. "Yes, ma'am."

"Updates every hour." Hayes spun on her heel and marched back to the car.

Hanson watched until she pulled away, then said, "Barbieri asked specifically for you two. Not only was Sandra one of the best prosecutors we had, we all take it very personally when anyone so much as looks at one of our own sideways. We want this fucker caught—we need to make sure the message is sent loud and clear that nobody fucks with law enforcement in Oakhurst County. So we want it done fast, but we also need it done right, and you two are the ones who can do it. Hayes doesn't have a damned thing to say about it."

Childish satisfaction surged up through Jo, much to her chagrin. She pushed it back down. "We'll get it done."

"I'm surprised Barbieri didn't show up himself." Arnett peered down the road as if he might materialize.

"He's in Maine, attending his father's funeral." Hanson turned to Jo. "Hayes' skepticism aside, Sandra just got the indictment for Ronnie Loren. He has a strong motive to want her dead."

"Ronnie Loren?" Arnett asked. "The guy responsible for ninety percent of the fentanyl and iso in western Mass?"

"That'd be the one," Hanson said.

Jo took a deep breath. "It's possible, I suppose. But if this is a drug-lord hit, a sniper hidden in the woods would be safer. Even if they were trying to send a message with an execution, it's strange they shot her first, *then* blindfolded her."

"Maybe they were trying to throw us off?"

"Could be. But everything I've heard about Loren, he's smart enough to know that just because he takes out an ADA, an investigation of that magnitude isn't just going to fall apart."

"So, what are you thinking?" Hanson asked.

"The up-close nature of this feels more like revenge after the fact than someone trying to stall a case. We'll also need to take a look at the other cases she's currently prosecuting, and any that have wrapped recently. Has anybody threatened her, anything like that?"

"Defendants never put us on their Christmas card lists, but nothing specific." Hanson held out the folder he was carrying. "I brought a list of her current cases, and her logins for her work systems. How far are you going to go back?"

Jo glanced at Arnett. "As far back as we need to. But my guess would be two, three years?"

"Sounds about right," he said. "Anything farther than that, it seems strange they'd suddenly act out now."

"Unless it's someone who was recently released from prison, so we'll check that too," Jo said.

"I'll get you access to her paper files too," Hanson said.

"We also have to consider this has nothing to do with work. I hear she divorced recently?" Jo asked.

Hanson's brows rose. "Yes, and despite her usual circumspection, I overheard a few heated conversations. The divorce wasn't his idea, and he wasn't happy about it."

"Any idea why she wanted it?"

"Same old." Hanson shrugged. "You know how it is with the kind of work we do."

Jo nodded. Long hours. Heavy workload. Facing the worst in human nature every day, and having to make a choice to bring the horrors you'd seen home and inflict them on the person you love, or bottle it all up to protect them, which inevitably pushed them away and created a pressure-cooker of unprocessed emotions that leaked out in some unhealthy way— most traditionally, alcohol abuse and difficulty with personal relationships. Jo had managed to avoid the former, but had plenty of struggles with the latter.

"Any idea why she went in for early retirement?" Arnett asked.

Hanson's eyes shot to Racinsky and his voice dropped. "She told me she needed to get out while she still believed in the justice system."

Jo dropped her voice, too. "Was she referring to something specific?"

"Not that I know of. When she told me she was leaving, she waved me into her office, closed the door, then pulled out a bottle of Maker's Mark. Told me over three fingers that she'd 'had it.' Guilty men going free, innocent men going to prison, hundreds upon hundreds of victims she tried to help but couldn't. Said the nightmares that came to her at night were starting to take over."

The desperation in the words tugged at Jo. She had nightmares of her own where injustice was a tsunami crashing down on the legal system's fragile attempts to maintain order.

"Got it." She cleared her throat. "If you can keep your ear to the ground, we'd appreciate it. We'll do everything we can on our end, and we'll give you regular updates."

Hanson nodded grimly, his voice tight. "Much appreciated. Sandra was a damned good ADA. Whoever did this, I want them locked up and the cell soldered shut."

———

As Hanson drove away, Jo pulled out her phone. "I'm alerting Lopez that we'll need her help going through everything as soon as possible. Work accounts and schedule, cell phone records, and Sandra must have a laptop somewhere."

"Isn't Lopez off somewhere with her boyfriend?"

"Yep, they went to some B&B up in Maine. But this is urgent, and with one of our ADAs involved, she'll want to take the lead on anything tech related anyway. She's not going to trust anyone else with this."

Arnett grimaced. "You ask me, we're doing her a favor. Can you picture Lopez in a B&B? It's like Charles Bronson at a doll's tea party."

Jo half-smiled. "I cannot. But apparently this is a very special B&B. Rather than cats and flowers and birdwatching, it specializes in vampires, zombies, and anarchy. Tony's been wanting to go for quite a while, and they both love long drives amid the fall leaves."

Arnett looked at her like she'd sprouted an extra head. "Let me guess—it's near Stephen King's house?"

"For all I know, it *is* Stephen King's house. I heard he was turning part of his property into some sort of retreat."

Arnett's brows telegraphed his befuddlement as he shifted his gaze to the CSIs' grid search of the property. "Help them out, or stay out of their way and tackle the house?"

"House."

They put on fresh PPE and headed up. "Security camera midway up, and another over the door. That should help." But as she squinted for a better view as they climbed the stairs, her hopes plummeted. "Except they're pointed to capture activity on the deck, not out to the pier."

Inside the house, sleek, Scandinavian-modern furniture and accents in shades of blue and brown gave an overall impression of clean precision. The house showed signs of habitation—a teakettle by the side of the sink—but no signs of disturbance. They quickly located Sandra's laptop, iPad, and an old-school day planner. Jo flipped through the calendar, taking pictures as she went, careful to touch as little as possible despite her gloves. "Just basic work appointments. Nothing that jumps out at me as unusual, except..."

"Except?" Arnett shifted over from the entertainment center he was checking to look over her shoulder.

"A countdown of some sort..." She continued to flip the pages. "Ah, to her retirement. She was literally counting the days."

Arnett's brows rose. "You think she was running from something?"

"Based on what Hanson said, she was absolutely running from something. The only question is whether that something was external or internal."

Arnett stiffened. "She wouldn't be the first ADA to just burn out."

"Nope. And if she hadn't shown up dead, that would be my first assumption. But I don't like how sudden and dramatic the decision seemed to be."

Jo closed the planner, then bagged and logged it. They finished up with the rest of the house, noting places to have Marzillo's team check for prints, then made their way back outside.

"I'd like to take a closer look at the foliage," Jo said. Arnett nodded.

They proceeded slowly, systematically scouring the ground, shrubs, and trees. About halfway down the road, several feet back, she spotted two patches of green fronds bent toward the ground. She pointed. "Look at this."

As Arnett leaned in, Jo glanced around for the nearest CSI. A few hundred feet away a short woman searched the underbrush, glimpses of pale skin and red hair peeking out from under the clear portions of her gear. Jo recognized her—an experienced, thirty-something CSI who'd recently moved from the Boston area—but struggled to remember her name. It came back to her in a whoosh, and she blurted it out. "Sweeney. Alicia Sweeney."

The woman straightened. "That's right, Detective."

"You can drop the 'detective.' I'm Jo. Can you help us?"

"Jo." Alicia hurried over to them.

Jo squatted into the underbrush. "See it? There and there? Can you photograph it for us so we can take a closer look?"

"Of course."

As she worked, Jo continued to analyze the terrain. "There's another." She pointed to a patch between two trees with several trampled plants.

Sweeney followed her gesture. "More traces go up the hill."

Jo stared up. The hilly ridge was about twice the height of the house; on the other side of it the larger, main road they drove in on ran parallel to the one that dead-ended in front of the house. "Could it have been some sort of animal?"

Sweeney wagged her head from side to side. "Could be a bear, I can't rule that out without actual footprints or tracks. But if it's a bear, why here? She's got raspberry bushes on the other side of the house and there are some grasses over by the shore that bears might want to eat, but nothing here. And, you can see the pier clearly from here."

Jo turned to face the lake. "Clear line of sight to the house, too. If the killer hid right between these two trees, they'd be able to see everything."

"And if they walked from here to where she was doing yoga, they'd be out of range of the security cameras." Arnett gestured a path across the road.

"Done. Go on in." Alicia stepped out of the way.

Jo squatted down in the space, testing the cover of the underbrush. "My first instinct is to use the trees to balance myself." She raised her arms, but stopped short of touching them. "Can you measure how high that is? Assuming our killer is my height or taller, if they weren't wearing gloves, we might be able to get some prints or some touch DNA from that area on up."

Sweeney examined the tree anxiously. "I'd have to swab several areas on the off-chance of DNA, and Hayes doesn't like it when we do tests unless we have good reason to think we'll get something. Too expensive."

Jo's jaw tightened. "An ADA has been shot. If there's a problem, I'll take it up with DA Barbieri directly."

Sweeney reached for her kit. "Will do."

Jo stood and pointed a trajectory up the hill. "What do you think, could you climb up and over the hill to get away?"

Arnett squinted as he considered. "Could *I*? No. Could *you*? Probably."

Jo nodded. "Alicia, can you follow this up, see if there's more? Also, can you have the team check the road on the other side, look for any evidence of a car parked along the shoulder?"

"Yes, ma'am."

"Thank you."

"Our killer is clever *and* athletic," Arnett said as they turned away back down the road.

"But not invisible or invincible. They left a trail and a trace, and we're damned well gonna find it."

CHAPTER FIVE

Jo and Arnett strode past the intersection of the T, waiting for the Nelsons' house to come into view between the vast clouds of orange and red leaves. Smaller than Sandra's house, the cottage was half fronted with brick, and half with white-trimmed gray paneling.

Arnett gazed up at it, shaking his head. "What d'you think, a cool million?"

Jo put on an incredulous grimace. "Oh, at least that. Can you even imagine? Must be nice."

"I know you're mocking me, Fournier," he grumbled.

"It's reassuring to know that even in the midst of a tragedy like this, there are some things in life you can always count on. Your masochistic fascination with housing prices is one of them."

Blue-checked curtains flicked open, and a concerned white woman with a sporty brown haircut peered out at them. Jo spotted a security camera and followed its trajectory outward, but the view was too obscured to capture anything at Sandra's house.

The front door opened before they knocked, revealing the

entire figure of the woman: On the lower end of her forties, medium height, solid build, dressed in ruggedly outdoorsy clothes that Camilla Parker Bowles could wear to a hunting party.

Jo shifted her blazer to show her badge. "I'm Detective Jo Fournier and this is Detective Bob Arnett of the Oakhurst County State Police Detective Unit. Officer Racinsky says you and your husband found Sandra Ashville this morning?"

The woman stepped back and motioned for them to follow her. "That's right. I'm Marianne. My husband Jeff's in the kitchen."

They followed her through a combined front room and dining area decorated with an abundance of sky blue, slate, and white. Rope accented everything, and a large sign on one wall proclaimed *If It's Not Lake Life, You're Not Living!* The kitchen was a cozy conglomeration of white and stainless steel, with an anchor motif that carried over from the dish towels to the mug Jeff clenched between his hands.

He stood to greet them, eyes wide and face pale. Tall and barrel-chested, his bushy brown beard, ruddy complexion, and blue-checked flannel shirt brought an image of a lumberjack flashing through Jo's mind.

"Please, sit down," he said. "Can we get you some coffee, or...?"

"No, thank you." Jo selected the Windsor-back chair directly across the table from him, and Arnett sat to her right. "We know you've been waiting to talk to us, so let's jump right in. How was it you found Sandra Ashville?"

"We'd planned to go out before dawn because that's when the fish bite best, but we got a late start." Jeff shot a glare at Marianne, whose lips tightened. "So we went out right after the sun came up. Sandra was on her pier, but didn't look right and didn't respond when we called out."

"What looked wrong?" Jo asked.

Marianne took over. "From our dock, she just looked like she was in some yoga pose, and I didn't think much of it, 'cause that's how she does these days. But when we drove past she still hadn't moved, and she was twisted all weird. When we got up close I saw some sort of cloth covering her head, and what looked like blood." The final words rushed like bullets from a machine gun.

Jo watched her carefully. "Did you try to revive her?"

Marianne clenched her hands together on the table in front of her. "No, ma'am. It was pretty clear she was dead, and I know better than to mess with a crime scene."

"How well did you know Mrs. Ashville?" Arnett asked.

"Not super well. They moved in, what, five years ago?" She turned to her husband, who nodded. "They were only here weekends at first, and not all the time. Then about a year ago he stopped coming and she moved in full-time. I guessed they must have divorced and figured she might be depressed, so I invited her to our Fourth of July party, but she didn't come—"

"Memorial Day party," Jeff interjected.

"No, it was—oh, no, you're right, because Fourth of July was when she had that dust-up with Mitch and Frieda."

"Dust-up with Mitch and Frieda?" Jo asked.

Marianne's face dropped. "Oh. You don't think—but then, somebody killed her, so I guess it's just as easy them as anybody else, and it makes sense with the rat—"

Jeff cut her off. "Mitch and Frieda Hauptmann, the neighbors on Sandra's other side." He noticed the questioning look on Arnett's face. "You can't see their house from Sandra's and you have to take a different road to get to it. Anyway, they had a big family reunion that day and everybody started drinking before noon. They had the music blasting and were getting careless with their Jet Skis, and she took that personal."

"That was later," Marianne cut in. "She just went over and asked them to turn down their music after sunset."

"Not after sunset. She didn't ask until after eleven, that's what Tiff told me."

Marianne glared at him. "Eleven *is* after sunset."

He returned a withering glare of his own. "*After sunset* means *right* after sunset, like eight thirty or nine in the summer, not eleven."

Marianne flicked a hand at him. "Same difference."

"No it's *not*, especially on Fourth of July when you have to wait until dark to set off fireworks. Asking someone to turn their music down at eight thirty at night on Fourth of July is just damned rude. After eleven, people have a right to go to sleep—"

Jo cut in—normally she'd let diversions run their course, but she was in no mood today. "Who's Tiff?"

Jeff jerked his head southward. "Tiffany and Dat Vo, our neighbors on the other side."

"They were at the party?" Jo asked.

Jeff looked at her like she was speaking Martian. "Tiff and Dat wouldn't've been caught dead over at the Hauptmanns' place. Neither would we."

Jo called up her reserves of patience. "Then how did they know?"

He shrugged. "Scuttlebutt."

Sure. She should have guessed. "I take it the Hauptmanns didn't respond well to Sandra's request?"

"Not unless you consider turning the music up *higher* responding well," Jeff said.

"Morons." Marianne sniffed. "Everybody knows not to mess with lawyers."

"None of us knew she was a lawyer 'til later," Jeff said.

Jo hurried to preempt the spat. "What happened then?"

"Sandra called the police, and that's when it got ugly," Jeff said. "Of course there were 'recreational drugs' at the party, and as soon as the cops pulled up, they went bat-crap crazy." He made finger quotes around *recreational drugs*.

"Funniest damned thing I ever saw." Marianne slapped her thigh. "Scattered like cockroaches when you turn the lights on."

"And Mitch was sitting on his Jet Ski, had it turned on and everything, and of course he was drunker than a skunk." Jeff paused to sip from his mug, and, Jo suspected, for dramatic effect. "They arrested him on the spot for operating under the influence."

"Tiff told you about all this?" Jo asked.

Jeff gave her the scathing look again. "*That* part we could see from our dock."

Jo took a deep mental breath. "Then something else happened? You said something about a rat?"

"Late July, Sandra put up two security cameras," Jeff said. "We asked her why all of a sudden, and she just said she'd been meaning to for a while. But what we heard from a couple different people is she found a rat on her doormat. Some said its throat was slit, some said it wasn't. All I know for sure is about a month after *that* the Hauptmanns moved out. No notice, all in a day. Movers showed up, and they were gone by the end of the day after living here for twenty years."

"And you think that was connected to the party and the rat?" Arnett asked.

"Maybe so, maybe no." Jeff shrugged, palms up, and leaned back in his chair. "Timing is odd is all I'm saying."

"Did she have any other trouble with anybody in the neighborhood? Anybody else who didn't like her?" Jo asked.

Both Jeff and Marianne shook their heads. "Not that I know of," Jeff said. "She kept to herself, but she was nice enough. Said hi and gave us chocolates at Christmas."

Jo nodded. "Did you see anything else strange this morning? Any strangers around your property or hers, or strange cars?"

"Nothing," Jeff said. Marianne shook her head.

"And you didn't hear anything out of the ordinary?" Jo asked.

"You're talking about the gunshot. No, we didn't." Jeff smirked. "But maybe the gunshot is what woke Marianne since she forgot to set the alarm."

Marianne flashed him another glare.

"It didn't wake *you*?" Arnett asked.

"I sleep like the dead," Jeff said.

Jo stood, and Arnett followed her lead. She handed one of her cards to Jeff. "Thank you for your help. If you remember or hear anything else that might be related, please let us know."

"Glad to help." Jeff stood and walked them to the front door, with Marianne following behind.

"Oh, one last question," Jo said when they got to the door. "Do you happen to know where the Hauptmanns moved?"

"Don't know, don't want to know. Good riddance to bad garbage."

———

"What do you think about that Mitch Hauptmann story?" Jo asked as they strode back to the crime scene. "Just neighborhood gossip, or something to it?"

Arnett glanced back to the Nelsons' house. "Hard to say. If she really did find a dead rat on her mat, I can't see her letting that go."

Jo nodded. "It's a pretty pointed response to her calling the cops on them, if so. But since they pulled up and moved overnight, something more happened after that. We need to talk to Mitch Hauptmann."

"Agreed." As the crime scene came back into view Arnett's face dropped. "Shit."

Jo saw the woman at the same moment. An average-height black woman most likely in her early forties, wearing a short black bob, trainers, and a faux motorcycle jacket over jeans, stood jotting notes as she talked to Racinsky.

Jo didn't recognize the woman, but she recognized the interaction. "Press?"

"Pretty sure. But everyone kept this quiet, how did she get here this fast?"

Jo grimaced. "Maybe the Nelsons? But why is she the only one here?"

Racinsky lifted his arm and pointed at them. The woman turned, then headed toward them with long, sure strides.

"Detectives Fournier and Arnett?" she asked when she reached them. "I'm Lacey Bernard, with the *Springfield Gazette*. I understand Assistant District Attorney Sandra Ashville has been murdered?"

Jo slipped on her stern publicity face and kept her pace steady, passing Bernard. "We don't have any comment at this time. Our lieutenant will be making a statement later."

"There were reports of a gunshot called in at six fifty-five. Was she shot?"

Jo calculated quickly what the Nelsons seemed to know and how much she could afford to put on the record. "I can confirm that a woman was found dead on this property this morning, and that we're in the early stages of our investigation."

Bernard kept up with Jo's stride. "My sources show no police activity dispatched to this location until forty-five minutes later. Was the gunshot unrelated?"

"We won't have more details to give you until the press conference." Jo clenched her jaw shut.

"She was found with some sort of cloth over her head. Was she asphyxiated? Was she tortured? Does this have to do with one of her cases?"

Jo's stomach churned. That was a detail she and Arnett would have held back from the public, but with the Nelson's fondness for gossip she should have realized they'd pass it on. Still, the way Bernard had worded it was wrong—maybe they hadn't realized what they were looking at. She had to figure out how much damage had been done, and do some damage control, quickly.

She stopped, met Lacey Bernard's eyes, and smiled. "I don't think we've met before. I thought I knew all the journalists from the *Gazette*."

Bernard's eyes bounced between the two of them, seemingly trying to figure out this sudden shift in response. "I just started there a few months back. I can show you my credentials if that'll help."

"No need." There wasn't, because Jo would verify everything later. But she needed a moment to think, and see if she could turn this into an opportunity. "How do you like working for George Mazar?"

Bernard's face turned wary. "Everyone at the *Gazette* has been wonderful to work with."

"That's good to hear." Jo studied her face. "How did you manage to get here so early, before the rest of the crowd?"

Bernard's eyes shifted away for the smallest moment. "Early bird gets the worm."

Jo leaned in slightly and lowered her voice. "So, the Nelsons told you about the bag over the victim's head?"

Bernard's eyes widened so briefly Jo would have missed it if she hadn't been specifically hoping for it. Bernard jotted a note as she answered. "They did."

Jo's glance dropped just long enough to read the note upside down: *bag over head*. "Here's the deal, Ms. Bernard. We need to keep that piece of information off the record for reasons of public safety, at least for now. Can you do that for me?"

"I'm all about public safety. But I need to bring something to Mazar that has more substance than 'a woman was found dead on a dock at Lake Pocomtuk.'"

"Fair enough. In exchange, I'll make sure you get first access to any information we're allowed to release."

Bernard searched her face, probably trying to judge how

likely Jo was to keep her word. Jo pulled out one of her business cards. "This is my direct line."

Bernard glanced at the card, buried it in a pocket, and produced one of her own. "I'm always happy to work with people willing to work with me."

Jo slipped the card into her blazer. "Sounds like we have an agreement. I'll be in contact as soon as I have anything."

Once they'd climbed back into her car, Arnett turned to her. "Nicely done back there with the bag-over-the-head decoy. In one swoop you managed to confirm she, and thus the Nelsons, didn't realize it was a blindfold, *and* misled her so if she does go rogue and print it, our proprietary information is still proprietary."

"And if the information gets out, we know exactly who leaked it. If it doesn't, we know we can trust her." Jo glanced at Bernard in the side mirror as they passed, watching her carefully. "Because as it stands, I don't understand why the Nelsons would call the *Springfield Gazette* and not the local Pocomtuk paper."

CHAPTER SIX

After a quick pit stop for very large coffees, Arnett looked up Bruce Ashville's address, then started the hunt for the Hauptmanns while Jo drove. Half an hour later, Jo pulled into the driveway of a nineteenth-century farmhouse with Victorian elements that looked like a strange mash-up between American Gothic and Addams Family. "What would you call that color?" she asked.

He glanced up at it. "Early-American Drab."

She laughed. "I'm going to land on day-old-avocado green. Remind me what Bruce does for a living?"

"Some kind of doctor. Podiatrist? Private practice, I know that much."

"That explains how they can afford two homes."

While waiting for Bruce Ashville to open the door, Jo searched her memory trying to remember something about him, but the best she could come up with was a vague, shadowy image from some past holiday function. She barely recognized him even once he'd opened the door; around six-foot tall and lean, his blond hair was now artificially boosted, and his eyelids now sagged around the edges of his blue eyes. His tanned skin was paling toward a winter white, making the dark circles under his eyes more pronounced. His tan-and-banana golf clothes felt both too casual and at odds with the storm on his face, as though he'd thrown on someone else's outfit without realizing.

His eyes shifted continually between Jo and Arnett as she reminded him of their names. "Right, right. Come in," he said when she finished.

He escorted them into an open living room with a sleek Scandinavian-modern aesthetic nearly identical to the one at Sandra's lake house—and that completely mismatched with Bruce's loud personal style. Did he just not care enough to redecorate, or was he holding on to the past?

Bruce sat on one of two blue modular couches and pointed toward the other. "What happened to her? Officer Racinsky would only tell me she'd been killed." Bruce's voice was thick, and wavered.

"That's what we're trying to figure out," Jo evaded as she sat. "We're so sorry for your loss, and we're hoping you can help us. But ADA Hanson mentioned you and Sandra divorced recently. When exactly was that?"

"We separated April of last year. The divorce was finalized at the end of August."

"Who filed?" Jo asked.

"She did. I didn't contest."

Arnett jumped in. "We heard you weren't enthusiastic about signing the papers."

He reached for a tinted highball glass on the end table and sipped. "I'm a busy man. I couldn't always get to things as quickly as Sandra liked. Given her too-busy schedule was the reason for our divorce, you think she would have understood that."

Jo pushed down the defensive rejoinder that rose up in her throat—long hours came with the job, and he should have realized that—and weighed his expression behind the glass. What was in it? Orange juice? Bourbon? He was hiding emotion, she was sure of that. But was that emotion frustrated sadness or angry bitterness? "But you said she was the one who filed."

"I'm not a quitter, Jo. I still loved her, and I fight for the things I want."

The too-casual use of her nickname grated. "How literally?"

Bruce turned to stare out of the window. "Purely figurative. But our verbal exchanges became increasingly tense."

"Only about the long work hours?" she asked.

He suddenly leaned forward. "I'm a doctor, Jo. I understand long hours and middle-of-the-night patient emergencies. Yet I was the one telling her she should rein it in. Doesn't that tell you all you need to know?"

The assumptions rubbed her the wrong way. Possibly Sandra really had worked longer hours than he had, but he'd known what she did for a living when he married her. She'd seen it too many times in her own life—men who just couldn't deal with a woman's job being as important as theirs. The self-centered arrogance suggested the real problem was Sandra refused to bend and reschedule around his needs.

"So, you tried to talk her out of the divorce?" she asked.

"Repeatedly."

"When did you stop trying?"

"I never stopped. I called her the day the divorce was final and told her I still believed we could work things out."

"How did she respond to that?"

His eyes flashed to the window, and he took a gulp of whatever was in the glass before he responded. "She told me that if I still couldn't accept it was over, she'd get a restraining order against me."

Jo allowed her eyebrows to pop up. "That seems dramatic."

"Funny, that's what I said." His voice turned to sarcastic steel.

"And you let it drop after that?"

"Considering she knows every judge in every court in the county and has personal relationships with several of them? That's not a fight I had a chance in hell of winning." He took another gulp from the glass, and tears welled in his eyes. "One of them probably advised her to threaten the restraining order in the first place. Or maybe it was the brainchild of her new boyfriend."

"New boyfriend? Who's that?" Arnett asked.

He shook his head, expression tight. "No idea, she wouldn't tell me. But the point is, I loved her and I never wanted to be without her. And I wanted to be with her in actuality, not just in theory."

Jo forced herself to soften slightly. "That's what I don't understand. She was planning on retiring in two months. Wouldn't that have solved the problem between you?"

Anger flashed across his face. "The very definition of irony, isn't it?"

Jo waited, but he didn't say more. He crossed his legs and picked up his drink again, sending the clear message that he didn't intend to.

Arnett cleared his throat. "Where were you this morning?"

He stared back out of the window. "I woke up at six and went for my run. I came back, showered, and met Dr. Ralph Prinz for a round of golf. We teed off just after eight." He pulled his phone out of his pocket and recited Prinz's phone number. "That's where I was when I received the call."

"Where did you go for your run?" Arnett asked.

"Around the neighborhood. It was dark, so I doubt anybody noticed. But I have security cameras that automatically record any time there's motion. You're welcome to check them. In fact, you can take the micro SD cards with you when you go."

"We'd appreciate that, thank you." Jo shifted in her chair—even if the cards backed up his story, there was still time for him to have killed Sandra. "Do you know of anybody who had reason to be angry with Sandra?"

He tossed back the remaining contents of the glass and set it down with a clank. "Other than the upstanding citizens she prosecuted? That ADA, Patricia Flynn, had it out for her. She put in a hostile work environment complaint with the chief operations officer against Sandra a few months before we separated."

Jo leaned in. "What happened with it?"

He shook his head. "No clue."

"What about the incident with your neighbor at the lake house?" Jo asked.

Bruce's brow creased. "Which neighbor?"

"The Hauptmanns," Arnett said.

Bruce's jaw clenched. "Why am I not surprised? White-trash hicks."

Jo bristled. "White-trash hicks with a million-dollar home?"

He shot her a withering glare. "*White trash* is an attitude, not a socio-economic status. What did they do?"

"Something about loud music?" Jo asked.

"Must have happened after I became persona non grata." He shook his head and stood up. "I'm happy to answer your questions, but if there's nothing more, I have a hundred phone calls to make. She doesn't have family in the area, so I'll be handling the funeral."

Jo and Arnett stood, and Jo handed him a card. "We're sorry again for your loss. Thank you for talking with us. If you can think of anything else, please let us know."

CHAPTER SEVEN

"Something isn't adding up," Jo said once back in the car. "On the one hand, she's so eager to retire she has a literal countdown in her calendar. On the other, she's so dedicated to her work she's willing to let her marriage crumble despite her husband's objections."

"My guess is she had other reasons for divorcing him," Arnett said. "With the level of resentment he demonstrated, I have no problem seeing him get violent, and she did threaten him with a restraining order."

Jo fired up the engine and pulled out. "But if there was a deeper basis to it, why did he tell us about the threat? We'd never have known otherwise. He was more concerned with not taking blame for the divorce than with how we might see that."

"He made a point of saying one of her judge friends suggested it. He probably knows they did, and knows it's only a matter of time before we find that out."

Jo grimaced. "Maybe—but he seemed to genuinely think her threat was inappropriate."

"How many people who get served with a restraining order argue it's inappropriate?"

"Fair enough," Jo said. "And I definitely didn't get the sense he responded well to the rejection. He was clearly upset when he mentioned the new boyfriend. We need to figure out who that was."

Arnett rubbed his chin. "So, you think when she threatened the restraining order, he gave up hope and decided to take action?"

"He wouldn't be the first person to decide if he couldn't have the one he loved, nobody could, but I think it's more complicated than that. You saw his reaction when I mentioned the early retirement. Once she did that, he'd have had to come to terms with the fact that the problem wasn't just her job, it was also *him*."

"It's possible," Arnett said.

"Then there's what Hanson said about why she was leaving the job, her loss of faith in the legal system. I wonder if that has anything to do with Patricia Flynn's hostile work environment claim."

Arnett's eyes scanned the dashboard. "You think she was taking out frustrations on her co-workers?"

"Maybe." Jo signaled a lane change. "Either way, I think we need to find out exactly what went down there."

"Lemme call Hanson. He'll know something about it." Arnett tapped at his phone.

"Bob." Hanson's voice burst through Arnett's speakerphone almost instantly.

Arnett explained why he was calling.

"Flynn, right. What a steep mountain of bullshit all that was," Hanson said.

"Bruce Ashville didn't seem to think so," Arnett prodded.

"Bruce Ashville wouldn't know his ass from a shaved monkey," Hanson said.

Jo tried to keep the smile out of her voice. "Enlighten us."

"Our jobs aren't for everyone, I don't have to tell you. The things we see in this job, and the choices we have to make? Watching someone we know for a fact murdered little girls go free because of a technicality? Having to compromise with plea deals to even get minimum prison time for violent offenders? We all come in thinking we're going to change the world, and we all get the idealism smacked out of us fast. The ones who can do the job learn to focus on one case, one victim, one victory at a time. But some people can't let go of the losses and the failures and the compromises. That was Flynn's problem."

"But Flynn claimed there was a hostile work environment?" Arnett asked.

"She made her own hostile work environment. Wouldn't listen to anyone and butted heads everywhere. Took risks we all warned her not to take, lost cases and watched criminals go free, then claimed it was because we hadn't supported her enough even though we told her exactly what would happen and why."

"So why did she name Sandra Ashville in particular?" Jo asked.

"Because Flynn had been learning the ropes by sitting second chair on Sandra's cases before we cut her loose to prosecute her own."

"So Sandra was her mentor?" Jo asked.

"Pretty much. Sandra was the most senior female ADA in the unit and the office, and Patty gravitated to her. Sandra didn't ask for it, and didn't treat her any differently than anybody else. That was the whole problem."

"How so?" Arnett asked.

Hanson gave a frustrated sigh. "After a couple of instances when Patty made some bad judgments, Sandra had a little heart-to-heart with her. Tried to let her know she was alienating everyone around her. Suggested she talk to a therapist."

"And Patty didn't like that advice?" Jo asked.

"She got defensive and nasty. After that, Sandra washed her hands of Patty."

"What did that look like?" Arnett asked.

"Nothing out of line. She just stopped going out of her way for her. No more special treatment."

Jo shot a glance at Arnett. "I thought you said she *didn't* treat her differently than anyone else?"

"She didn't, *after* that talk. Before that, she gave her all sorts of special considerations because she was new to the unit. You know how it is when someone's new. You explain things to them, walk them through it all. But after a while, you expect them to pick up their own slack. We all let it go on far longer than we should have because Patty was struggling. By the time Sandra had enough, everyone else already saw Patty as a troublemaker, so they'd become careful around her. Nobody was going out of their way or taking up her slack anymore."

Jo sucked air in through her teeth and rubbed her neck against the impossibility of the situation. From the perspective of everyone in the DA's office, Flynn was a prima donna who couldn't handle her job and tried to blame them for her failings. They'd become mistrustful of her and afraid of being the next person centered in her crosshairs, so kept her at arm's length. From Flynn's perspective, who didn't realize she'd been on an extended honeymoon, it would've felt like an arctic cold front had settled in. In essence, she'd built a wall around herself that she'd never be able to break back down.

"So she went to the chief operations officer," Jo said.

"She did, on the advice of another informal mentor of hers."

"Who?" Arnett asked.

"She claimed it was some friend of the family who was a judge." Hanson's tone was dismissive. "And apparently some detective she knew seconded it."

Jo shot Arnett a questioning glance, and he shook his head—he hadn't heard anything about it from among the detectives, either.

"What was the outcome of it all?" Jo asked.

"No misconduct found," Hanson said. "And she resigned a week later."

"Do you think she was still holding a grudge?" Jo asked.

"She was absolutely holding a grudge," Hanson said, tone somber. "As far as she was concerned, Sandra hated her and had gone out of her way to kill her career. And somehow, I don't think struggling to practice family law now in some Springfield fleabag to pay the bills would soften her resentment."

That triggered another question Jo wanted to ask. "What were the nasty things Flynn said to Sandra?"

"I don't know." His voice was frustrated. "She wouldn't tell me, but they must have been beyond the pale. Sandra had a thick skin."

"One last thing," Jo asked. "Do you know who Sandra was dating?"

"Dating?" he asked, confused.

"Bruce said she told him she was seeing someone, but he didn't know who."

"Really. First I've heard of it. I'll ask around."

Arnett thanked him and ended the call. "Sounds like we need to have a chat with Patricia Flynn."

Jo nodded grimly. "Three suspects and a mysterious boyfriend already, and we haven't even touched her case files yet."

CHAPTER EIGHT

Patricia Flynn's office was set in the sort of strip mall that proliferated in the late 90s, had taken a huge hit during The Great Recession, and had been all but abandoned during the pandemic. Anchored on one end by a Dollar Tree, a take-out Chinese restaurant on the other, and spotted with empty retail spaces in between, her office sat at the bottom of a small three-story building that seemed to include living areas above.

"You think she lives up there?" Arnett asked as they stepped out of the car. "That downgrade is motive enough to kill someone."

Jo laughed as the scent of beef-and-broccoli wafted past on the wind. "Don't knock it, it might be cozy. There was a little bakery we went to in New Orleans when I was a kid. Run by a husband-and-wife team who lived over the top of it, and I remember thinking how fun it would be to just roll out of bed right into work."

"Until the day it closed down because of the murder-suicide?" Arnett quipped.

"You're grim today. Not that I don't understand why." Jo's mind flew back to Matt, at that very moment moving things into her house. "And I admit, there is something to be said for personal space."

He picked up on the shift in her tone. "Moving day not going well?"

"No, it's fine." She waved him off. "Mostly. You know it takes me time to adjust to change."

"Right there with you." He pulled open the door and gestured her through.

Jo stepped into the surprisingly bright vestibule decorated with soft yellow walls and rust-colored trim. A twenty-some-thing Latina woman with curly brown hair and kind eyes sat at a sleek mahogany desk on the left side of the back wall, book-ended between two large potted bamboo palms; a large wooden door dominated the right half of the wall.

Once they identified themselves, she picked up the phone on her desk. "I'll let Patricia know you're here." She gestured vaguely to the rust-colored armchairs perched along the side walls, accompanied by several smaller wooden chairs meant for children.

Before they could sit, the internal door opened. Patricia Flynn looked to be in her mid to late thirties, with strawberry-blonde hair pulled into a stylish chignon and a slash of mascara highlighting blue, guarded eyes. Her slate-blue suit was poly-ester, and her black pumps were sensible.

She extended her arm ambiguously, looking from one to the other of them. "Detectives Fournier and Arnett. How can I help you?"

"Thanks for making time to meet with us." Jo pointed to the office behind her. "Can we talk inside?"

"Of course." Flynn stepped back and gestured them in. "Please, have a seat."

The internal office had the same soft-yellow walls and rust accents and the same mix of armchairs and children's chairs, but was nearly covered wall-to-wall with mahogany bookshelves and filing cabinets. Books and Duplo blocks dotted the bottom shelves, and two framed pictures perched on the desk, one of two young girls, and one of Patricia and an Asian man smiling for the camera.

Flynn noticed the direction of her gaze. "Me and my husband on a trip to Nantucket."

Jo nodded and sat, then explained why they were there.

She met Jo's eyes. "I wish I could say I was surprised."

Jo's composure almost dropped. "That's quite a statement."

Flynn shrugged. "I told Sandra myself that the way she did things would eventually come back to bite her."

No way was Flynn naive enough to not realize she was a suspect. "Like the misconduct claim you made against her?"

Flynn scrutinized Jo's face. "My time at the DA's office was a nightmare, and that was largely due to Sandra Ashville."

Jo gestured around her. "And ultimately landed you here."

Flynn reached for a travel mug of coffee. "It did. I can't claim I was happy about it at first, but it's for the best. I became a prosecutor to do good in the world. I'm still able to do that here." She leaned forward. "I'm guessing you're here to ask about my alibi. What time frame do I need to provide for?"

"This morning. From about six until about eight," Jo said.

Flynn grimaced. "Ah, well, that's unfortunate. I woke up at eight, ate and got ready, and arrived here at nine for my first appointment. Weekends are busy for me since so many of my clients work Monday-through-Friday jobs. My husband was asleep when I left, but I have external security cameras here and at home that will show me leaving and arriving. But that's just a bit too late, isn't it?"

Jo considered the flippancy. Was it real, or a defense because she was scared? "You said Sandra Ashville made your life in the DA's office difficult. Can you tell us how?"

She leaned back in her chair. "I didn't like her approach to the job, and I called her on it. That hurt her ego, so she iced me out. But the chief operations officer told me there was nothing I could do. From what I gather, unless someone physically assaults you, they can get away with anything."

Jo's brows bounced up at the raw bitterness. "You said you called Sandra out. What about?"

Flynn's eyes scoured Jo's face again, like she was judging whether it was worth telling her the truth. "I get that prosecutors don't have an easy job. Our hands are tied by all sorts of limitations, and the criminals aren't, and because of that a lot of people end up back on the streets that shouldn't be there. But that doesn't excuse taking the easy route."

Jo noted the use of *our*. "I don't fully understand. Can you give me an example?"

Flynn crossed her arms over her chest. "How about scaring a kid with the threat of a long stretch in prison so they'll take a plea for a crime they didn't commit? That was the last straw for me."

Jo felt Arnett tense up, and fought to keep her own expression blank. "Sandra put someone away for a crime they didn't commit? That sounds like a pretty strong motive for murder. What's their name?"

"John Huertas."

"And you confronted her about that?" Jo asked as Arnett jotted down the name.

"I did. I'd only recently been given my own cases, and asked her advice. She used Huertas as an example of what she thought I should do. I looked her right in the eye and told her I wasn't going to threaten some kid just to keep my record looking good."

Jo's eyebrows popped again. "How did she respond to that?"

"As you'd predict. Gave me a lecture about how this isn't a *TV show* and how in the *real world* we don't always have clear-cut fingerprints or DNA, and that two eye witnesses to a crime was far better evidence than you were likely to get in most cases."

"She's not wrong," Jo said. "Two eyewitnesses is a gift."

Flynn pushed her coffee away and leaned forward again. "The witnesses both gave vague descriptions, and his father swore they were together the night of the burglary."

"That's what juries are for, to weigh the evidence, or lack thereof," Arnett said.

Flynn's eyes flashed to him. "Right. Except when you intimidate the suspect into taking a plea deal, they don't get a jury trial."

"Didn't he have a defense attorney to advise him?" Arnett said.

Jo jumped in, surprised at his vehemence—they weren't going to get what they needed by alienating her. "I get what you're saying. They're hard decisions to make, and it sounds like Ashville drew her line in a different place than you did. I take it she didn't respond well to being challenged?"

Flynn's face flushed red. "She laughed at me. Told me when I had more than a day's experience under my belt, I could come back and apologize to her over a beer."

That was a far gentler reaction than Jo had anticipated from Sandra—not really angry or hostile, and far closer to what Hanson had argued. "And then you filed the complaint?"

"No. *Then* I told her that I didn't appreciate being condescended to, and that between her style and mine, I thought the chief operations officer would prefer mine." She leaned back in her chair.

"Telling a defendant about the potential sentence he's facing and offering him a plea isn't illegal or even immoral," Arnett said.

"How about conspiring with a detective to create a fake confession from a defendant's supposed accomplice? And keeping that confession in his file? Is that immoral?" Flynn spat.

"Ashville did that to get the plea?" Jo asked.

"Different case. She did it to get a confession." Flynn's voice was clipped.

Jo struggled to keep her face impassive. It wasn't illegal to lie to a defendant in an interrogation, in fact, it was a fairly common, if controversial, practice. But producing a faked confession and putting it in a case file was pushing a different line altogether. "And that's when you went to the chief operations officer?"

"No. That's when she retaliated against me. Not only her, but the other prosecutors in the office. And once they started retaliating against me, *that's* when I reported everything, including the detective who faked the confession." She stabbed her pen in the air to accentuate the word.

"How did she retaliate?" Jo asked.

"Barely spoke to me when she didn't have to. Left me dangling completely on my own, an impossible place to be." Anger flashed through her eyes. "Isn't that what we're supposed to do? Call out prosecutors and detectives who are getting too jaded and cynical to do their job correctly?"

Jo noted Arnett's posture tense, and purposefully softened her expression. "You were trying to do what you believed was right."

Flynn relaxed slightly, leaning back against her chair. "Thank you. And to be clear—I do believe Sandra thought hers was the best way to get justice."

"But?" Arnett asked.

Flynn stood up. "But the road to hell is paved with good intentions."

CHAPTER NINE

As soon as Sandra hit the ground, the clock had started ticking. There'd be no turning back now until it was all finished.

The gunshot would be hard for anyone to locate precisely, but I couldn't count on that giving me more than a few minutes. Between the dim light and my ski mask, anyone scanning the area with binoculars would have only the most generic of descriptions for the police, but I couldn't risk some good Samaritan showing up to intervene—something just ironic enough to happen.

So I had to push down what I was feeling and act. Gun in pocket, gloves snapped on.

I posed the arms first. Both out to the side, one palm toward the lake, one toward the road. Then I grabbed a hank of hair from the side that wasn't bleeding, lifted her head, yanked the blindfold down over her wide, open, blindly staring eyes.

I allowed myself a moment to take in the sight of her, and stored the picture in my memory, next to the snapshot of the fear on her face.

Then away back to the trees, removing the gloves and

shoving them into the Ziploc left from the blindfold. I snatched down the two cameras I'd hidden, then bolted up, over the hill and down again into the non-existent traffic.

Only then, in the car and safely down the road, could I allow myself a moment to take everything in.

I'd played it out in my head a hundred times beforehand. Picturing the expression on her face. Imagining how it would feel to pull the trigger. In my simulations, I never once felt the remotest sense of hesitation, but that was no guarantee. I'd never killed anyone before, so I couldn't know what I'd actually feel when the moment came.

I read about it once, how soldiers react the first time they have to shoot the enemy. Some freeze, unable to pull the trigger even if it means they'll be killed. Some manage to force themselves but spend their lives agonizing over it, pouring alcohol or drugs or sex on top of a guilt they can never quite bury. Still others never think twice about it, before, during, or after. It's nearly impossible to predict who will do what, the article said.

So the most nerve-wracking thing about killing her was not knowing what would happen when I came face to face with her. Would I freeze up, unable to pull the trigger? Would I kill her, but be instantly filled with remorse? Or would I feel nothing?

But I didn't feel any of those things. What I felt was alive—more alive than I'd ever felt in my life. Like a weight had been lifted off of me that allowed me to breathe again.

It killed me to stay below the speed limit on my way out of town—I wanted the car to fly along with my spirit, happy and free and energized for the next steps of the journey I'd just embarked on. I flipped on the radio and found a happy upbeat song and let loose, singing off-key at the top of my lungs. I pictured the police arriving, taking in the scene I'd left for them, trying to figure out the significance of it all. It killed me not to be able to leave a clear, bold declaration for them about what was *happening and why—but I just couldn't risk them putting all the pieces together before I saw the whole thing through.*

In the meantime, I smiled like a teenager in love, wondering if he'd be at the scene, stumbling blindly through the field of clues, completely unaware of what was coming for him.

CHAPTER TEN

Jo's phone rang as they buckled themselves back into the car.

"Hayes," she said to Arnett, then connected the call.

"Fournier, Arnett," Hayes said. "The press are hounding me for a statement and I can't put it off much longer. What do we have?"

Jo caught her up on Bruce Ashville, Mitch Hauptmann, and Patricia Flynn, then summarized. "Three suspects, two so far with no alibis."

"I can't give any of that to the press without evidence. At the lake, you made it sound like you thought the killer was someone she'd prosecuted."

She rubbed her eyes. "We're on our way back to HQ to work through her case files now."

"I'll tell the press we believe a previous defendant is responsible, and we're on their trail. I want a name to go along with that by the end of the day." She hung up.

"Okay, then." Jo tossed the phone aside and started up the car. "In the meantime, back to Flynn."

Arnett shook his head and stared out the window. "She's veering close to delusional. In an ideal world, we'd have DNA and fingerprints for every case. And perpetrators would walk in off the street and handcuff themselves while unicorns flew through the air sweating winning lottery tickets. Until that day, we have to settle for getting some of the bad guys off the street for only a year or two via a plea deal."

"Right, no, that's true," Jo said as she pulled out into traffic. "But what worries me is her accusation that Sandra faked a confession. I don't like the picture that's coming together."

Arnett turned to her, surprised. "What do you mean?"

"I mean that sort of behavior doesn't fit with what I thought I knew about Sandra, and it changes what we're looking at. Now we aren't just looking for a disgruntled defendant. We may be looking for one who has *valid* reason for believing they were treated unfairly. And when I look at the Mitch Hauptmann case through that lens, it makes me wonder what exactly happened to make him disappear overnight after tangling with her."

Arnett's brows knit. "Who says Flynn is even telling the truth?"

Jo nodded. "She may not be. We need to find out. And that means the Huertas file and the Hauptmanns just became my top priority."

———

Half an hour later they settled into their desks, diving into the bags of Sal's meatball subs they'd picked up for dinner on their way. "You want to take Hauptmann, or should I?" Jo asked.

"Already typing it in," Arnett said.

"Great. I'll call Lacey Bernard with the information I promised her ahead of the press conference, then dive into Sandra's files, starting with Huertas."

It took mere seconds for Jo to find what she was looking for. "Yep, here it is." She pulled it out and handed it to Arnett. "A confession from his alleged accomplice. Nothing on it or around it indicates whether it's genuine or not."

Arnett's brows shot up. "Maybe Flynn's wrong. Maybe the kid did actually confess."

"I'll track him down and ask."

He wasn't hard to find; his information hadn't changed in the two years since Huertas had been investigated. When she got him on the phone, he staunchly denied ever having confessed to anything.

"What did you expect?" Arnett said when she relayed the response to him. "Of course he's not going to risk going to prison over it now."

As Arnett turned back to his computer, Jo studied his face surreptitiously. Was it her imagination, or was he going out of his way to disbelieve everything Flynn had said? She understood the instinct to defend a colleague, but one of the reasons she valued Arnett as a partner was that he never closed his mind on possibilities, and this was veering strangely close to him doing just that.

She mentally shook her head and returned to the file in front of her. Silence fell as she searched, until Arnett announced he'd found Hauptmann a few minutes later.

"Sure enough, he was arrested for operating under the influence this past Fourth of July. But that wasn't his first mix-up with law enforcement by a long shot."

Jo swiveled toward him. "Do tell."

"Started out small with some possession of marijuana back before it was legal and a bar-fight assault or two. But a couple of years back he was indicted for sexual assault. Allegedly raped a woman."

Jo's eyes narrowed. "Allegedly? He wasn't prosecuted?"

"Nope. Hang on." Arnett tapped some more. "Charges were dropped—after they got an indictment from the grand jury. Looks like Nguyen was the ADA on it. I'll give him a call."

The connection rang several times and went to Nguyen's voicemail; while Arnett left a message, Jo fed in Hauptmann's information to find his current location. "Not only did Hauptmann and his wife skip town, they skipped the entire county. They live out in the Berkshires now, not too far from the New York border."

Arnett glanced up at the clock on the wall. "About what, an hour away? Seems to me it'd be smart to make sure they'll be around before we head out."

Jo called the numbers she was able to find for the Hauptmanns, two mobile lines on a shared account. She left messages on both of them identifying herself and asking for a callback, without referencing the reason for the call.

"Jo, Bob." Christine Lopez's voice rang out behind them.

Jo and Arnett both whipped around to find her striding toward them, her expression grim. Dressed in yoga pants, trainers, and an over-sized Walking Dead sweatshirt, her normally long, sleek black ponytail was mussed, and she had bags under her eyes. She clutched a backpack in one hand and a Rockstar in the other.

"I got here as fast as I could." She dropped the backpack next to Jo's desk. "No way I'm sitting out someone killing one of our ADAs on my watch."

"How did Tony take you leaving early?" Jo asked.

Lopez scrunched her nose in a half-grimace. "He'll get over it. They're having an all-night *Zombicide* marathon tonight, and he'll probably sleep until four tomorrow before heading home. He'll barely even notice I'm gone."

But Jo detected traces of tension as Lopez set her Rockstar down on Jo's desk, cracked it open, then took a gulp. Tony was far less happy about it than she was letting on.

"Nothing like that first sip of the day," Arnett said, eyebrows drawn together.

Lopez waved him off scornfully. "Took one to get me out of

bed and another to make it through the drive. Last night was a *Vampire: The Masquerade* marathon."

"Well. I'm surprised you were able to break away from The Kindred to come help us," Arnett said.

Lopez choked on the second gulp of Rockstar she'd been taking and gaped at him.

He raised his eyebrows at her. "I know things."

Jo laughed. "I didn't realize how serious you and Tony got about the board games, I thought you were more of the video game set. Either way I'm grateful you were able to break away."

Lopez started to reply, then gasped and pointed at Jo's desk. "Is that half a Sal's meatball grinder? I'd kill or die for half a Sal's meatball grinder right now."

Jo shoved her forgotten sandwich toward her. "A far lesser sacrifice than you just made. Tuck in while we catch you up."

Lopez ate, perched on the edge of Jo's desk as she listened, then swallowed the last bite and crumpled the sandwich wrapper. "So, from what I'm hearing, we already have several suspects with strong motives: the ex-husband, the neighbor, the newbie prosecutor, and possibly this Huertas guy. There's also this mystery boyfriend we need to find. But I agree that the killing style smells suspiciously like disgruntled defendant." She tossed the wrapper into Jo's garbage can.

"We're waiting to hear back from Marzillo, and from the officers canvassing the area," Jo said, and tapped on the stack of files. "In the meantime we have to deep-dive these suspects' lives, starting with Huertas, and identify any suspicious defendants she's prosecuted recently. While we're doing that, can you start digging into Sandra herself? Her work and personal email accounts, phone records, financials, anything and everything? I know you could probably use a nap, but time is of the essence here. Until we bring someone in, the message we're sending to every criminal out there is it's okay to take out members of law enforcement."

"I can sleep when I'm dead. Her work stuff is easy-peasy with the access info Hanson gave you. And I'll have her personal stuff cracked before I finish this Rockstar." She took another large gulp, accentuating her point, and winked. "Trust and believe I won't rest until we have this bastard."

CHAPTER ELEVEN

Jo eliminated Huertas almost immediately. Not only had the charges against him been dropped, he now lived in Wisconsin and had a solid alibi, as did his alleged confederate.

After that, the work was slow going. In theory, every case a prosecutor won made them an enemy, and there weren't many ways to easily narrow down the field. Even those in prison couldn't automatically be ruled out, since many criminals still had reach that extended far outside their cells. The process became an exercise in educated guesswork; Jo ignored for the moment anyone who'd received a sentence of under a year and repeat criminals whose sentences were more of the same, assuming both sets would be least likely to hold the intense sort of grudge needed for Sandra's murder. She paid close attention to red flags, especially those who had personal circumstances that might put a different spin on their incarceration. Then, after making a few calls out to confidential informants asking them for any information they could gather, she began verifying alibis one at a time.

She didn't realize how late it was until her stomach growled, and she looked up to see the sun had set. As she checked the time, a call came through from Marzillo. She put it on speakerphone.

"Jo. Just wanted to let you know that the diving team is still working. It'll probably take them until tomorrow morning at least. So far they haven't found anything except a very aggressive snapping turtle. One of their divers had to go to the ER."

"Snapping turtles are no joke," Arnett said.

"The grid search is almost done, and, in the meantime, Sweeney found something interesting when she was processing those trees you told her to check out."

"The ones where the killer possibly stood?" Jo asked.

"Yes. She had the stroke of genius to try luminol. She found a small smudge of possible blood."

Jo sat up in her chair. "Where? At the base or higher up?"

"About shoulder height. But don't get too excited just yet. It might not even be blood, and even if it is it may have been left by a deer or a bear. Even an injured squirrel."

"Consider my expectations managed," Jo said.

"Also, the ME confirmed the only injury Sandra sustained was the bullet to the head. Caliber of the bullet is a twenty-two. That's all I have for now; I'll call back when I know more."

"Thanks," Jo said, and hung up.

"Good to have a clear-cut cause of death," Arnett said.

"Yes." Jo fingered her diamond necklace.

"What?" Arnett asked.

"I'm not sure. The twenty-two. It feels... off for someone executing an ADA. Like they'd use something with more heft."

Arnett shrugged. "Criminals use whatever illegal guns they can get their hands on. Plenty of twenty-twos circulating out there."

"No, right." Jo shook her head and tapped at the phone. "I'm sending Hayes an update. Then should we compare notes?"

"I'll call Lopez."

As soon as they had her on the line, Jo started. "I've managed to eliminate quite a few suspects, but I have a list of about ten possibles I can't track down by phone."

"I've got about seven myself," Arnett said.

Jo rubbed the bridge of her nose in frustration. "Well, that'll take, what, two to three weeks to sort through? How about you, Christine, anything more concrete to help us save time?"

"I got a whole lot of nothing on my end. Nothing in her emails, phone records, or calendar that's even the least bit suspicious. No threats, not even angry contacts. I found a smattering of emails between her and her divorce attorney, and all indications are it was a fairly smooth divorce. Bruce may not have wanted to divorce her, but he isn't one of those assholes who fight over every asset just to make their soon-to-be-ex's life miserable."

"No surprise. He was still trying to get her back, up to and including the day he signed the papers," Arnett said.

"Yeah, well. We do have a case of the dog that didn't bark in the night," Lopez said.

"What's that?"

"You asked me to see if I could figure out who she was dating. I couldn't find anything even remotely romantic. No texts, no phone calls I couldn't account for, no emails."

Jo shot Arnett a questioning look over the phone. "Does she have another phone?"

"Not that I can find. And why would she bother?" Lopez asked.

Jo tapped a nail on her thigh. "Maybe she was lying to Bruce about dating someone to get him off her back?"

"Been there." Lopez yawned. "Anyway, guys, I'm wrecked. I think that's all I'm going to be able to do until the morning."

"You? Too tired to work?" Arnett asked, feigning surprise.

Lopez sighed. "Turns out I'm getting too old for all-nighters around board games followed by four-hour drives and a full day of staring at tiny print on monitors and documents. Catch you guys bright and early in the a.m." She hung up.

"Dammit." Jo shoved her notepad. "How can there be nothing helpful in Sandra's accounts? We need something to narrow this down, now, before Hayes pops a gasket. Should we check out the names on each other's lists, see if we can pick up on something the other missed that might help?"

"I'm right there with Lopez." Arnett checked his watch. "It's almost eleven. I say we send her the list of names we have and let her do what she wants with it, then get some sleep so we can think clearly and take a fresh look in the morning."

Jo winced, and dropped her head into her hands. "How did it get that late? I never texted Matt."

"Oh, that's right, isn't this your first night living under the same roof?" Arnett asked.

Jo rubbed her lips together. "Technically, yes. But we've slept under the same roof many nights."

"You know what I mean." His voice took on a teasing sing-song. "Not a great way to start things out..."

Jo felt herself tighten in a way she didn't like, and forced herself not to react. He was teasing, something he wouldn't do if he thought there was any truth to what he was saying—if he thought she was screwing up, he'd tell her straight out.

She stood, and grabbed her coat and her car keys. "Now, now, let's not create problems where there aren't any."

———

Despite her best efforts to ignore it, the nerve Arnett had scratched was still humming when she pulled up to the house. She slipped in as quietly as she could, thinking Matt was most likely in bed. But he was up, sitting on her couch—their couch—one leg crossed over the other knee and supporting a book thicker than the Bible, one hand gently flipping pages while the other rested on a glass of red wine.

He smiled and closed the book when he saw her. "Hey there. Long day?"

Something panged inside her. "Hey. I'm sorry, I should have texted you and told you not to wait up."

He patted the couch. "Not a problem. I wanted to see you before I went to bed. Can I pour you a glass of wine?"

She flicked a glance at the clock. If she hurried, she could manage a quick shower and about six hours of sleep before she got back up for work. Enjoying a glass of wine with him would take at least an hour—and most likely would turn into something that took far longer. Something she'd greatly enjoy in the short term, but that would leave her overtired tomorrow morning when she needed to be at her best to solve a colleague's homicide.

Not a great way to start things out...

Arnett's words kept echoing through her head, stirring a cabal of worries and experiences she'd hoped she'd dealt with, but which had apparently just been hibernating. *This is why*, those voices said to her. *This is why you've guarded your space so carefully. So there were no hard choices to make and nobody's feelings got hurt when your priorities had to be elsewhere.* Except someone had always gotten hurt, regardless. And by inviting Matt into her life, she'd made a promise to him that she'd find a work/life balance that included him.

She dragged up a smile. "That sounds lovely. I'll get the glass."

Once the wine was poured, he grabbed one of her hands and gently ran his thumb over the top of it. "How did it all go?"

She caught him up as she sipped the pinot noir. "So, the good news is, we have suspects. The bad news is we need to be moving faster. So I'll be up early in the morning again."

He continued to stroke her hand. "It's good the DA has confidence in you."

"Sure, absolutely, except Hayes doesn't want to be overshadowed by me, so that ticks her off. What I really need is a calm, neutral, middle-of-the-road place to hang out in until she finds another outlet for her angst."

Matt swirled his wine. "People like that don't get distracted from feeling threatened. They dwell in that space, and can only feel better by pushing you down. You're going to have to find a way to pull her over to your side."

"Yeah, well, for now I'll have to put that miracle on hold, since I'm going to need every ounce of ingenuity I have to narrow down this suspect pool." She raised her glass. "Here's hoping the blood Sweeney found on the tree wasn't left by some wounded raccoon. Or that the underwater team pulls up a gun with fingerprints intact. And, hell, while we're at it, why not hope he engraved his name right on it, too?"

He laughed as he clinked her glass. "Sounds like I may not be seeing much of you for the next few weeks. And that's what's so great about living together—whenever you get home I'll be here waiting, and we'll be able to curl up together for at least a little while."

"Mmm." Suddenly she felt like someone was encasing her in shrink-wrap. She tried to hide it behind another sip of wine. "How was *your* day?"

"I finished the unpacking, and I got in touch with David. He didn't have much, so he's already in."

"Good to hear, I think?" She rubbed the bridge of her nose.

Matt stroked her hand. "Don't worry, everything's going to work out. Your sister will figure this out, and you'll catch this bad guy."

That was the thing about Matt—somehow when he said it, she believed it. And a wave of guilt washed over for feeling anything other than complete joy at coming home to him, because if she couldn't find a way to get over herself when it came to *him*, she'd never be able to get over herself with *anybody*. The problem resided well and truly within *her*.

She smiled up at him, letting the warmth of the wine seep through her. Then she stood and held out her hand to him. She'd regret it in the morning—but what the hell.

DAY TWO

CHAPTER TWELVE

Winnie Sakurai's eyes popped open minutes before her alarm went off—they always did. She'd asked herself a thousand times why she even bothered to set it, but deep down she knew the answer. She'd never been able to take the chance that tomorrow was the morning when her early-bird nature would fail her, and she'd find herself in a desperate race against time.

Not that she had to race these days. People had warned her about retirement, that when you had a long, fulfilling career that formed the basis of your personal identity and gave your life meaning, the empty days could be a death sentence. Everyone had an example of a loved one who'd slipped into a depression and died within a year of retiring. So, during the year prior to her retirement, she and Nate had written out everything they wanted to do together, now that they were both free. Big things like vacations, yes, but more so all of the little things. Places they wanted to take their grandchildren. New recipes to try over moonlit dinners in their backyard. Books they'd never had time to read, hobbies they hadn't had time to indulge, documentaries they'd never gotten around to watching. New rituals to establish, like solving crosswords together over morning coffee and taking strolls to pick wild blackberries in the woods.

Which meant she woke every morning happy and excited, mind brimming with possibilities for the day. But Nate was an inveterate night owl, so most days she'd bake and read and wake him with fresh muffins for breakfast. But twice a month on the days when Burkefeld Gardens was open, she'd sneak off for a glorious early morning of birdwatching.

She slipped out of bed, careful not to wake him, and pulled on the waiting clothes in the dark. Downstairs she hummed to herself as she filled a Thermos with strong coffee, then slipped a leftover muffin into her pack next to her binoculars and her journal. The temperatures had turned cold, so she chose a heavier coat and gloves. She always seemed to be hot these days, but it was better to be safe—she could always take off the coat if she needed to.

As she clicked the front door into place behind her, she let her mind wander over the magical birds waiting for her.

———

I've always been invisible.

The sort of person people don't notice. The one people cut in front of at the Costco food court, not because they're rude but because they truly don't see me. When I object, they glance around confused, realize what they've done, then turn red and apologize profusely. When I smile and reassure them, they smile back, grateful to be let off the hook and happy to forget me again. If you asked them half an hour later to describe me, their brow would crease and their mouth would wiggle like a fish gasping for air.

And not just visually forgettable. I was the student whose name the teacher couldn't remember until it was nearly time for Christmas break. The cousin nobody remembered when making up their wedding-guest lists. The co-worker people would walk right past in the supermarket, unrecognized. I came to expect it, and learned there are benefits to it, too. People say and do things around you that they shouldn't, give you insights into their real states of mind.

And since they don't find you either consciously or unconsciously threatening, stalking them is insultingly easy.

Except Winnie Sakurai. No, that's not accurate—stalking *her had been easy. But figuring out how to kill her had been a challenge, because she was almost never alone. Her relationship with her husband bordered on codependent, and he rarely left her side. They went to the gym together and they went for walks together and they did charity work at the community food bank together. They played endless games of backgammon and cribbage together. They even did their solitary activities together*— *she read while he watched the news, and painted vases of painstakingly arranged flowers while he sat just feet away in an armchair reading historical biographies.*

I could find only one opening. Every other week, as regular as her disgusting morning-fiber-stirred-into-water eye-opener, she came to Burkefeld Gardens alone at the break of dawn and lost herself in its fifteen acres.

She had several favorite spots, so I arrived earlier and waited near the entrance, watching for the tiny figure with the bold gait, silver-streaked black hair bobbing as purposefully as if she were late for an important meeting. I followed her, careful to keep my distance, breathing in the smell of dew and dirt and decaying leaves, pulling my coat closer against the burgeoning bite of the fall air.

Today she chose the topiary Zen garden, and I had to laugh— *so perfectly symbolic in so many ways. Lined with hedges almost like a maze, the sections set aside for dry waterfalls and raked sand and shaped conifers made convenient cover with easy visibility. She selected a spot at the far end of the grotto, near a* topiary shaped vaguely like a dragon. I judged the angles and the distance as she settled onto a bench, organizing her notebook and pen next to her, then lifted her binoculars toward the copse of elms that bordered the grotto.

Then I waited, watching her face with my own binoculars.

A bird flew up and out of the copse. She jotted something in her journal.

When she looked back up, it was there—the look of pure peace on her face. Watching them transported her, and for the final time, I pondered why. Was it their tiny, unspoiled innocence? Their freedom, the ability to soar unhindered over fields and mountains and trees? Or was it the intimacy of observing habits and rituals she had no right to be party to? I understood the magnetic pull of all those things.

But then, the why didn't matter. I soaked her expression in, allowing it to feed my anger and stoke my resolve. It built and swelled and magnified, and when I felt my fingers clench so hard I thought my bones would crack, I began.

She didn't look up as I approached, or even when I stopped behind her. Finally, when I didn't move for a full minute, she lowered her binoculars and glanced over her shoulder at me.

She flinched when she realized I was staring at her, and the peace dissolved into confusion. When I explained why I was there, the confusion gave way to fear.

I lifted the stone I'd selected and smashed it into her skull. And I didn't stop until she was still, and silent.

CHAPTER THIRTEEN

Jo stood under a stream of warm water, eyes closed, silently regretting both the wine and the late-night aerobics session she'd had with Matt the night before. The cruel reality was that with each year that passed, biological necessities like regular sleep became harder to deny.

An eddy of cool air announced Matt's entrance into the bathroom. She forced her eyes half-open and smiled.

"Hey, beautiful." One of Matt's hands poked into the shower and handed her a cup of coffee.

She gulped greedily before replying. "You didn't have to get up just because I have to. You deserve your Sunday sleep."

His face, blurry through the fogged glass, shifted into a smile. "I kept you up far too late. The least I can do is help ease your entrance into what's likely to be a very stressful day."

"It's gonna be a busy one, that's for sure." Jo took another large sip of the coffee, then reached out of the shower to set it on the sink.

"I got that feeling. Your phone is blowing up," he said.

Her eyes flew the rest of the way open. "What's happening?"

He looked playfully offended. "I'd never read your texts."

She hurried to rinse off. "The most recent should show on the home screen. Can you read it to me?"

He disappeared, then returned with her phone a moment later, expression now somber. "Someone else has been found dead. Winnie Sakurai?"

Jo froze in place. "*Winnie* Sakurai?"

He glanced up and searched her face. "You know her?"

"My God." She snapped off the faucet and snatched up her towel, hands shaking as she tried to dry herself. "She's a judge."

CHAPTER FOURTEEN

Arnett's somber demeanor as he climbed into Jo's car hit her with the frightening déjà vu of a recurring nightmare.

"It could be a coincidence," she said after a minute of saturated silence.

He turned from the window to glare at her. "How likely do *you* think that is?"

She didn't reply.

They hurried into Burkefeld Gardens twenty minutes later, following signs to the Zen topiary garden. A tall, late-twenties Latina officer, hands lightly resting on her belt with a tense confidence as she scanned the perimeter, spotted them instantly. Her nameplate identified her as B. Rivera.

"What do we have?" Jo asked after introducing herself and Arnett.

"Late-sixties Asian woman believed to be Judge Winnie Sakurai, found dead this morning near the dragon topiary." She pointed to the tree in question. "Inner perimeter set up around that section."

"We're not sure yet that it's Judge Sakurai?" Arnett asked.

"The crime-scene investigators seem sure, but the official ID hasn't been made," Rivera said.

"Has her husband been notified?" Jo asked.

"An officer is on his way now." She glanced at her watch. "Should be there soon, if not already."

"Who found the victim?" Arnett asked.

"A man who'd come to the topiary garden to meditate."

Jo glanced around. "Where is he?"

"You passed him on the way in. He's waiting on the other side of the hedge."

"Nearest security cameras?" she asked.

"They have one on the visitor center and one each on the front and back main entrances. They're putting together the footage for you."

"*Main* entrances. Are there more?" she asked.

"Several one-way exits that don't have cameras."

Jo gritted her teeth in frustration—that meant their perpetrator would only have hit a camera on the way in, when it was almost certainly still dark outside.

She nodded her thanks and ducked under the tape. She and Arnett wound their way through the hedges and trees that marked off the separate sections of the topiary garden, and provided an evergreen enclave amidst the autumnal colors of the rest of the park. Clipped, precise landscaping alternated with elaborate, sculpted dry waterfalls and sandy areas stocked with rakes. "I've never been here before. It's beautiful."

Arnett's eyes scanned the area. "I've been, a long time ago. I remember it being sparser." He pointed to a peacock topiary. "I guess things like that don't happen overnight."

Jo nodded, considering his words.

They stopped at the inner tape to outfit themselves in PPE. Jo spotted Marzillo again heading the investigators with Peterson again at her side—given the likely relation to yesterday's crime scene, Marzillo would want to make first-hand contrasts and comparisons. Despite three additional CSIs combing the grounds, the scene was again unnaturally silent, with no casual chit-chat, no instructions called back and forth, and none of the gallows humor that normally allowed the techs to keep their psychological distance while facing the horrors of the job. The implications of two murdered members of law enforcement cast an oppressive net that disabled all their defense mechanisms.

As Jo slipped on her hair covering, a familiar figure appeared from around the far hedge. She prodded Arnett with her elbow. "Hayes."

Arnett responded without moving his lips. "Must've used a light bar to get here this fast."

As they approached Marzillo and Jo caught her first sight of Winnie Sakurai, the fledgling hope she'd been nurturing that Sakurai's death was a coincidence instantly shattered. On the ground between an ornately carved bench and a pristinely trimmed hedge, Sakurai lay flat on her back, a strip of off-white fabric wrapped around her face, sticky from the dark pool of blood matting her thick hair and soaking into the packed dirt. Her mouth, the only visible portion of her face, slashed diagonally in an exaggerated moue, like she'd been frozen amid a scream she'd never finish.

"Jo, Bob." Marzillo's expression was grim as she followed Jo's gaze. "I'll do an official comparison, but I can tell you right now the blindfold is made of the same material. The edges are raw, so my guess is it was cut off the same larger piece of cloth."

"Also shot in the head?" Jo asked, bending for a closer look. A pair of binoculars lay about two feet away on the right, while a Thermos and a journal sat arranged carefully on the bench.

Hayes joined them, planted her hands on her hips, and answered before Marzillo had a chance to. "Beaten to death."

Marzillo waited a beat before continuing. "Skull fracture. Bludgeoned on the back of the head, most likely with that." She pointed to a rock several feet away that Peterson was currently photographing.

Jo stepped toward Peterson, then squatted down to examine the rock. "Smooth, flat, oval-shaped. It looks like one of the rocks in the stacked sculptures."

"It could have come from anywhere," Hayes said. "You're making assumptions."

Marzillo's words became clipped. "We'll do a comparison to determine."

Arnett squatted down next to Peterson and pointed. "Looks like blood all over that end of it."

"And if I'm not much mistaken, several strands of hair," Jo said.

"The ME will have to determine if it fits the damage done to the skull," Hayes said.

Jo forced herself to nod, then stood back up and rotated to take in the scene as a whole. "You said the damage is to the back of the head, but she's lying on her back. So either she didn't die right away or the killer moved her after she was dead?"

"Until I get the ME's report back, I can't tell you how many times the killer struck her, and thus can't tell you how likely it was she was instantly knocked out. Either way we know the killer put the blindfold on after the injury, so my guess is he moved her in the course of tying it or slipping it on."

Arnett tilted his head. "Seems like it'd be easier to just lift the head and put on the blindfold than flip her over and still have to lift her head to put on the blindfold."

"Exactly right. So either Winnie fell that way, or she was moved to that position for some other reason. But—hang on. Something about this is familiar." Jo took a step back for a more bird's-eye view.

"The blindfold isn't enough for you?" Hayes sniped.

"The arms. Look—both away from her sides, one palm up and the other down." Jo gestured to each.

"Probably just how the body naturally fell after the killer put on the blindfold," Hayes said.

Jo pulled up a picture of Sandra Ashville, and held it out to Arnett. "See?"

Marzillo and Hayes stepped in to peer at the phone.

"You're right. Left arm up, right arm down in both cases, at very similar angles." Arnett turned to Marzillo. "How likely is it that she fell that way?"

Marzillo didn't hesitate. "Extremely unlikely for even one person. For two to fall the same way? Astronomical odds against it."

Hayes' face reddened. "We'll test it out with a lab dummy."

Jo decided not to push the point. "Other than that, this murder is substantially different from the first. Sandra was shot, Winnie was bludgeoned. Public versus private location. The killer didn't even try to hide the murder weapon here, but we haven't found one at Sandra's scene." She paused to confirm with Marzillo.

"Nope," Marzillo interjected. "The divers finished early this morning and found nothing except a few empty beer bottles."

Arnett squinted down at Winnie. "Ashville was shot from the front, but in this case, the killer attacked from the back."

"I'm not sure it's clear he meant to attack from the back," Marzillo said. "The site of the fracture isn't centered in the back of the head, it's off to the left."

Visualizing Winnie sitting on the bench, Jo mimed a series of gestures. "Maybe a left-handed person came up behind her. Or maybe she was having a face-to-face conversation with her killer, realized she was in danger, and tried to get away."

"Second possibility makes more sense," Arnett said. "Sakurai didn't have earbuds like Ashville, she would've heard someone coming up behind her."

"And in a setting like this a gunshot would have received immediate attention," Jo said.

"So why pick here to do it in the first place?" Arnett asked.

Jo chewed on her lip. "Excellent question—there has to be a reason. No point mixing up your MO if the blindfolds are going to flag that the killings are related regardless."

"Could be he didn't have control over the setting, and used the blindfolds to make sure we connected them? We've seen that tactic before," Arnett said.

"If that's all it is, why pose the arms?" Jo asked.

"And it's almost unavoidable that you'd get blood on yourself putting on the blindfold," Marzillo said. "Why take that risk if you don't have to?"

"Let's keep this moving." Hayes checked her watch. "We need to get this scene processed as quickly as possible, Barbieri's waiting for my call. And we're keeping it as under wraps as possible, but the press will find out about it soon and will be all over it. I need something concrete to tell them, and we need someone we can bring into custody. So get to work and do the chatting later over tea."

Jo forced her hands not to curl into fists. "Do we have an approximate time of death?"

"My best estimate, based on core temperature and blood coagulation as best I can estimate, is somewhere between four and seven thirty this morning. But since the park opened at six thirty and the body was found at seven forty-five, that may be a more accurate window," Marzillo said.

"We'll see if we can narrow it down more based on when she entered," Jo said. "Anything else you can tell us?"

"Not yet. Until we undress her completely it's hard to tell if she has other injuries we can't see, and we have a large area to search. But if there's even an errant gum wrapper here, my team will find it."

———

Once Hayes left the site, Jo and Arnett interviewed the man who'd found Sakurai. He'd stopped on the way into the gardens to get a map from the visitor center, and chit-chatted with the attendant and bought a birdwatching guide before going directly into the Zen garden. He produced the receipt, the time on which verified it would have been nearly impossible logistically for him to kill Sakurai. They took his identifying information regardless, and verified he had an alibi for the time of Ashville's murder.

Next, they located the one-way exit closest to the topiary garden, a metal contraption akin to a revolving door, but with a set of bars on one side that prevented entrance back into the park. Jo examined the clearance of the doors and bars. "Should we have the team fingerprint this? God only knows how many people push out of here in a day. They'll be fighting through hundreds of prints even if our killer was stupid enough to forget his gloves at home."

"Yeah, it's a long shot, but I think we gotta take it," Arnett said. "Who knows, might be the final piece of the puzzle that gets us a conviction."

"One hundred percent of shots not taken don't go in," Jo said, face grim. She made a phone call to Officer Rivera, who promised to send someone to cordon off the exit ASAP.

"So, next steps," Jo said as they waited. "We'll need to make an appeal to the public for anybody who was in the park this morning. We already have a hotline set up for Sandra's death, right? We can put this on the same one."

"And we'll need to review that security footage," Arnett said. "Good news is, this narrows down our suspect list. We're looking for someone with a connection to both Sandra Ashville and Winnie Sakurai."

Jo tapped on her phone. "And since Sakurai retired just

under a year ago, she hasn't had anyone on her docket in at least that long."

"We can also cross off Sandra's husband." Arnett flashed his badge at an approaching jogger. "Exit's closed."

The man's eyes widened, and he made an abrupt U-turn.

Jo watched him check back over his shoulder. "I'm not a hundred percent sure about that. If there was a domestic violence issue in the marriage, Sakurai may have known about it. And something weird is going on there, with an alleged boyfriend we can't find any trace of."

Arnett grimaced skeptically. "Feels like a stretch."

"I agree it's more likely someone Sandra prosecuted and Sakurai sentenced, but we should at least follow through. And it should be easy enough to check if Sakurai ever came into contact with Mitch Hauptmann," Jo said.

"As far as Flynn," Arnett said, "her mystery mentor could've been Sakurai. Judges don't necessarily stop giving career advice once they've retired."

"And if she's angry enough about the death of her career, she might spread that blame to the person who gave her the career-ending advice."

"Easy enough to check. If they were in contact, there'll be some record. Email, phone calls, texts."

"I keep going back to the blindfold and the posing. Like Marzillo said, if you're just looking to tie the cases together, why pick a way that risks getting blood all over yourself? And why blindfold someone after you kill them? That and the posed arms—it's too strange *not* to be significant. But what does it mean?"

Arnett shook his head, frustrated. "Beats me. Hopefully something will pop out when we go over the case files."

A late twenty-something white male officer approached at a rapid pace. "You here to secure this?" Jo asked.

"Yes, ma'am," he answered.

They left him to it, striding quickly back across the park toward the front entrance.

"I've walked enough today to count for a week," Arnett deadpanned as they reached the parking lot. "Laura will be ecstatic."

Jo half-smiled. Arnett's wife had been on a mission to improve his health for a decade, with varying levels of success. She'd managed to get him to quit smoking, and he rarely drank alcohol anymore. But he was still far too fond of junk food and far too averse to exercise. "I'm surprised she hasn't bought you one of those Fitbit things to track your daily steps."

He wouldn't meet her eyes.

"She did buy you one?" She glanced to his wrist. "Where is it?"

"After I *lost* the third one, she gave up." He put finger quotes around the word 'lost.'

Jo started to laugh, but the sound died in her throat as a car pulled into the parking lot. "Dammit."

Arnett followed her gaze. "Lacey Bernard. How in hell did she get here so fast?"

CHAPTER FIFTEEN

Bernard strode up to them. "Detectives. A judge has been murdered?"

Jo kept her face impassive. "Ms. Bernard, the prodigal early bird. We don't have verification of identity yet. What makes you think the victim is a judge?"

Something flashed over Bernard's face, quickly replaced by annoyance. "Come on, Detective. You said you'd play straight with me if I kept your secret. Did you see anything in yesterday's reports about a bag over Sandra Ashville's head? No, you did not. Ball's in your court."

Jo called over to Officer Rivera. "Has the husband confirmed identity yet?"

Rivera's eyes flicked to Bernard and back to Jo. "He has."

Jo reoriented to Bernard. "Judge Winnie Sakurai, retired. The manner of death has not been confirmed by the ME, but we suspect homicide."

"And the cause of death?"

"Still TBD."

Bernard gave her a pointed glare.

"Not negotiable until I hear back from the ME. They're the

experts for a reason. But what I *can* tell you is the ME confirmed Sandra Ashville's death was the result of a gunshot wound to the head in an apparent homicide."

Bernard scrawled on her notepad. "Weapon caliber?"

"No comment."

Bernard grimaced, but shifted gears. "So in the space of just over twenty-four hours, an assistant district attorney and a judge have been found dead, likely murdered. Does the SPDU believe the deaths are related?"

"It's too early to draw any conclusions," Jo said.

"Suspects?" Bernard asked.

Jo stepped toward her. "Actually, we could use your help with that."

Bernard's face turned wary, but her postured perked. "How so?"

"When our lieutenant holds our press conference later, we'll be asking anyone who was at the park earlier today to contact the SPDU. We'd like to talk to them, and look at any pictures or video they took. Since I've confirmed the identity of our victim for you ahead of everyone else, I'd appreciate it if you could also get our appeal for information out as soon as possible."

Bernard nodded. "Any particular details you want included? Items of clothing you're looking for? And I'm guessing an emphasis on people who were around the Zen topiary garden?"

Jo went rigid. "I didn't mention anything about the topiary garden."

Bernard's eyes flicked down and up. "My source must have."

"Who's your source?" Jo asked.

"You know I'm not going to tell you that."

Jo watched her face carefully. "Your source asked for anonymity?"

Bernard pushed her bobbed hair behind her ear with the hand holding her pen. "Something along those lines."

The word choice pinged Jo's radar. "Here's the problem I have with that. You managed to arrive at both crime scenes well before other members of the press. Even if you're listening to the police scanners at all hours, we've been circumspect about this because of the nature of the victims. Only the general location would have gone out over any publicly interceptable transmission. That means your source has inside information about this crime scene. And *that* means they're either a cop, a dispatcher, or the killer himself."

Bernard held her gaze. "You gave me information you said you wouldn't give anyone else. Is it so strange someone else would, too?"

Jo's eyes narrowed. "The detectives in charge determine which information gets withheld and which is disseminated. And law enforcement gets extremely insular when one of our own is murdered, let alone two of us in two days. Whoever's feeding you information has an agenda."

Bernard remained silent.

Jo studied Bernard's face. Her gut told her Bernard was being deceptive, not just being professionally evasive. Still, Bernard had made good on her end of their deal so far, and it was too soon to completely alienate her as a potential ally. She made a quick decision.

"Hopefully we'll know something more by the time we hold the press conference." Jo turned and strode away, raising her hand where Bernard couldn't see to signal Arnett not to say more.

They were halfway to the car when Bernard called out. "Detective Fournier—I need to show you something."

Jo stopped and turned around. "Show us what?"

Bernard pulled out her phone and tapped at it as she closed the distance between them. Then she held it up to reveal a text:

Assistant District Attorney Sandra Ashville was shot outside her home on Lake Pocumtuk this morning. One down.

An aching chill gripped Jo. "Whose number is that?"

Bernard glanced around. "I have no idea. I tried to trace it and couldn't. But there's more." She tapped again, then displayed another text:

Judge Winnie Sakurai was killed this morning in the Zen topiary garden of Burkefeld Gardens. Two down.

Jo again checked the source. "From a different number."

"Yes," Bernard said. "I couldn't trace that one, either."

Jo met and held her eyes. "Failing to inform us of this could be seen as obstruction of justice."

"That's why I'm informing you now." Fear showed in Bernard's eyes. "When I got it, my first instinct was not to look a gift horse in the mouth. I was thinking more in terms of *my* agenda rather than what agenda *they* might have until you just pointed that out."

Jo found that awfully naive for a journalist, but didn't have time to push her on the issue now. "Screenshot those and text them to me," Jo said. "Our tech expert will track them. And she may need to see the actual phone and your phone records."

Bernard frowned. "I have sources for other stories I need to protect."

"And we have a killer who's counting down their murders to a journalist, with language that strongly suggests they're going to kill again. And with two murders in two days, that gives us less than a day to find them before the killer does."

CHAPTER SIXTEEN

"Both burner phones," Lopez told them back at HQ. "Let me guess. You're shocked and stunned to hear it."

Jo half-smiled—she would in fact have bet her retirement fund that's exactly what they'd find. "Any chance you were able to trace them to place of purchase?"

"One from a Walmart in Worcester, the other from a Walmart in Boston. Both with cash, so the trail ends there. One about two months ago, the other a few days after that, so the security footage for both purchases is long gone."

"Also not a surprise," Arnett said. "Can we get data on where the phones pinged at the relevant times?"

Lopez cracked the knuckles of one hand. "Already submitted the requests."

Arnett pointed at her hand. "Where'd you pick that nasty habit up? You'll get arthritis."

Lopez scrunched her brow at him. "First of all, *thanks, Dad*. And second of all, that's a myth."

"You're deluding yourself," he said.

"Google it." Lopez purposefully cracked each knuckle on the other hand one at a time.

"Disgusting," Arnett grumbled.

"She's right, I was talking to Matt about that the other day. And, she's been cracking her knuckles for years," Jo said. "But she only does it when she's intensely stressed. Just like you get crabby when you're frustrated. In this case, by murdered colleagues and mystery texts."

"You've been spending too much time with that therapist," Arnett mumbled under his breath.

Jo chose to ignore him. "So. Why would someone send texts to a journalist alerting them to the crime scenes?"

Arnett pulled up the screenshots Jo had forwarded to him. "In Sandra's case, the gunshot was reported around six fifty-five, and this text was sent at eight that morning. In Judge Sakurai's case, she was found at eight fifteen, and Bernard received the relevant text at nine oh five. So each within about an hour of when the crimes were discovered."

"Long enough for the killer to be safely away from the crime scene," Jo said.

Lopez said, "Judge Sakurai's husband confirmed she was alive at six thirty that morning?"

"Not only that," Arnett said. "He had security camera footage that showed him kissing her goodbye when she left at six thirty, him coming out half an hour later to pick up the paper, then leaving just after eight to go to the gym."

"Always good to be able to rule out the significant other," Lopez ran a hand down her long ponytail. "Maybe they wanted to make sure the press was on top of it."

Jo shook her head. "We all know the press are going to show up sooner rather than later, so what's the benefit for half an hour earlier? They sent the first text before Bob and I had even reached the scene. No, I think the countdown is the crucial part."

"Why not just notify us?" Arnett said.

Jo shook her head. "Maybe they hoped the press would be

stupid enough to report the countdown and get the public in an uproar?"

Lopez pulled her legs up under her. "What if it's someone close to the killer who's trying to alert us without putting themselves in danger?"

"That's interesting." Jo's brows popped up over the coffee she was sipping. "But people don't keep a stash of burner phones around without a pre-existing reason."

Arnett shrugged. "If they're involved with someone doing something illegal, it's not far-fetched they're doing something illegal themselves."

Lopez pointed her Rockstar at him. "That. And maybe that's why they didn't want to reach out to law enforcement directly."

Jo wrapped her fingers around the diamond at her neck. "Fair enough. So then why Bernard? She's new to the paper. If you were going to risk passing information to the press, wouldn't it be to someone you knew and trusted?"

"We need to know more about her," Arnett said.

Jo nodded and tapped her pen on her notepad. "The good news is, we should be able to knock two-thirds of the suspects off our case-files list since we'll only be looking at cases Judge Sakurai presided over."

"I'll start in on Sakurai's emails and phone records," Lopez said.

Jo gave a sharp nod. "Let's go."

———

Fortified with large coffee refills, Jo and Arnett dove into the surveillance videos from Burkefeld Gardens. Because of the early hour, there wasn't much to see; only four other people entered the park before Sakurai had been found, and six more entered after. Because of the darkness, even the clearest screenshots they were able to take showed only human shapes with little distinguishing detail.

Once they'd worked through their suspect lists, they came back together.

"So," Jo said, "I've got two possible suspects that involve both Sandra and Judge Sakurai and have situations extenuating enough they might be harboring a grudge."

"I only have one," Arnett said.

Jo gave a not-bad smirk. "Sounds like we're making progress. Hit me with yours first."

"Dantay Brown. Twenty-seven-year-old male in state prison for felony homicide while operating a motor vehicle under the influence. Killed two people and was tried for both, ended up with a total of fifteen years. His wife gave birth to a baby girl just a couple of months before the accident, and has gone on record with the press that she feels it's a miscarriage of justice. She argues that he hadn't had that much to drink that night and there must have been an error with the blood alcohol test, and that since her husband never had any prior incident he should have been given a far lighter sentence."

"I'd be willing to bet the families of the two people he killed don't agree," Jo said.

Arnett tapped his nose. "They've made it pretty clear they don't. I tried calling her listed number, but she's not picking up. I didn't leave a message, because I suspect she's not interested in talking to us. We'll need to pay her a visit. How about yours?"

"My first is David Wheedan. He was involved in a road-rage incident at a McDonald's drive-thru with someone who purportedly cut him off. He tried to bait the other driver into getting out and fighting, and when he didn't, Wheedan rammed the car multiple times. The man exited his vehicle at that point, and Wheedan ran him over. The man survived, but will be in a wheelchair for the rest of his life."

"Sounds pretty clear-cut?" Arnett said.

"Oh, it is, especially since Wheedan has a history of anger mismanagement and a penchant for revenge. He's still incarcerated, but he's got a couple of brothers on the outside who also have a similar approach to problem-solving. I made a round of calls but didn't leave messages for the same reason you didn't."

Arnett made a note. "Adding them to the list."

"My second is Cooper Ossokov, but I'm not sure how likely he is. He was just exonerated with the help of an Innocence Project. Originally convicted of murdering and raping Zara Richards, but a confession and an analysis of touch DNA identified the actual killer as Dale Kranst, who had also raped and murdered several other women since."

Arnett nodded, expression blank. "Right. I've been keeping up with that. I was one of the detectives on his investigation."

Jo did a double take. "How is that possible? We were partnered during that time."

"Remember when you broke your leg and were on desk duty for a few months?"

"I completely forgot about that." Jo had been invited on a ski trip by a romantic interest, and had learned the hard way that a few trips down the bunny slope as a child did not a ski expert make. "Or maybe I repressed it. What was that, fifteen years ago?"

"About that."

Jo sagged back against her chair. "Safe to say fifteen years in prison for a crime you didn't commit could make you bitter."

"He claims he's not." Arnett shook his head "Supposedly found Jesus in prison or some such?" Arnett said.

"Buddha," Jo said. "And, sobriety."

"Whatever it takes."

Jo tapped her notepad. "The point is, he's out now. But why would you risk going right back?"

"Depends whether he's really okay with it."

Jo sat back up and swung around to her monitor. "Either

way, due diligence. So that makes three new people we need to check out in addition to Hauptmann. I'm hoping something in Bernard's background will point us to the identity of our mystery texter and save us some time."

"While you do that, I'll see if I can dig up any sort of aggressive history for Bruce Ashville."

Jo started with the basics. Lacey Bernard had no criminal record, and had grown up in a small town on the west end of Oakhurst County. Once she graduated high school, she moved to New York where she attended SUNY Buffalo for her degree in journalism; she got married shortly after she graduated and her name changed to Grandin. The only employment listed was for a small paper in Buffalo, where she worked until 2018. At that time, she divorced her husband, changed her name back to Bernard, and settled in Springfield. She didn't show any employment again until she was hired by the *Springfield Gazette* at the beginning of 2021.

Jo paused to consider. Thousands of people left their hometowns to go to college, stayed in the new location because they fell in love, then returned home when the relationship fell apart. But to leave the job without having another one lined up? Whatever happened must have been dramatic.

Hoping for something more personal, Jo turned to social media. Bernard's Facebook page was set to private, and her Instagram was carefully polished and curated to create a 'brand' rather than give insight into Bernard's personality. Jo continued scrolling, and as the months passed in reverse, the feel of the feed shifted—fewer professional shots and more candid, personal ones. By the time she made it back to the beginning of the account, opened in 2018, she found a few pictures of Bernard's sister, who'd recently been diagnosed with breast cancer. There were also several graphics for causes near to her heart—breast cancer and sexual assault awareness were recurring themes.

Twitter turned out to be a goldmine. Bernard posted her own stories and retweeted others several times a day. For nearly the past year, regular links to articles in the *Springfield Gazette* appeared, all police-blotter oriented: Murders, robberies, break-ins, car-jackings, drug arrests, some with follow-ups, most without. Then Jo stumbled on a familiar name.

"Well, well, well," Jo said.

"What?" Arnett asked.

"Bernard wrote a series of articles about Cooper Ossokov."

CHAPTER SEVENTEEN

"Coincidence?" Jo asked.

He rolled his chair over to her desk and followed her finger to one of the tweets. "Hard to say. His release was big news. I'm sure everyone on these sorts of beats went nuts over it."

"Right. But read, say, this story"—she pulled up an article—"then compare it with this one about Ossokov."

After skimming the openings, his brows rose. "The other is perfunctory. In this one she has an agenda. You think there's a personal connection?" he asked.

She tapped her nails on the desk. "Maybe. But she doesn't just argue that Ossokov was harmed. She makes the case that Dale Kranst wouldn't have been able to kill the other women if he'd been caught at the time, and that Zara Richards' family were harmed because her actual murderer had been allowed to live a free life for all of those years. She argues all of them should sue."

Arnett's jaw clenched. "So, what, every time we don't catch a killer, the commonwealth should be liable for it?"

Jo swung her chair to fully face him. "How much do you remember about the investigation?"

He scooted his chair back to his desk and rapped his knuckles on a file lying on his desk. "I just refreshed my memory. Zara Richards was reported missing by her boyfriend when she didn't come home after her night shift taking messages for on-call doctors. Turned out she never showed up for work that night. Richards' boyfriend told police she usually stopped by the local Starbucks to caffeine up for her night's work, because she went to school during the day and struggled to stay awake at night. We found her car behind the Starbucks, driver's-side door open, her extra-shot latte on the ground next to the car. A couple of kids out mountain biking found her body a week later, abandoned in the woods. ME said she was strangled, and suspected she'd been raped, but the body was decomposed to a point where he couldn't be sure."

"Why did they link Ossokov to the killing?" Jo asked.

"His Starbucks account verified he'd been charged for a drip coffee two hours before Zara came in, and they had him clearly on their security camera."

Her brow knit. "Wait. I'm sure dozens of people were at the Starbucks around the time she was there. What made him a particular suspect?"

"He was already being investigated for two other rapes."

Jo nodded. "So, when another woman turned up possibly raped, he was an instant suspect."

"Correct." Arnett flipped through the pages. "Our theory was he'd been enjoying his coffee in the interim at one of the outside tables where they had no security cameras, and spotted Richards. He then forced her into his car somehow, probably at gunpoint, drove her out to the woods, then raped and killed her."

"He didn't have an alibi?"

Arnett wagged his head. "He claimed he was with his girlfriend at the movies after he left Starbucks, then went back to her place. But the girlfriend said he was lying."

Jo's head snapped up from the notes she was taking. "Why would—"

Arnett raised both palms. "No idea. And since we subsequently found traces of Zara's blood in his car, that was that," Arnett said.

Jo tried to match that up with what she'd just read. "But he was released because DNA found on Zara's body matched up to someone else? How does that work?"

Arnett grimaced. "Because it was never that clear-cut. Zara Richards' wrists had been secured together with duct tape, and the CSIs found an unidentified male DNA profile on it, one that didn't match Ossokov."

Jo sucked in air through her teeth. "That's reasonable doubt if I've ever heard it. Was his defense team incompetent?"

"Only one defense attorney, and nope, she hit that point hard. But the DNA on the tape was touch-transfer DNA, not from blood or semen. And, the same DNA profile was found on the Starbucks cup found next to her car."

Jo's eyes skated across her desk at the implication. "Let me guess—the prosecution claimed it was transfer from the barista who made Zara's drink. That he left skin cells on the outside of the cup, and when she grabbed it, some of the cells transferred to her hands. Those cells would then have attached to the adhesive on the duct tape when the killer placed it on her hands."

"Not only did they argue it, they showed it." Arnett sipped his coffee. "Got samples from each of the baristas on shift when she got her coffee, and came back with a match to Starbucks employee Dale Kranst. And since they didn't pick up any DNA from anywhere else they tested her, they argued that the actual killer must have been fully clothed, with gloves."

"Because how would the killer leave DNA on her cup, which he had no reason to touch, but not on her clothes or skin?"

"Bingo. And people had barely heard of touch DNA then,

so the clear-cut case of Zara's blood found in Ossokov's car was far more compelling."

She pointed her pen at Arnett. "That's where you lose me. If Zara's blood was found in Ossokov's car, how did he manage to get a judge to overturn the conviction?"

Arnett rubbed the back of his neck. "It's all a huge mess. Turns out, Dale Kranst, the barista in question, had been raping and murdering women throughout New England in the years since. The condom broke during his last assault."

Jo barked a bitter laugh. "Finally a broken condom I can get behind."

Arnett continued. "When Kranst realized he was going to prison for a very long time, he agreed, if the ADA would take the death penalty off the table, to give details about his other murders, whose bodies he claimed had never been found. In the process he also admitted to Zara's murder, as he went into detail about how he used his work as a barista to pick women and learn their routine. Zara came in every weeknight, so on that day he made special arrangements to time his meal break. Once she came in and he made her drink, he took his break, forced her into his tarp-lined trunk, and drove her out to the woods."

"He raped her and killed her all on a thirty-minute meal break?"

"Turns out he regularly combined one of his shorter breaks with his meal break, so he had forty minutes. He laughed and said racing the clock made it 'more exciting.'"

Jo winced. "Charming."

"Oh, yeah, quite a guy. So, ironically, the prosecution was right—his DNA was on the cup and on the tape because of transfer."

"Okay, sure, but it's still possible Ossokov was an accomplice," Jo said.

Arnett shook his head. "Kranst lost it when they suggested

he hadn't done it on his own, and Ossokov had rock-solid alibis for the times of the other murders."

"Okay, so Kranst only had an accomplice for that one murder, then."

Arnett shook his head again. "Except there was nothing to show any connection between Kranst and Ossokov. And also, by then the girlfriend came forward and said she'd lied, that she *had* been with Ossokov on the night of Richards' murder."

Jo leaned forward in her chair. "Oh, come on. How did any judge take that as credible?"

"She said she'd lied because she'd caught him having sex with a friend of hers right after the night they went to the movies, and was pissed."

Jo scrunched her face skeptically. "And she just woke up one morning and decided to tell the truth?"

"She was heavy into meth and alcohol back when she lied. Went into rehab and Narcotics Anonymous and found God. Part of the program and her new born-again life was making amends for her wrongs. The fact that she was willing to risk a perjury charge lent credibility. Initially the judge ruled that her testimony wasn't likely to have changed the outcome of the trial, but once it combined with Kranst's confession, that changed, and Sakurai overturned. She didn't see the point in subjecting everyone to a second trial when there was no way the prosecutor would get a conviction."

Jo sat for a minute, trying to straighten out the twists—something still wasn't making sense. "If Sakurai was the judge that overturned his conviction, he'd have no reason to bear her a grudge. And wait—how could Sakurai know for sure it would have changed the outcome of the trial when Zara's blood was found inside Ossokov's car? It had to have gotten there somehow."

"The new defense attorney argued it was a lab mistake, that there had somehow been cross contamination between the tests.

The amount of blood found in Ossokov's car was tiny, just a smudge. When the CSI swabbed it, they took all of it and used it in the analysis and it couldn't be rerun."

"And no way to confirm equals reasonable doubt." Jo blew out a long puff of air. "Fifteen years behind bars for an innocent man."

"That's one way to look at it," Arnett said.

That struck Jo as an odd response. "What's another way?"

Arnett started to respond, but his phone rang. He glanced down at the screen. "ADA Nguyen returning my call about Hauptman."

———

Jo pulled her chair over to Arnett's desk as he put the phone on speaker.

"Arnett. I'm returning your call."

The brisk, mildly irritated voice pulled up an image of Steve Nguyen in Jo's mind: his receding line of black hair, medium-brown eyes, and jittery demeanor always seemed to fit better in a room of over-caffeinated stockbrokers than a DA's office.

"I appreciate it. I'm here with Jo Fournier. You have a minute?" Arnett asked.

"I'm at the wife's mother's house for Sunday lunch, so take all the time you need."

Jo and Arnett both smiled. "We need to talk to you about Mitch Hauptmann. About six years ago you got the grand jury to indict him for rape, and were lined up for trial in front of Judge Sakurai when the witness bowed out. Does the name ring a bell?"

"You have to be kidding me. What is it with this case that I have people calling me every few months, like I have nothing better to do than relive the most frustrating experience of my life?"

"Who else called you about it?" Arnett asked.

"Sandra Ashville did, a few months back."

Jo raised her brows at Arnett, and he raised his back. "Why?"

"The guy had given her some trouble, and she was looking into his record. Wanted to know all about the rape case, and why the witness bailed."

"We'd like to know that, too."

Nguyen blew out a puff of air. "Yeah, well, I don't know for sure, but I have my suspicions. We had as solid a case as you can have without DNA. Victim was a young, widowed church-going librarian named Arlene Wharton, would have been next to impossible for the defense to drag her through the mud. She described him down to a birthmark on his arm, and appeared fearless, at least at first. I gave her my standard prep talk about how the defense would try to attack her any way they could, and she looked me directly in my eyes and told me she wouldn't be able to live with herself if he did the same thing to anybody else. I went home that night and had happy dreams about Truth, Justice, and the American way. Then the very next morning she called and told me she wasn't willing to testify."

"What reason did she give?" Arnett asked.

"She didn't. Wouldn't say a word, no matter how much I pushed her. But she didn't have to, because the quiver in her voice told me all I needed to know."

"She was afraid? You think Hauptmann threatened her?" Jo asked.

"Her? No. She had one thing that meant the world to her—I think he threatened *her daughter*."

Jo's stomach flipped, and her mind flew to the times when the people she loved had been put in danger because of her— most recently her own niece, and Matt. "That makes sense."

"Once I realized that, I knew I had a gnat's chance in a vat of frogs of getting her to testify, so I had to drop it all. And let me tell you, it killed me to let it go. Then Sandra called and dragged the whole thing up again. After I told her what I thought happened, she made some cryptic remark about having a little chat with Hauptmann. I told her there was no point in talking to either Hauptmann or Wharton, but she just thanked me and hung up."

Jo sent another significant glance to Arnett.

"Got it," Arnett said. "Thanks."

"There's more," Nguyen said.

"More?" Arnett asked.

"I ran into Sandra about a month ago. Since I never heard anything about it again, I figured I'd razz her a bit about how talking to him hadn't worked. She laughed and said, 'Oh, it worked alright.' I pressed her about what she meant, and she told me she'd gone to Hauptmann and told him that there were nine years left on his statute of limitations for that rape, and if he didn't move out of Oakhurst County by the end of the month, she'd put Arlene Wharton and her daughter into witness protection so they could testify safely, add charges for intimidating a witness, and threatening an ADA, and put him away for the next twenty-five years."

Jo's mouth dropped.

Arnett winced. "No way she'd get approval for witness protection in a case like that. We don't have nearly enough funding."

"Exactly what I told her," Nguyen said. "She just smiled and said, 'Hauptmann doesn't know that.'"

CHAPTER EIGHTEEN

Jo's stomach flipped again; from the look on Arnett's face, his had, too.

"Well," Jo said, trying to get her feet back under her. "Sandra was right, he apparently didn't. Hauptmann sold his house and moved to the far side of Berkshire County, almost to the New York state line. Frankly, I'm surprised he didn't leave Massachusetts entirely."

Nguyen whistled. "She always did have bigger balls than most guys I know. Almost makes me wish I'd thought of doing that. Look at her, scaring him straight even though it wasn't her case."

"I'm sure he'll be on his best behavior for the next nine years," Jo said.

Nguyen didn't catch Jo's scornful undercurrent. "Got that right. I asked her why she suddenly got a wild hair about the case when she's in a different unit, but she wouldn't tell me."

"I can tell you," Jo said. "Hauptmann was her neighbor up at her lake house. The annoying kind that makes life unpleasant, with loud music and rats dumped on her porch, and she apparently decided she didn't want to deal with it anymore."

"Holy shit." Nguyen let out another whistle. "Talk about bringing a nuke to a slap fight."

As Arnett thanked him for his help and hung up, Jo rubbed her temples, wondering if Nguyen was missing the point or just didn't care. "Holy shit is right. I can't even count the number of lines Sandra crossed with that."

Arnett tensed. "Intimidation and blackmail, at least. Whatever you call it, it gives Hauptmann a clear motive for murder."

"I don't even know how to process it. I always thought Sandra's integrity was unassailable."

Arnett's face went blank. "Nguyen might be right about her motives. She may have seen it as a win-win: get rid of the pain in her ass and scare him enough to keep him on the up-and-up at least until the statute of limitations ran out."

Jo shook her head in disbelief. "And it lends credibility to what Flynn told us, that Sandra was willing to bend the rules past the breaking point of integrity. Between that and the faked confession, it definitely changes my perspective on her ex-husband."

"How so?" Arnett asked.

"I don't find it at all hard to believe she'd threaten him with a non-existent boyfriend and a non-provoked restraining order if that would get him to go away. Do you?" she asked.

Arnett's eyes skimmed the desk in front of him for a moment before he answered. "Not in light of this, no."

She pushed her chair back to her desk. Her mind was reeling, and she needed to rein it back in. "Recap our suspects and make a plan?"

He nodded, face still drawn tight. "First up, Flynn. Potential motive is she believes Sandra Ashville destroyed her career. If Sakurai is the mentor who advised her to file the complaint, she may think Sakurai tanked her with bad advice."

"Hopefully Lopez will be able to clarify if there's any personal connection between them. We can also ask Sakurai's husband directly. He'd know if they were close." Jo jotted it down. "Then there's Hauptmann, with an even clearer motive, at least for Sandra. He may have decided he didn't want to spend the rest of his life wondering when she'd show back up at his door. But what about Sakurai?"

Arnett shrugged. "Maybe he assumed Sakurai is the one who talked to Ashville about it. Or maybe Sakurai made it clear to him at the time that she knew he'd tampered with a witness even if there wasn't anything she could do about it, and he didn't want to risk that Ashville had talked to her about reopening the case. Hell, maybe he just snapped and decided to kill everyone involved. If that's the case and he does intend to kill again, Nguyen might be next."

"We need to call him back and let him know that, right now."

She waited while he made the call; Nguyen's voice mail picked up and he left a message.

Jo tapped her pen on the notepad. "Next up. Dantay Brown, simple motive. He and his wife are resentful that he's in prison, and Sandra and Sakurai are the ones who put him there."

Arnett nodded. "Ditto for David Wheedan."

"And Cooper Ossokov may be angry he was wrongfully imprisoned. He says he isn't, but that's just what you'd say to the press if you were planning a murder spree," Jo said.

"Last but not least, Bruce Ashville. I didn't find any history of aggression for him, but that doesn't mean it's not there. And if Sakurai knew about some physical threat to Ashville, it would have come out in the investigation."

"So, six suspects. Any favorites?" Jo asked.

"Hauptmann and Flynn have the strongest motives as far as I can see, since they both had strong, recent vendettas against Ashville that may have extended to Sakurai. Ossokov could be lying about being okay with his time in prison, but even if he's willing to go right back to prison, I agree that I'm not sure I understand why he'd go after the judge that freed him. For Wheedan or Brown, in both cases a relative or spouse would have had to commit the murders, and since that wouldn't even get their loved one out of prison, it's harder for me to believe they're our killers."

"I agree. We need to check them out regardless, but since time is of the essence we need to go after our top priorities first."

"So we prioritize Hauptmann, Flynn, and Ossokov. We've already talked to Flynn and Lopez is checking into her background, so we need to talk to Hauptmann and Ossokov ASAP."

"Bring them in or pay them a visit?" Arnett asked.

Jo stood and grabbed her blazer off the back of her chair. "The faster the better. The clock is ticking."

CHAPTER NINETEEN

Once Judge Sakurai collapsed onto the dirt, the same surge of freedom I'd had with Sandra overtook me again. Slipping the blindfold over Sakurai's head and posing her arms felt like severing the ties that bound me. I embraced and relished it as I strode out of the garden.

The lightness wasn't quite as strong and it didn't last quite as long. Not surprising that the reaction would be tempered, because the easy part was over. The moment the police found Judge Sakurai, their suspicions would have narrowed considerably, so I was now walking the fine edge of a very dangerous dance in order to complete my list. I'd spent months carefully plotting out the order of everything, picking the locations and methods that would keep them from zeroing in on me for as long as possible. But it was absolutely imperative that each of my targets looked me in the eye and understood what would happen to them. From here on in the balance would be infinitely harder: while I had layers of back-up plans, keeping all the balls in motion would require all my concentration.

Once the adrenaline wore off, I was starved and fatigued. A quick trip through a McDonald's drive-thru addressed both. As I sipped my large coffee and ate my burger and fries, I pulled out my phone and checked in on my next target. At her desk, chipping away at the tasks in front of her, her professionalism front and center.

I had mixed feelings about that. I knew she'd be busy at work today like so many days, but I preferred the rare weekends when I could watch her with her partner. They cooked together and chatted, and when they finished eating, they sipped coffee together. Smiling and laughing, with no cares in the world. Stabbing a knife through my abdomen.

Because why did she get the opportunity to build a relationship, to be loved by someone? She took it for granted, working late hours, staying away far too often. Chugging coffee and slaving away, always serious. Always stressed.

But today she had a different look to her: she looked afraid.

Had she made the connection? Had she realized I was coming?

A warm feeling settled over me like a cozy blanket and a blazing fire on a cold winter's night. Watching her own peace be destroyed was a balm to my own, so much so I almost wished I could postpone killing her to revel in the sensation. Maybe shuffle the order of everything so I could watch her a little longer? Maybe send an ambiguous letter, or call her and hang up a few times to poke at the wound? But no. All the pieces were in place, and everyone was looking where I wanted them to. Changing anything would only get me caught, and that would weaken my message.

So, I refocused my attention on the next step of the plan. Like Sakurai, she was rarely alone, in this case because of her busy schedule.

Luckily, I'd found the perfect way to exploit that. One she'd never see coming.

CHAPTER TWENTY

Mitch and Frieda Hauptmann's house turned out to be an oddly sprawling ranch-style home with three distinct connected sections each made of different material: one section covered in navy clapboard, the next in gray slate, and the final, which appeared to be the garage, in natural wood. All together it gave the impression of a caterpillar changing form as it struggled across the green lawn toward the dense surrounding trees.

"Looks like the construction team went with whatever was on sale that day," Arnett said as they exited the car.

"My guess is if the Hauptmanns had to uproot quickly, they didn't have much chance to be picky about their new place," Jo said.

The front door opened as they crossed the lawn. A muscular white man in his late forties, well over six feet tall, with a blond buzz cut, angry blue eyes, and a black Korn T-shirt over his jeans, peered through the screen. Definitely not the sort of man you wanted to meet in a dark alley, and most likely very much used to making things go the way he wanted them to.

"Can I help you?" he barked.

Jo doubted he had any intention of helping anybody with

anything, and she watched his face as she slid her blazer aside to reveal her badge. His eyes widened, and he took a physical step back from the screen.

"Mitch Hauptmann? I'm Detective Josette Fournier and this is Detective Bob Arnett of the Oakhurst County State Police Detective Unit." She emphasized *Oakhurst County*.

He started to speak, but a woman who must have been Frieda appeared next to him. Also white, blonde, and in her late forties, her muscularity was stringy despite the fact that she was far shorter, to the point of being almost petite.

"Oakhurst County?" she said.

"Correct. We have a few questions we'd like to ask you."

Jo watched the wheels turning in her head.

"This is about that district attorney," Frieda said scornfully. "Sandra something."

Jo hid her surprise at the tone—she'd been expecting feigned sadness or pretend ignorance. "Sandra Ashville. That's correct."

"And if we say no?"

"Then we'll have you brought in."

A series of emotions flickered over Frieda's face before she responded. "Fine, ask your questions."

"May we come inside?" Jo asked.

"No way in hell I'm gonna let you in here to plant drugs or whatever you got on you." Frieda stood straighter and braced her feet. "We've been harassed enough."

Jo considered her approach, and decided she only really had one course open to her. "I'm here because two women are dead, both of whom your husband had a grudge against. I need to know where both of you were yesterday morning between six and eight, and this morning between seven and nine."

"Who's dead?" Frieda asked.

"You just said it yourself. Sandra Ashville. And Winnie Sakurai," Arnett said.

One hand flew to Frieda's hip and she spat out a laugh. "Sandra Ashville's *dead*? I'm surprised it took so long."

Despite the bold reaction, the fingers of Frieda's other hand were plucking at the seam of her jeans, and Mitch's eyes had widened. They were nervous—because they were guilty or because they were afraid of being falsely accused?

"Where were you this morning, and yesterday morning?" Arnett asked.

"I work over at the Atomic Raccoon, just off the pike," Frieda said. "It takes an hour to close up the place and it's a twenty-minute drive home, so I don't get home 'til at least a little after three on Friday and Saturday nights. In bed by four, and then I slept 'til noon."

Jo's eyes flicked to Mitch. "And you?"

"I was working Saturday, starting at six. This morning I slept in."

"Do you have anybody besides each other who can confirm that?"

"Nope." Frieda's eyes blazed.

"Where do you work?" Arnett asked Mitch.

"My brother and my cousin have construction companies, and I work wherever they need me to."

"What's the name and number of the one you were working with yesterday?"

Mitch jerked a phone out of his pants, tapped at it, then read off a name and number.

Jo turned back to Frieda, who was now gripping the seams of both legs. "One of the neighbors at your previous residence told us Sandra Ashville called the cops on you during a Fourth of July party?"

Frieda's face came alive. "Who does that on the Fourth of fricken' July? Yes, the music was loud. We were celebrating the *birth of our nation*. I could see it if it had been like one in the morning. But it was *eleven*. Give me a break."

"She didn't come talk to you first?" Jo asked, putting on a veneer of incredulity.

"Oh, she did. I told her she needed to relax and have a drink, or something stronger. You should have seen the puss on her, like she'd been sucking on a lemon. She just turned around and left, and next thing we know, the cops show up. They made up some crap about how Mitch had the Jet Ski turned on when he was intoxicated, and hauled him off."

"It wasn't turned on?" Jo asked.

"Hell no, the Jet Ski wasn't turned on," Frieda said, warming to her subject. "He wasn't even *on the Jet Ski*. The cop came in with an agenda."

"And you think Sandra Ashville was responsible for it?"

Both hands found her hips now. "I *know* she was. She told us herself, later."

Jo was careful to keep her face blank. "You confronted her?"

"No, *she* confronted *us*. Told us what she did for a living and threatened to— threatened us."

"What did she threaten?" Jo asked.

Frieda's eyes shifted to Mitch and back. "Just that she'd have the cops make up something else and put us in jail."

Jo made a show of looking confused. "I thought there was something about a rat?"

Frieda's eyes widened—she hadn't been expecting that. "We lived on the lake, in the woods. There were plenty of rats, one coulda crawled out of the woods when it was dying. That's when we knew we were in trouble, if she was going to blame us for stuff like that."

So that was the line Frieda was going to stick to. "What did you do when she threatened you?"

"We got the hell out of there before she could do anything else to us." She gestured both arms in a circle around her. "Completely broke our hearts. That house had been in Mitch's family for years. His grandfather built it with his own two hands."

Jo popped her brows. "You just up and moved from a family heirloom?"

Frieda warmed to the perceived sympathy and bobbed her head up and down. "That's how terrified we were."

Jo put the confused expression back on, and turned to Arnett. "Didn't you say you heard something about a rape charge?"

The color drained from both Frieda's and Mitch's faces, and Frieda's voice tightened. "The cops invented those charges—"

Jo threw up her hand. "If you don't mind, I'd like to hear what Mitch has to say about it."

"I do mind," Frieda said, but fear now tinged her voice. "That was very traumatic for him—"

Jo reached toward her back pocket. "If you're not willing to let him speak, we'll separate you."

Frieda gritted her teeth and nodded to Mitch.

"The cops in Pocomtuk have always hated me," he said.

"Why?"

He shrugged. "Small town. I broke up with the sister of a guy who ended up a cop. He never forgot it."

"But you didn't go to prison?" Jo said.

"Of course not, because it was all bullshit." He shifted from foot to foot "They got some junkie to say I raped her, but I guess last minute she got a conscience and they had to drop the case. But maybe next time I won't be so lucky, so it was better to get out of the county where I can get a fair shake."

Jo decided it wasn't worth pointing out the inconsistencies with his version of the story and shifted back to Frieda. "You said you were surprised it took so long for Sandra Ashville to show up dead. Do you know of someone who wanted to harm her?"

Frieda's chin jutted out. "Not specifically, but people who

think they rule the world don't just act like that once. Looks like she finally messed with the wrong person."

Jo watched both their faces carefully before asking the next question. "Do you own or have access to any firearms?"

Frieda cleared her throat. "All our guns are registered. We have a right to protect ourselves and our property."

"List them." Arnett's pen was poised over his notebook.

Mitch took over. "They're mostly mine. I have a Glock 19, a Luger, and a SIG Sauer 522 LR."

Jo nodded as Arnett jotted them down. "You said mostly yours. Anything else?"

"I have a Beretta," Frieda said, voice far quieter.

"What caliber?" Jo asked.

"Twenty-two."

CHAPTER TWENTY-ONE

Jo scanned the flaming red, yellow, and orange trees whizzing past her window as Arnett drove back toward Oakhurst. "I'm amazed they were willing to let us take the guns without a warrant."

"They know the writing's on the wall. We'd've been back with a warrant for more than just the guns."

"We still will if I have anything to say about it," Jo said. "Marzillo can put a ballistics expert on the two that are the same caliber as the gun, and hopefully we'll have a match to the bullet and a warrant by the end of the day."

"Seems unlikely to be the rifle given the close-range nature of the entrance wound," Arnett said. "But the pistol fits."

"Mitch could have used her gun, but after meeting her, I think we have to consider she may be the killer. She definitely seems to be the one in control there."

He scratched his chin. "And we only looked at him. Very sexist of us."

"No time like the present," Jo said, and tapped into the MCT. "Interesting version of the story they told."

Arnett sped up onto the pike. "How stupid do you have to be to not realize we have access to all the facts? Junkie, my ass."

Jo reached for her necklace. "It would be one thing if Ashville had just done what she'd threatened—gone to the witness and asked her to testify again, gone to the DA and asked for witness protection. But to use another person's victimization to get what you want? When waters get murky like that, scary things hide below the surface."

Arnett nodded, but kept his eyes on the road.

"And I'm wondering about the cops who showed up on the Fourth of July. Did she just make a noise complaint and the cops were over-aggressive, or did she specifically ask them to send a message? Frieda's posture completely shifted when she was telling us that part of the story, and her anger was different. I think she might have been telling the truth."

"Either way is possible. But it's not like the officer's gonna admit it one way or the other," Arnett said.

Jo's phone rang. She glanced at the screen, hoping it was Marzillo or Lopez with an update. But the picture of her brother-in-law's dark hair, blue eyes, and too-charming smile popped onto the screen. "Oh great, it's David. What the hell could he possibly want?"

Arnett shot her a sympathetic look. "Sounds like a fun call. You going to take it?"

"Whatever it is, putting it off isn't going to help." She took a deep breath and raised the phone to her ear. "David. What's up?"

"Hi, Jo. Is now a bad time?" David's voice floated over the line with a practiced nonchalance.

Jo reached for the right balance between *so-nice-to-hear-from-you* and *die-in-a-fire-you-cheating-ass*. "No, actually, we're in transit and I may not have another chance for a while. What's up?"

"Oh, well." He hesitated, then dove back in. "I'm calling to thank you for giving me the OK to move into Matt's place. I wasn't sure you'd be willing to allow it."

It was Jo's turn to hesitate—she hadn't anticipated hearing from him directly. And, she was fairly sure he wasn't just calling to say thank you. "It doesn't do anybody any good to have you out on the street."

He laughed awkwardly. "Well, I appreciate it more than I can say, especially since Matt's place is furnished. I'd really hate to have to squander the girls' college fund on furniture that'll just end up on the sidewalk in a few months."

She bristled. "You're assuming quite a lot. It might be better to get yourself settled into a new life sooner rather than later."

She caught Arnett's wince—apparently she'd erred too far on the side of *die-in-a-fire*. She cleared her throat and made a stab at civility. "How are you settling in?"

"All finished." His voice was artificially light—her words had stung. "I only had a couple of suitcases. But now that I'm not in a hotel I'll have room to bring over a few more things from home. Quite a situation, isn't it?"

"It sure is."

Cue moment of awkward silence.

"Was there another reason you called?" Jo finally asked.

"Jo, you and I have always gotten along well, right?" His words came out in a rush. "I've always been fond of you and I've always felt you were fond of me."

Jo pinched the bridge of her nose as she forced back the snarky comments popping through her brain like kernels of corn. "I always considered you a good guy, David. But I can't lie, you impregnating another woman did put a dent in that."

"Deservedly so. What I did was wrong, very wrong, and I'll regret hurting your sister for the rest of my life."

"But?" Jo prompted.

"I've heard you talk about infidelity before, especially your father's and Bob's. About how it's rarely one person's fault when someone philanders."

Jo shot a sideways glance at Arnett and said a silent prayer of thanks that she hadn't put the call through the car's speaker-phone. About nine years before, Arnett had discovered his wife Laura was cheating on him. He loved her more than life itself, so when she asked him to go to counseling, he'd agreed. He also listened carefully to what she'd said there: that he'd been emotionally absent in their relationship for years thanks to the demands of his job, and she was lonely. Bob agreed to change that, and they'd managed to save their marriage. Jo's parents' story was the same, but with the opposite outcome, because her father had refused to hear her mother. David knew very well the implications of the scenarios he was invoking.

"*Philanders*," Jo said. "That's a quaint word for it."

"Cheats, then. Has an affair. Fucks around."

Jo flinched at the profanity. David rarely swore, and only in moments of very heightened emotion.

"*Philanders* works fine," she mumbled.

He seized onto her shift in tone. "You of all people know that Sophie isn't the easiest person to live with."

"So this is Sophie's fault?"

"My choices are my own fault. What I'm trying to say is those choices didn't spring from nowhere."

Jo gritted her teeth. Her rampant, automatic ability to see things through other people's eyes was part of the reason she was a good detective. But right now, it was a curse rather than a blessing because as much as she didn't want to see his perspective, she couldn't help it. For most of their lives she and Sophie had gotten along like cats in a burlap bag. Sophie resented that Jo's dedication to her work left Sophie taking care of family obligations alone, and Jo rebelled against Sophie's martyred barbs. Jo knew all too well the sort of arctic frostbite Sophie could inflict, she had to admit David had probably lost more than one toe to it. But there was also no way on God's green earth she was ever going to admit that to him.

"I don't know what went on inside your marriage, and I don't really want to," she said, hand tightening around the phone. "She's my sister, and I'm on her side. Period."

"And I wouldn't expect anything else. But I know you want what's best for her. Do you really think divorcing me is what's best for her?"

Jo stared out at the trees lining the highway. "I have no idea what's best for her." As it was, she couldn't even figure out what was best for herself, especially when it came to men.

"Look, I'm not trying to get you to think well of me. But I love your sister and I think the best thing is for us to be together. I made a mistake, but I learn from my mistakes. I truly believe we can come back even stronger for having gone through this."

Jo sighed. "Tell that to her, David. Even if I was inclined to lobby on your behalf, she wouldn't listen."

"Whether she admits it or not, she values what you think. If you encourage her to consider reconciliation, she'll consider it. But at the very least, I'd appreciate it if you wouldn't sabotage whatever chance I might have with her."

Jo bristled. "I would never sabotage you."

"I'm relieved to hear that. Thank you."

Somehow Jo felt she'd just been manipulated into agreeing to something she didn't want to. "Anything else you needed to talk about?"

"Just that the faster we get this sorted out, the better. It's not good for the girls."

Jo bit back the response on the tip of her tongue: *too bad you didn't think about the girls before you jumped in bed with another woman.* "Rushing Sophie isn't a good idea. The girls are strong, and they're not the first children to have to deal with divorce. They'll be fine."

She hung up the phone and sagged back against the car seat. "I can't believe he had the nerve to call me."

"Is your sister taking his calls?"

"She's limiting their exchanges to texts so she won't be swayed by his 'sexy' voice."

Arnett shot her a wide-eyed TMI glare.

She broke out laughing, grateful for the tension relief. "Yeah, that's pretty much how I feel about it. I wish I could tell if he's sincere about wanting to repair the marriage."

Arnett wagged his head. "I'm not sure that's the right question to ask."

She turned to him. "What do you mean?"

He cleared his throat. "One of the things our marriage counselor said that stuck with me was the difference between expectations and boundaries."

Jo raised her brows but remained silent; Arnett rarely talked about anything to do with therapy, and she didn't want to derail him.

"You can't control or guarantee other people's behaviors, so you can't have any expectations about them. You can only stand firm in your own standards of how you will and won't be treated, and walk away if those standards aren't met."

"So, you think she should walk away because he cheated."

"That's not what I'm saying." He raised a hand at her. "I'm saying there's no way to know if he's sincere, and even if he is, he might change his mind tomorrow. She can't put her faith in that. She has to decide what *she* wants. And if she decides to give him another chance, she has to make her boundaries clear and not let him cross them. And I don't just mean the cheating, I mean whatever they agree on. Marriage counseling, whatever."

Jo nodded. "Good advice for all of life."

His face went blank and he turned back to the highway in front of him. "Ain't it just."

CHAPTER TWENTY-TWO

As Arnett drove, Jo familiarized herself with the media coverage of Ossokov's appeal and release. She skimmed a couple of print articles that each gave quotes from Ossokov vigorously denying he was bitter about his incarceration. Skeptical, she clicked on a link to a video interview—seeing a suspect's expressions and hearing the tone of their voice always put her on firmer ground.

After a brief intro, the clip turned to a one-on-one interview, with Ossokov sitting in a brown, cushioned chair. About Jo's age, he had blue eyes, medium brown hair, and the pale skin of a prison pallor.

"It's everybody's nightmare," the blonde woman interviewing him said. "Being locked up for fifteen years for a crime you didn't commit. You must have been angry."

Ossokov smiled a small, seemingly genuine smile. "I was angry when I was incarcerated for a crime I didn't commit, at least at first. It's deeply frustrating to be unable to get anyone to believe what you know is true. You feel desperate and hopeless."

The interviewer nodded gravely. "So how did you manage to stay sane through it?"

"I've always loved books and learning, and the only time I ever felt worth something in life was when my teachers rewarded me for doing well in school. So, when I was struggling to face living the rest of my life in prison, I tried to find some meaning in it. I started reading everything I could find on the meaning of life and why we're here. Among other things I studied several Buddhist traditions, and they spoke to me. I began meditating, and I came to understand that my incarceration was a gift. I had no direction in life before I was put in prison, and now I do. Those fifteen years behind bars was the price I had to pay to find it."

"What is the direction you found? A new career?"

"Yes and no. I'm writing a book about everything I've gone through and I'm hoping it will be able to help others find their way through hard times. I was very self-centered before, very lost in my own head. Now I understand that we're put on this planet to make the journey easier for others. That's the only real lasting contribution we can make to society."

Arnett snorted. Jo paused the video and looked over to him.

"He's writing a book? Gimme a break." Arnett waved a dismissive arc.

Jo tilted her head. "He sounds like a poster boy for rehabilitation. And that's what everyone in the prison system wants to believe will happen to the men and women behind bars."

"Any man with half a brain can figure out the smart thing to say." Arnett signaled a lane change.

"But to what end? He's not trying to convince a parole board."

Arnett pointed toward her phone. "He said it himself. He's trying to sell the book."

Jo examined his face. Arnett certainly leaned more toward cynical than she did, but there was something else underlying his response that she couldn't quite put her finger on. "It would be hard to keep up that level of quality BS for an entire book."

Arnett laughed derisively. "Really? With some of the hyper-intelligent psychopaths we've met?"

"You make a good point," she said. Psychopaths took all forms, but the smart, charming ones could convince almost anyone of anything they wanted to. "And I suppose it's possible he prepped for this interview so he could come across as genuine, but—he seems sincere."

Arnett shrugged.

Jo closed out the video, and after a long minute, spoke again. "When we were discussing this earlier, I said an innocent man had gone to prison for fifteen years, and you said 'that's one way to look at it.' What's another way?"

Arnett shifted in his seat. "Ossokov was already under investigation for two other rapes when we brought him in for Zara Richards' murder. The ADA even had a DNA match from one of the rape kits, so he'd likely have been sentenced to the maximum sentence times two for those alone if the cases hadn't been put aside in favor of Zara Richards. He's well aware he served far less than the thirty years he was facing otherwise, and the statute of limitations for those other rapes has expired. So no, I don't find it hard to believe he's okay with how things turned out. He knows he got the best end of the stick, and that makes it hard for me to see this as anything other than playing the situation for all it's worth."

Jo shook her head. "Why didn't they prosecute the other rapes?"

He frowned. "Sandra was worried the other rapes would taint the jury because they weren't clear-cut, and since Richards' case involved a murder anyway, she felt prosecuting it alone was the stronger way to get a conviction. And if they hadn't gotten a conviction for Richards' murder and rape, the office could have prosecuted the other cases after the fact. They still could, except the statute ran out."

Jo nodded. "And once he was already in prison for life

without parole, there was no reason to waste resources by prosecuting the other cases after they'd already won the Richards conviction. Nobody considered his conviction might be overturned."

"Yep. One in a million thing."

Jo chewed on her lip. It made sense, and fell under the hard choices prosecutors had to make. They didn't have an infinite number of chances or resources to make a case against someone, and they had to be strategic about when they had enough evidence to make a conviction stick.

And, she realized—if he really had raped two other women, he had quite a good reason to hide any residual anger he might be harboring. He didn't need any additional eyes on him—because once rapists and murderers started, they usually didn't stop.

———

Rebecca Ossokov's house in Chicopee turned out to be a small red-brick duplex with twin white-stone driveways leading up to each side of the house. Well-trimmed bushes lined a well-mown lawn. When they knocked, a sixty-something white woman, dirty-blonde hair streaked with gray and dark blue eyes ringed with heavy liner, yanked open the door.

"What the hell do you want?" she demanded.

Arnett's expression tightened. Jo shifted her blazer to reveal her badge. "I'm Detective Josette Fournier of the Oakhurst County State Police Detective Unit, and this is Detective Bob Arnett. Is Cooper at home?"

Her eyes blazed. "I know a plainclothes cop when I see one. Haven't you all done enough?"

A small tendril of guilt tugged at Jo. If Ossokov wasn't their killer, the visit would feel invasive, at best. But she had a job to do, and very little time to do it in. "We just need to speak with him briefly. Is he at home?"

A voice from inside the house called out to her. "Just let them in, Ma."

Her jaw clenched, but she shoved open the screen door and stepped back.

The entryway opened onto a crowded living room. Two brown couches kissed each other diagonally around the edge of an oak coffee table, all perched on the edges of a burgundy Agra rug. Ossokov straightened as they entered, pushing the throw pillow lodged behind his back to the end of his couch.

He clicked off the television and gestured to the other couch with the remote. On the inside of his forearm, Jo spotted a yin-yang symbol tattoo, applied in telltale blue prison ink. "Please sit."

Jo sat on the side closer to Ossokov. "Thank you for talking with us."

Ossokov's eyes followed Arnett. "Detective. It's been quite a while since I've had the pleasure."

Arnett's expression remained blank. "We have some questions we'd like to ask you."

"About the Assistant District Attorney who was killed yesterday?" Ossokov asked.

"Yes." Jo hid her surprise at his candor, and made a snap decision to jump right in. "And the judge killed this morning. Can you tell us where you were both mornings?"

This time his eyes stayed with Jo, and something flashed in them before his brows rose. "Judge Sakurai."

"You haven't seen the news yet?" she modulated her surprise. "Judge Sakurai was also murdered."

"I'm sorry to hear that." His gaze shifted to Jo as she spoke, then slipped back to Arnett. "Yesterday I was here, asleep. I'm a janitor for Denton Dental. I clean up after they close for the day, about seven on Fridays. I finished my work in just under five hours, and was back here a little past midnight. I watched a movie until about two, then slept until ten. Today my morning was as uninteresting as yesterday's. I was here, in bed, asleep, until about ten this morning."

Jo glanced at Rebecca, who was still standing. "Do you have anybody who can verify that?"

Ossokov's chest rose and fell in a steady rhythm. "My mother was asleep when I got home both days. I can tell you the movie I watched yesterday was *John Wick*."

"Do you or your neighbors have a security camera that you know of? Maybe they caught you coming home," Jo asked.

"Not that I'm aware of." Ossokov's index fingernail raked over the battery compartment of the remote, flicking back and forth. "But maybe. I'll ask."

Jo measured his body language and his cadence—he was choosing his words with care. Why?

"I've read a few of your statements to the press. You've been careful to say you don't harbor any ill will toward anyone involved, and that you're just glad the ordeal is over. So you have no lingering resentment?"

The flicking stopped, and he leaned forward—toward Arnett. "Of course I struggle with lingering resentment, I just don't allow myself to give in to it. How would you feel about someone who had you locked up for a crime you didn't commit?"

Jo spotted the twitch in Arnett's temple, and raised the fingers of her left hand just enough for him to notice: *Let me handle it. Every word you say is a potential land mine.* He remained silent.

"I know I'd be angry," she said. "The rational part of my brain would understand that Sandra Ashville had been assigned to my case, that a grand jury had made the indictment, and she was just doing her job to the best of her ability. But the emotional part would be screaming that someone needed to pay."

Ossokov's gaze slid to her, then back again to Arnett. "I just want to live what's left of my life, Detective. In peace. Without the same people who put me away showing up at my door looking to lock me back up." Ossokov set down the remote and picked up his phone from the coffee table. "When I saw Detective Arnett coming up my driveway, I hoped he was coming to deliver some sort of apology to me for what he'd done. I suppose I should have known that was a ridiculous thing to hope for, but considering I've had nothing but a bureaucratic 'apology' through attorneys, I thought perhaps it was possible. But it's clear now you're here to harass me, so I think it's best I contact my attorney."

Jo stood, and Arnett slowly rose to her side. "That's certainly your right. But whether you feel harassed or not, two women who played a role in your incarceration have been murdered, and the SPDU can't ignore that just because it might hurt your feelings. If it *is* just a coincidence that those two women turned up dead shortly after you were released from prison, it would be in your best interest to help us eliminate you as a suspect."

Ossokov also stood, his face still passive, but now he spoke directly to her. "The SPDU could have sent out any detectives in the unit to talk to me, but they sent *him*. Do you expect me to believe *that's* a coincidence? Whatever it is he's doing here, I can assure you, it's a very, *very* big mistake."

Jo very gently raised her eyebrows. "Mr. Ossokov, that sounds very much like a threat. I don't respond well to threats."

He stared directly into her eyes. "Neither do I, Detective. Now please leave my home."

CHAPTER TWENTY-THREE

A chill settled through Jo as they climbed back into the Crown Vic—the way Ossokov had looked at Arnett penetrated to her bones. He hadn't just been annoyed, or tired of dealing with the situation. The look had been pointed. Calculating. "He didn't respond well to seeing you."

"No, he didn't," Arnett said as she set the GPS. "I should've anticipated that and had you go with someone else."

"There was no reason to think he'd respond that way with all the love and light he's been feeding to the press." She turned to him. "Did something happen when you were investigating him that led to some sort of rancor?"

Arnett turned up his palm in a frustrated gesture. "Me specifically? Not that I'm aware of. I was nowhere near the shit storm."

"Shit storm?"

He scrubbed his hand through the back of his hair. "I already told you. The other ADA—Grace Bandara, I think?—already had the prior rapes up in front of a grand jury. It was a battle royale between her and Ashville over who was going to prosecute him when Zara Richards' murder came in. With multiple detectives and ADAs looking to make sure he ended up behind bars, I'm sure he spent quite a lot of time at HQ having a variety of conversations."

"Right. So why was it that Sandra was worried the other rape cases would drag down her case?"

His brows knit. "If I'm remembering correctly, in the one case, the witness couldn't pick him out of the lineup, and while they had a DNA match in the other case, Ossokov claimed the sex had been consensual. From the start the case was going to hang on the one witness's testimony."

"But they had DNA in the Richards' case. Pretty clear cut."

"I think she was worried Ossokov would argue the sex had been consensual with Zara, and that someone else had killed her after. You have sex in a tight car, the possibility of scraping something that's not usually bare and getting a tiny swipe of blood on the dash is pretty high."

"And with someone else's DNA on the cup and tape, the defense would have reasonable doubt." Jo shook her head.

"We've both seen defendants get off with far more convoluted defenses."

Jo sighed. "I keep forgetting to ask. Who was your partner on that case?"

A call from Marzillo preempted his response. She connected through speakerphone.

"Jo." Marzillo's brisk, efficient tone came over the line. "Just touching base. Dr. Krug made the autopsy her top priority given the situation. She's running a tox panel, but can say with confidence that Judge Sakurai was killed by at least two blows to the head, possibly three, that fractured her skull. There are no other injuries anywhere on the body. She confirmed that the contours of the rock we found at the scene, particularly the portions covered in blood, are a match for the fracture. Even without knowing the rock was several feet from Judge Sakurai, she also determined that manner of death was homicide—Sakurai couldn't have fallen and sustained such injuries."

"What about the blood and hair on the rock?" Jo asked.

"Too early for DNA, but blood type matches Sakurai's and several hairs attached to the rock match hers as well."

"Safe assumption then," Arnett said.

A second call flashed on the screen—Lacey Bernard. Jo declined the call and made a mental note to call her back later.

"We didn't find anything in our grid search. However, thanks to your suggestion that the killer may have taken the murder weapon from one of the rock sculptures, we checked all the ones in the garden for footprints and found an impression in the gravel of one."

Jo grimaced—gravel could be finicky when it came to preserving any sort of impression. "How good?"

"Useless for our purposes. It appears to be a depression from the front side of a right foot, but doesn't show any tread or anything to help us get an accurate read on shoe size or type."

"And it could have been left by anybody at any time, even the night before," Jo said.

"Correct. But people don't usually walk on those spaces, so I thought you'd want to know."

"I appreciate it," Jo said.

"I'm heading back to the lab while the team wraps up to compare the fabric on Sakurai's head to the fabric on Sandra's," Marzillo said.

Jo glanced down at the GPS. "We'll be there in about twenty minutes, and we have some guns from the Hauptmanns we need tested. Any chance we can come take a look when you do the comparison? Something about the blindfold seems strangely familiar and I wouldn't mind a closer look."

"Sounds like we'll be back right about the same time. Head on over."

———

Marzillo was typing notes in at top speed when they arrived at the lab, but otherwise looked as cool as a frozen cucumber despite the crushing workload.

"Amazing," Jo said. "No matter how much you have going on, your desks are always pristine, with everything in clear, functional stacks."

"She's the second coming of Adrian Monk," Lopez said without looking up from her computer screen.

"It's not OCD, it's organization." Marzillo cast a withering glare at Lopez's desk. "You should try it sometime."

Lopez waved both arms over her area like she was conducting an orchestra. "I also have a system. It's called controlled chaos."

"Uh-oh," Arnett said. "We interrupted Felix and Oscar in the middle of a spat."

"Yes, very funny." Marzillo grabbed the evidence bags with the guns and set them on a cleared table. "I was just lining up the blindfolds if you want to see."

"Very much." Jo made a warning face at Arnett as they followed her to another table.

"The cloth on this side is from Sandra Ashville, and that one is from Judge Sakurai, hence the identifying pictures."

Jo peered over. Marzillo had placed a picture of each victim next to the cloth in question as a reminder to show how they'd been originally placed. She bent for a closer look, her stomach flipping at the sight of the blood patterns over each.

Marzillo pointed from one to the other. "I want to see if their edges line up. I'm not ready to risk cross contamination yet, so I can't let them touch each other. But I took a picture of the edges, and Lopez is matching them up virtually." She pointed toward a nearby monitor.

Lopez jumped up, eyes gleaming. "I got a new toy, and it's the wave of the future. You know how careful we have to be about rulers at crime scenes, making sure they don't cross contaminate? Well, check this out. It's called a FreeRef, and it's new technology out of the Netherlands, and it's completely badass. They just started field testing it, and I know a guy who knows one of the guys on the team, so I was able to convince them to let us help test it."

"What's FreeRef?" Jo asked.

Lopez picked up a camera. "Short version is it's a laser projector you put on the lens of your camera that accurately measures size so you don't need a ruler. The software figures out all the relevant measurements for you. From there it's easy for me to calibrate these two to be the same scale." She pointed to the pictures on the monitor. "And, hey presto, you can see these two edges match perfectly."

Jo examined the monitor. The line Lopez had matched up seemed deceptively straight until she magnified the images; then slight warping became visible. "So this was one piece of cloth cut into two."

"Yeppers." Lopez beamed down at the camera lovingly. "Now I just have to convince Upstate Ursula to snap us up a few more of these babies."

"The cloth is muslin." Marzillo pointedly ignored her. "There are four grades of muslin, and this is sheeting. Turns out, there are nineteen muslin suppliers in this country, so I'm going to see if I can figure out where this muslin originates and where it's sourced to. But I have to be honest with you, I'm not optimistic. If we had the selvage edge, it might contain some identifying information. But muslin itself is incredibly common."

Jo glanced over the fabric again, then at the pictures. One shot was taken from the waist-up only, focusing on the torso and face, and the other was a shot of the whole body. As she glanced back and forth between them, she realized with a gasp what was so familiar about the poses.

"Oh my God, I can't believe I didn't see it before now," she said.

"What?" Arnett asked.

"She's posed like Lady Justice." She gestured over the pictures. "Look at the arms, one extended up, the other extended down. That's how justice is usually pictured, one arm up holding the scales of justice, and the other down, holding the sword that will execute justice. And she's always wearing a—"

"—blindfold," Lopez finished for her, and grabbed her phone.

"Exactly," Jo said.

"And that would explain why he positioned Sakurai face up, even though she fell face-down. He was trying to leave a very specific visual."

Lopez thrust out her phone, now showing image results for the word 'justice.'

"I'll be damned," Marzillo said. "Nice catch, Jo."

Jo grabbed at her necklace. "But what's the point? We already knew from the choice of victims that this had something to do with the justice system. It seems redundant to label members of the justice system with an overt marking of the justice system."

Lopez smoothed down her ponytail. "Could just be a case of crazy is as crazy does."

"No." Jo continued to peer closely at the pictures. "They're making a statement. You don't take that time and risk getting blood on yourself unless it means something to you. It's the key to this, I'd bet anything. And we've got to figure it out before they kill again."

CHAPTER TWENTY-FOUR

I spent the day watching and waiting, because there wasn't anything else to be done. I'd be fine if she did the same thing she'd done every Sunday evening week after week, but you never knew—people were unpredictable creatures. If she changed up her routine, I'd be scurrying like a rodent on a flooding ship to get everything back in line. So I waited and watched obsessively not because it would make her any more likely to cooperate, but to keep my mind busy lest the hamster on my mental wheel drove me to distraction.

Because my own mind was my enemy, and my existence was a continual struggle to keep myself safe from it.

It never used to be that way—I'd been a happy person before my life was ripped away from me. My childhood was a solid, happy one overall. I can't call it idyllic; I didn't scamper along the prairie and I wasn't greeted when I got home from school by a plate of fresh-baked cookies from my pearl-laden mother. We didn't have much, but we had enough. And yes, I had the typical childhood and adolescent stressors like everyone else: unrequited crushes, disappointments, intermittent bullying. Nothing that permanently scarred me. Nothing that foreshadowed my future.

Admittedly I was a quiet child, but not due to any issue with my mental state. Both my parents worked, so I was a latchkey kid. The only way they could make sure I was safe was to call me at home—kids didn't have cell phones back then—so I spent my afternoons safely at home. I did my homework, and sometimes I watched TV. But mostly I read, because books have always been my greatest friends. You can visit a thousand worlds via books, from past eras to far-off planets to fantasy realms, and you can learn anything you want. How to build a bridge, how to play poker, the thoughts of famous thinkers throughout history. I happily wiled away the hours learning and entertaining myself until my parents came home.

Not that I didn't ever go outdoors, because I did. My father took me up to Quabbin for little fishing trips all the time. We'd head up early in the morning—before the fish woke, he'd say— and row ourselves out to whatever section caught his attention. My mother never came. The idea of "skewering" a worm onto a hook horrified her, and she felt "killing a creature by shoving a sharp mini-harpoon through its mouth and then bashing its head on a rock" was cruel. So my father and I went alone. Very low-tech, without sophisticated rods and reels. We didn't even have bobbers; my father taught me to wrap the fishing line around my finger so I'd feel if a fish bit. And we didn't talk, so as not to scare the fish. We just sat in the boat together, one hand wrapped in the fishing line, the other holding up a pocket paperback, and we'd lose ourselves in separate worlds until a fish tugged at one of our lines.

Periodically I'd look up from my book and peer out over the water, watching and listening. To all the little sounds and all the little movements. I didn't know it then, but it was a form of meditation. And I didn't know how fragile a thing it was to feel safe, happy, and at peace.

I glanced back to watch as she worked—that was a lesson she'd be finding out herself in a few short hours.

CHAPTER TWENTY-FIVE

Jo pulled out her phone. "I think at this point we have to err on the side of caution. Whatever the blindfold and the pose mean, our killer has made it clear they feel they have a vendetta against the justice system. We've already let Nguyen know he might be the next target, and we know Bob was involved in Ossokov's case, but given we still have several suspects, it could be anybody, so we have to get the word out. They've already taken out their prosecutor and their judge, so what do we have left that's probable? Detectives, CSIs?"

Lopez bent over her own phone. "I'll send a blast to the lab."

"Thanks." Jo finished sending her own text out to the rest of the unit. "Next steps. Christine, you keep on with Sandra's and Sakurai's personal files and phone records, Marzillo will keep processing evidence to see if we can come up with anything, and Bob and I will dive back into our suspects. We have it narrowed down enough we can start requesting search warrants."

Marzillo threw up a hand. "Actually, with two crime scenes

in thirty-six hours, I've only managed a protein bar and twelve cups of coffee. I need food, and I need to clear my head for a few minutes. I'm gonna go grab a carnitas plate over at Fernando's to fortify myself, then come back here and work through the night."

Jo's mind pulled at her to dive back into research, but her stomach rumbled at the thought of Fernando's—she also hadn't eaten anything except a muffin she'd grabbed on the way out of the house that morning. If she didn't eat soon, she'd crash. "If you want company, I'm in."

"Please. It'll give me a chance to catch up on Matt moving in," Marzillo said.

With a longing gaze at her monitor, Lopez jumped up and pulled her coat off her chair. "Woman cannot live by caffeine alone. A heaping plate of nachos will soothe my jangled nerves and fire up my flagging energy reserves. You in, Bob?"

He shook his head. "Bring me back a burrito. I want to jump into my research on Frieda Hauptmann, and check in on the tip line."

Jo shot a worried glance to Marzillo and Lopez—Arnett never delayed food, no matter how urgent a case. Lopez mouthed 'what's happening' and Marzillo gave an I-have-no-idea shrug.

"Chicken?"

"Carnitas, with all the trimmings."

———

October at Fernando's injected a dose of much-needed perspective that helped steady Jo's mind amidst the chaos of the previous thirty-six hours. The restaurant was modeled after a Mexican cantina, with faux-stuccoed walls, tiled accents, and chairs in bright, happy colors. But during October, they also decorated in a *Día de los Muertos* theme, with multicolored *papel picado* banners, ornate sugar skulls, and elaborate skeletons throughout. An odd contradiction, she thought as she glanced around, that the theme of death should carry connotations of celebration and fun. But maybe that was the whole point of holidays like *Día de los Muertos* and Halloween—to take back the power that death held over people, if only for a few days. To use the grim reality that mortality is inescapable as a reminder to eat, drink, be merry, and love the people in our lives while possible.

After adding her own and Arnett's order to Marzillo's and Lopez's, she handed her menu to Alma, Fernando's twenty-something daughter, and thanked her.

Lopez attacked the chips and salsa Alma had left behind. "So, what's up with Bob?"

"We had a run-in with a suspect today." Jo filled them in on Ossokov's reaction to Arnett during their interview, but left out his overly cynical responses beforehand.

"Yeah, that'd probably rub me the wrong way, too." Lopez sighed. "Some days it all gets to be too much as it is, let alone with a psycho breathing down your neck."

Jo's brows popped in surprise—that wasn't like Lopez, at all. "Everything okay?"

"You mean besides the mind fuck of someone taking out law enforcement?" She cupped a hand under her chip to keep the salsa from dripping on the table during the trip to her mouth.

Jo took a sip of the Diet Coke Alma set in front of her. "You already looked a little strained when you got here yesterday."

"Not gonna lie, Tony threw a little hissy fit." She paused for a sip of her own soda. "I don't know how you guys manage healthy relationships with this job."

A sarcastic laugh burst out of Marzillo, almost sending iced tea out of her nose. "Whoever said we did? I'm hanging on to my marriage by the skin of my teeth."

"Yeah, but you managed to get yourself married. At this

rate, I'll be past my childbearing years before I even move in with a guy," Lopez said.

"I never pegged you for a married-with-children type." Jo batted down an image of Lopez standing next to a husband and two kids in a Sears family portrait, all made up like zombies.

"Just a figure of speech," Lopez grumbled into her next chip. "And *you* just moved in with Matt. Everybody has their shit together except me."

"It took Jo twenty years to get herself together," Marzillo said.

Jo swiped at a drop of condensation on her Diet Coke. "And I'm not sure I did manage to get it together. As soon as he started moving in furniture and boxes, my skin felt like it was shrinking down too small for my body."

Lopez waved a hand at her. "I feel like that every time I move. That's just hating change."

Jo tapped her finger on the side of her glass. "I hope so. But Janet's right. This is a process. Lots of people don't want to talk about rape and murder over dinner. And even the ones who say they're okay with it turn out to not be able to handle it. But if you can't talk with your partner about what you're going through, you bottle it up until it explodes into something self-destructive. All that makes our dating pool pretty damned small."

Marzillo waved a chip in the air. "Everybody says they want a partner with a meaningful career. But then when they have to put the time into the relationship because of that, it's a problem."

Lopez sighed. "Maybe he's right. Maybe I need to learn how to say no. I mean, look at Sandra Ashville. Her whole life was work, and she ended up divorced, then dead before she could retire. Is that what we all have to look forward to?"

They all stared down at their drinks as the comparison hit home.

Alma appeared, and set steaming plates of carnitas, chile rellenos, and nachos in front of them. They silently began to eat.

A text buzzed Jo's phone. "Dammit, it's Hayes. She wants to know when we'll have the guns tested."

Marzillo's cheeks flushed. "We're up against it enough as it is without her popping up to raise our cortisol levels. A good manager knows the best way to get things done is to back off and trust their team."

Jo's shoulders crept up toward her neck. "She's pissed because Barbieri asked specifically for me. She wants them to know they made a mistake, and you're caught in the crossfire."

A voice rang out a few feet from the table. "Detective Fournier."

Jo tensed at the familiar voice and looked up to find Lacey Bernard closing in on the table. She swore internally—she hadn't returned Bernard's call. But that still didn't give Bernard cause to track her down and disturb her meal.

"Ms. Bernard." Jo didn't keep the annoyance from her face. "How did you know where to find me? Or is this just a very strange coincidence?"

"I went by your building and they told me you weren't there. At first they wouldn't say more, but when I told them I had important information about the Ashville and Sakurai murders, they told me you'd gone for a meal break, and your favorite places were Sal's and Fernando's." She circled the table to Jo's side while reaching into her cross-body bag. "I have something I need to show you, and you need to actually see it."

Jo's annoyance faded, and she turned to Lopez and Marzillo. "This is Lacey Bernard, the journalist I mentioned."

They nodded, expressions professionally non-expressive.

Lacey extracted her phone, tapped it, and then thrust it at Jo. "A third text from a third anonymous number."

Jo glanced down at the phone.

Report the blindfold—or you're next.

CHAPTER TWENTY-SIX

Jo gestured for the check to Alma with one hand and gave Bernard's phone to Lopez with the other. "Christine?"

Lopez grabbed the phone, then pulled out her own. "On it."

Bernard stared at Lopez. "Who's your friend?"

"Christine Lopez, one of the best tech wizards in the Commonwealth of Massachusetts." Jo jutted her chin across the table as she reached for her own phone. "Janet Marzillo, who oversees our crime scene investigation lab."

Bernard's hand shot out to Marzillo. "Lacey Bernard, *Springfield Gazette*."

"Ms. Bernard." Marzillo didn't look up from what Lopez was doing.

Bernard refocused on Jo. "You weren't straight with me. You told me there was a bag over the victims' heads, not a blindfold."

Alma appeared with three take-out containers and Jo began shoveling her chile relleno into one. "Assure me all of this is off the record unless I say otherwise."

Bernard didn't blink. "All of this is off the record unless you say otherwise."

"I didn't know you, not even by reputation. I had to see if I could trust you." She looked up, dead into Bernard's eyes. "Just like *you* weren't sure you wanted to give up your advantage of texting with an inside source."

Bernard's face reddened. "So you lied to me?"

Jo threw up a hand. "Not a full-out lie. Nothing that would put egg on your face. Facts don't always come out one hundred percent accurately early in an investigation, and the difference between a bag over the head and a blindfold wouldn't have been significant. But if it had turned up in the press coverage, I'd have known the source."

Bernard's face shifted to a grudging respect. "Nice to know I passed the test."

"You're not out of the woods yet," Jo said. "What I'm about to say will put a big strain on your responsibilities as a journalist, since you seem to be officially caught in a conflict-of-interest situation."

"It's another burner," Lopez interjected. "*Quelle surprise.*"

"Did you find the source?" Jo asked.

"Another Walmart, this one in Connecticut. We're crossing state lines—now it's a party."

Bernard's eyes scanned the table. "Why would the killer want that information out in the public?"

Jo watched her carefully. "They have a message they want to send. I think the better question is why do they want *you* to be the one to send it?"

Bernard blinked at her. "I have no idea."

Alma appeared with Arnett's burrito and the check. "Well we need to figure it out, fast. Do you have any connection to either of the murdered women, or to the DA's office or judiciary?"

"Nothing different from any other journalist. I've interviewed people in the DA's office, but never Sandra Ashville.

And never Winnie Sakurai. Could it be as simple as me being relatively new to the paper?"

"That's possible," Marzillo said. "They may want someone hungry to prove themselves."

"Or naive enough to do something stupid," Lopez said, sending a glance at Bernard up over the phone.

Bernard caught the look, and narrowed her eyes. "If they have some statement they want to make, why not send a manifesto or some such to the paper?"

"Too risky. The police are reluctant to give a platform to a murderer. The FBI only released the Unabomber's manifesto in order to generate leads when they'd run out of options," Jo said.

Bernard pointed to her. "That must be it then—they want someone hungry enough to push their agenda."

"But why not carpet-bomb the media with the texts?" Lopez said. "Everyone they can get their hands on. That'd at least help justify the cost of dumping a burner every time they need to get a message out."

"And what are they going to do, threaten everyone? No, they wanted to give an advantage to one person, to guarantee that person had motive to react to the texts." Jo scoured Bernard's face, and made a quick decision. "After you told us about the other texts earlier, we looked into your background."

"You don't say," Bernard said.

Jo recapped what they'd learned. "You moved to Buffalo for university and got married there. After you graduated, you were a jack-of-all-trades for a small paper. In 2018 you left that job, divorced your husband, and your sister was diagnosed with breast cancer. If I had to guess at the causal order of those things, I'd say your marriage wasn't great, you had ambitions for a better career, and when your sister got sick, you reevaluated your life, pulled up roots, and moved back here to be with her."

Bernard tilted her head at Jo. "All that in less than a day. I see why you made detective."

"Once back here you freelanced. And a recurring topic we found among those pieces was Cooper Ossokov."

The significance of the name settled on Bernard quickly. "Sandra Ashville led his prosecution. And the judge was Winnie Sakurai."

"You win the bonus round." Lopez shot her a look as she boxed up her tamales.

"Your articles about Ossokov all had an underlying passion rather than the professional neutrality of your other articles. Given this"—Jo gestured to Bernard's phone—"I need to know why that is."

Bernard seemed to consider her answer, then took a deep breath. "No offense, but we all know the justice system isn't perfect, and even less perfect for some of us. I support innocence projects for that reason, so when I realized there was a case regarding someone from my own home county who'd been wrongly incarcerated, I decided to do what I could to help."

Jo pushed down her knee-jerk reaction. She was well aware of the problems with the justice system, and was a strong advocate for reform. But it was like family—you might want to strangle them, but when an outsider criticized them, your first instinct was to defend.

She cleared her throat. "I found your take on it interesting. You were almost more concerned about justice for the other people impacted than you were for him."

Lopez sat forward in her chair. "I read a few of those articles myself. You basically called out the families of the murdered women and told them they had a moral obligation to sue."

Bernard's chin lifted. "I surely did, and I still think they should."

"What we do isn't an exact science." Lopez's face went taut. "Should people sue every time we aren't able to put someone behind bars before they kill again?"

Bernard's gaze flitted around the table before she answered.

"No, of course not. In Ossokov's case, your unit made mistakes. Actual errors."

Now Marzillo's face turned dangerous. "You're referring to the purported cross-contamination of the blood evidence."

Bernard's eyes flicked between them all. "I'm sure it's easy to accidentally touch something you shouldn't when running a variety of tests, and I understand we're all human. But don't you think when someone's freedom hangs in the balance, someone should be held accountable?"

Marzillo sat disturbingly still. "Do you know how these tests are run?"

"I don't," Bernard said, palms up. "But I'd love to learn."

"The first thing you should know is that I don't test DNA in my lab; specialty labs do that. And depending on the backlog we have, which is usually considerable, it's often outsourced to facilities that are privately owned. Nothing whatsoever to do with the law enforcement agency in question."

Bernard's chin bobbed. "I did know that."

"And do you know who ran the test in Ossokov's case?" Marzillo asked, still not moving.

"I don't."

"Don't you think that, if your argument is whoever made that mistake should be held financially responsible, that piece of information would be a crucial place to start?"

"Fair enough." Bernard shifted in her seat. "But I'm fighting for a principle that transcends this one case."

Lopez took over. "If you want to fight for that principle, fight for more funding dedicated to adequate resources to enable accurate, timely evidence processing," Lopez said. "All over the country there are funding shortages and backlogs, so bad detectives and CSIs have to pick and choose what tests they request."

Bernard nodded vigorously. "The backlog of rape kits across the country is horrifying. I wrote several articles about that when I was freelancing, too, because it's absolutely shameful, especially when you're up against statutes of limitations. Which is another ridiculous truth—how does Massachusetts still have a fifteen-year statute of limitations on rape?"

Jo cleared her throat. "This isn't helping. Have you had any direct contact with Cooper Ossokov?"

"I interviewed him once, yes. There were several of us at the interview."

"Did he show you any particular interest?" Jo asked.

Bernard pushed out her bottom lip and shook her head. "Not that I remember."

As best as Jo could tell, she was being candid. "What about Mitch or Frieda Hauptmann, do you have any connection to them?"

Bernard searched the ceiling. "Those names aren't familiar, but I can check my records."

"Dantay Brown? David Wheedan? Patricia Flynn?" Jo asked.

Bernard's brow creased. "The last name *does* sound familiar, but I'm not sure why. I'll check that too."

"I'd appreciate it." Jo stood up. "We need to take this back to HQ and confer with my partner. My guess is we'll want you to do what the killer asks, to get out the information about the blindfold so they'll think you're on their side. In the meantime, if you get another message, respond to them immediately and see if you can get any information about them. Who they are, what they want. And contact us immediately. Can you do that?"

"I can." She stood, posture tight. "But I'm concerned that I've somehow been pulled into a murderer's crosshairs."

Jo blew a puff of air through her nose. "As long as you're doing what they want, you're safe. But I can't say the same for the rest of us, so I need you to think hard about why this person is interested in you. We need answers, fast, or more lives are going to be lost."

———

Arnett stared down at the screenshot of Bernard's new text message. "And she claims she has no personal association to any of our suspects?"

"That's what she claims, but there has to be something. She may not realize how she's connected, or she may be downright lying. Lopez is diving into her financials and other background as we speak."

Arnett jotted a note on his pad as he nodded agreement. "And I think you're right that we can let Bernard report about the presence of the blindfolds. We have enough proprietary information about them being placed after death and about the positioning of the arms to ferret out any false confessions."

Jo took back her phone and sent a text to Bernard. "Letting her know."

Arnett tucked into his burrito. "While you were gone I found out Frieda Hauptmann is squeaky clean. Not so much as a parking ticket."

Jo dropped into her chair. "Damn. But it doesn't mean she's not behind this."

"True. I also checked in with the local PD officers who've been canvassing. Several residents around Lake Pocomtuk noticed a vehicle parked by the side of the road near Ashville's house, but nobody got a license plate and none of the descriptions match each other. I followed up on a few calls that came through the tip line, but nothing panned out. None of my informants have heard anything useful. We have a smattering of descriptions from people at Burkefeld Gardens, also varied and useless."

"Great." Jo tapped her pen on her desk.

"I also managed to catch up with Dantay Brown's girlfriend; she works opening shift at a restaurant on the weekends, and has a solid alibi for both murders. Same with Wheedan's brothers, who are currently on a fishing trip up off the shores of Nova Scotia, and have been for three days. In both cases, those are the only relatives in the area."

"Well, that narrows things down to three," Jo said. "Hauptmann, Ossokov, and Flynn. We know Ossokov intersects with Bernard, so let's see if the other two do."

Jo went back over her original searches of Bernard, hoping what little they'd learned over the last few days would make something she hadn't noticed before pop out, and digging further as she went. Her ex-husband, Thomas Grandin, seemed to have a happy life back in New York; he'd remarried, and his Facebook page was filled with posts about his new baby boy. If there was a grudge between them, it seemed more likely to be Lacey against Thomas than the other way around.

Lacey's sister, Jacinda, had a sparse social media presence, with few pictures and interactions. At first, Jo suspected this had to do with her cancer diagnosis, but when she scrolled back to before the diagnosis, the posts were just as sparse. She'd almost given up when, two years before the diagnosis, her Facebook feed blossomed, full of spiritual memes and happy pictures with friends. She scoured her Instagram and Twitter feeds for any clue as to why she'd shifted so dramatically, but found none.

Jo switched gears, tackling possible connections from the suspects' sides. She brainstormed a list for each, jotting down everything she knew about them. Two possible commonalities popped up. In the first, Flynn, Ossokov, and Bernard had all demonstrated issues with the failings of the justice system; that alone could explain why Flynn or Ossokov would reach out to Bernard in particular if they were the murderer. For the second, both Hauptmann and Ossokov had been accused of rape; Jo's mind flew to the passion in Bernard's comments about sexual violence when they'd talked at Fernando's, along with the prevalence of articles she'd written on the topic and awareness posts on her social media. Jo knew the reason for her interest in breast cancer awareness and innocence projects, but where had her dedication to fighting sexual violence come from?

She considered the connections. It made sense in Ossokov's case, since he'd been wrongfully convicted of rape and murder —except the evidence seemed strong that while he hadn't murdered Zara Richards, he had raped at least two other women. It made no sense to engage a sexual-violence-awareness champion, unless he thought she wouldn't find out about the previous convictions? But that was a dangerous chance to take with a journalist.

The same objection went for Hauptmann, who'd moved to another county to avoid having his alleged rape brought back to public attention. Why would he want to reach out to someone with a history of activism against sexual assault?

Or maybe rape had nothing to do with it at all. She sighed, frustrated; she needed to know why sexual violence was a hot-button issue with Bernard to judge whether it mattered.

Her mind returned to Patricia Flynn, and something about the possibility pulled at her. What had Flynn said? *That doesn't excuse taking the easy route.* Had she been disillusioned enough by her time in the DA's office to kill Ashville and Sakurai in order to bring attention to what she considered inadequate justice? That fit with kitting the victims out to look like Lady Justice, and it would explain why she'd reach out to the press to make sure someone outside the unit and the DA's office knew about what was happening.

Lopez appeared at the desk with a stack of printouts. "Okay, I have a request in for any and all information about the new burner phone. But the first two had no activity other than the text to Bernard, so I'm expecting the same. I also have requests in for location information on each of the burner phones. At least we'll be able to tell where the user was when they sent the texts."

"Thanks so much," Jo said.

"Not done. There are no unknown or unexplained calls or emails on Ashville's and Sakurai's personal or business lines. Nada, zip, zilch, bupkis."

"Of course not. That would be far too helpful." Jo grimaced, and leaned back against her chair.

"But—" Lopez paused dramatically. "I did find some calls between Patricia Flynn and Judge Sakurai. Not recently, but still. They knew each other, for sure."

Jo leaned back forward. "How long ago?"

"The last call was about a month after she left the DA's office." Lopez flipped Jo's sheets and pointed to the relevant call.

"Very interesting." Jo jotted a note next to it, then shared her theory about Flynn. "If she's that disillusioned, she may be channeling her anger over her lost career into a misguided attempt to get supposed 'justice,' and convincing herself it's for others rather than for herself."

Arnett scratched his chin. "Still hard for me to picture a scenario where she kills Sakurai."

"Could be she was angry because she'd expected more from her mentor," Lopez said. "Some people get *wicked* attached in those situations."

Arnett considered. "It's possible."

"I also pulled the financials for Lacey. She got a fair amount of money from the sale of her marital home, most of which went directly into the mortgage on her current place. Other than that, her only income comes from the *Gazette*."

"Great work, thanks." Jo stared down at her watch. Ten o'clock already—how could that be? She pushed a vision of Matt's angry face out of her mind. "So Flynn is very much still in the running. How do we feel about Hauptmann? If he killed Ashville and Sakurai to try to bury the rape charge, why go out of his way to alert someone who'd drag it up?"

"People like that tend to assume everyone is too stupid to figure things out. He was dumb enough to harass an ADA," Lopez said. "What about the wife?"

"A pit bull with a perm," Arnett said. "Wouldn't even let him speak."

Lopez pulled her legs up under her. "Sounds like overcompensation. I don't see how anybody's okay with finding out their husband is a rapist."

"Maybe she's in on it, like the Ken and Barbie Killers." Arnett shrugged.

Lopez raised her brows in admiration. "Okay, good one. But what I'm saying is, maybe she's putting on an act so he won't kill her, skin her, and bury her in the backyard. That would fit with the random texts, if she's saying one thing and doing another."

"That's the best explanation for the texts I've heard so far," Jo said. "But then why tell us 'one down' and 'two down?'"

"Maybe that was just her way of warning us there will be more kills. Everyone knows intention is impossible to read in texts." Lopez tapped her temple with her index finger.

"Then there's Ossokov," Jo said. "The way he responded to Arnett, he's not as Zen as he likes to claim. Bernard is definitely a sympathetic ear, so maybe he pulled her in to make sure she gets his message out there."

Arnett's face went professionally guarded. "Could be."

Jo did a double take—he used that expression when maintaining distance with suspects, not when discussing them with colleagues.

"I don't think we can rule any of them out," Arnett continued. "You have the warrants for the phone records and emails?"

"In process," Lopez said. "Hopefully we'll find something that'll justify a warrant to search their homes."

"What's taking so long?" Jo glanced at her watch again. "I know it's a Sunday, but we're looking at another possible murder in less than twelve hours."

"We didn't know that when we put in the initial request. I left another message for the judge, stressing the urgency."

Jo reached for her phone. "Let me call Barbieri, he'll be able to move it faster."

Lopez's hand shot up. "I'd call Hayes first if I were you."

Jo winced. "Good point."

She put through the call to Hayes. "She's on the line with someone else. It's going to voice mail." After informing her about the texts to Bernard and the implications for further murders, she called Barbieri. "Same thing."

"Maybe they're on the phone with each other," Lopez said.

Jo left another voice mail, then stabbed the phone off and glanced frantically around her desk. "Dammit, dammit, dammit. We can't just sit around and wait for our killer to strike again."

"There's not much more we can do until we have access to at least some of those records," Arnett said. "We've sent out alerts to everyone here and at the DA's office that there's a pending threat against members of law enforcement, and we've contacted DAs and detectives we know are associated with these suspects directly to warn them. Everybody's on high alert. Whatever he tries next, our people are ready. With any luck they'll catch him in the act and we'll be done with all this."

Jo paused, not sure whether to speak. Which in and of itself worried her—when had she ever not felt comfortable saying what was on her mind?

"The way Ossokov looked at you today," she finally said, "wasn't good. If he's our killer, my guess is you're high on his list."

Arnett flapped a hand at her. "We all have a mile-long line

of perps who'd like to take us out. I know how to take care of myself."

Jo studied his face for a long moment, landing on the dark circles under his eyes, and the matching set on Lopez's. "We all need to get some sleep so we can stay sharp. You two should head home."

"What about you?" Lopez asked, indignant.

Jo stood. "Me too. But I think I'm gonna go have a little chat with Bernard on the way."

Arnett grabbed his coat. "I'll go with you."

She shook her head. "I want to probe her on her sexual-violence awareness advocacy. I think she might be more willing to open up to another woman, alone."

"See you tomorrow, then," Arnett said.

Jo didn't miss his narrowed eyes as she turned away.

CHAPTER TWENTY-SEVEN

Bernard's small, gray clapboard house was barely bigger than the detached garage that sat next to it at the end of the driveway. A tiny, quaint creek edged the property; the lawn was uneven, with a thick scattering of dead leaves built up amid the bushes that lined the buildings. The house also was in need of tender loving care, particularly the roof, whose tiles wouldn't make it through the rapidly impending Massachusetts winter.

Since she'd called on her way over, Jo wasn't surprised when the door opened before she reached it. Bernard wore yoga pants, an oversized SUNY Buffalo sweatshirt, and a deep crease in her forehead. She pulled the door back and gestured Jo in.

"Welcome to my humble abode."

The door opened directly into a room the width of the house, divided only by furniture into a kitchen and a living room. A tiny hall, barely big enough to hold its three doors, bisected the rest of the house into what Jo guessed was two bedrooms and a bath. The contrast with the outside of the home was astonishing—walls freshly painted in a warm yellow complemented the red and cream furnishings, creating a happy, cozy, yet sophisticated space. "You have a charming home."

Bernard glanced around distractedly. "Someday when I have the money, I'll do up the exterior to match."

"I hope someday is soon. You have a couple of roof tiles out there that are on life support." Jo smiled to take the potential sting out of the words.

"I have a guy coming next week for that. I put it off as long as possible because I refuse to run up a mountain of credit card debt. Interest rates are how the rich keep the rest of us down." Lacey half-smiled, then pointed to a bottle of wine on the glass coffee table. "Would you like a glass?"

"No, thank you," Jo said.

"Hope you don't mind if I have one," Bernard said. "*Another* one if I'm telling the truth. Today's been quite a day. Please, have a seat."

Jo surreptitiously studied Bernard as she slid into the red armchair diagonal to the matching couch. At Fernando's, Bernard's emotions had been largely masked by her professional demeanor. Now, no doubt aided by the wine, her facade had dropped and her tension was on full display, from the too-wide eyes to the knee that wouldn't stop bouncing. "Thanks for letting me stop by, I know it's late. I'm struggling to get a handle on why our mystery texter chose you. I can't help feel it's key."

"Something about this feels strange." She filled her empty wine glass. "When you have to put your nose where folks don't want it, you deal with more than a few threats. But this is different. My mind has been chasing circles around it, but I can't come up with a damned thing."

"I'll jump right in then. Why did you and your husband divorce?" Jo asked.

Lacey took a swig of her wine. "Lots of reasons. But mainly, he wanted kids. I couldn't have them."

"I'm so sorry," Jo said.

Lacey waved her off. "I'm not. At least, I'm not sorry I didn't have kids with *him*. I *am* sorry I can't have kids."

Jo hesitated—no matter which way this went, it wouldn't be pleasant. If she was wrong, her questions would be insulting. If she were right, the answers would be painful beyond words. She needed the most delicate approach possible. "No chance the problem was on his end?"

"None." Lacey gazed out across the room, face blank. "I know exactly what happened, down to nearly the minute. When I was nineteen, a sophomore in college, I was attacked and raped one night after a late class, walking across campus. As luck would have it, he impregnated me. I chose to get an abortion, and didn't have good health insurance, so I went to a—let's call it less reputable—place. As a result of the procedure, I came down with an infection that left permanent scarring. They never caught the guy. Not even close."

"Damn. I'm so sorry." Despite having guessed something along these lines, Jo felt like she'd been punched in the gut. Her mind flew to her own surprise pregnancy several months before. She remembered the agony of trying to decide whether to keep the baby before she miscarried—how much worse would that agony have been if the pregnancy had been a result of a rape? She couldn't even imagine, after enduring sexual trauma and making the hardest decision of your life, discovering you couldn't have further children as a result. "No wonder you wrote those articles about the statute of limitations for rape."

"Oh, there's more." Lacey laughed bitterly. "My sister was raped two years later. Thank the Lord, she didn't get pregnant. But she was afraid to go out of the house for months. And it really messed up *my* head, too. Like somehow it was my fault it had happened to her, even though she was in a completely different state, because it was so strange that it had happened to both of us. I knew in my mind that was ridiculous, but in my soul, I couldn't let it go." Her hands tightened into fists. "But as it turns out, it wasn't strange at all. Did you know that over forty percent of women experience some form of sexual violence?"

Jo nodded.

"Stupid question, of course you know." She rolled her eyes at herself. "I pushed the cops to find the man who did it, and so did my mom before she passed. And I know they did try. But they never found a suspect, so they never analyzed the DNA from the rape kit. As DNA databases got bigger, I pushed them to run it and check for a match, but by that time, it was a cold case and there were stacks of more recent cases that had a better chance of being solved. And then, the statute of limitations ran out, and there was no point."

A vice tightened around Jo's heart. "I'm so sorry that happened to her, and to you."

"Yeah, well. Like I said, we're not special."

"That doesn't make it okay."

"You know, it really doesn't. But I can't understand how any of it could be relevant."

Jo reached for her necklace. "Two of our suspects allegedly committed rape. Another has shown concern about cases not being prosecuted correctly. Our killer has left clear signals they're concerned about the justice system. Your interest in miscarriages of justice and your concern about rape could be attractive to any of them."

"Well, when you put it like that." Bernard took another sip of her wine. "You think there's any chance the killer only had two victims on his list?"

Jo shook her head slowly. "My gut's telling me this is only the beginning."

CHAPTER TWENTY-EIGHT

Matt greeted her at the door with a huge smile and a languorous kiss. "Hey, gorgeous. You had another long day. Are you hungry? Do you want me to make you up a plate of my abuelita's arroz con pollo?"

The thought of food reminded her of her barely touched chile relleno, forgotten on her desk back at work. She'd been battling nausea ever since seeing Bernard's text. But now, with Matt's arms around her, the thought of the meal sounded nourishing, emotionally as well as physically. "Yes, thank you," she said.

He led her by the hand into the kitchen, where the smells of sofrito, , sazón, and chicken lingered.

"You want some wine?" he asked. "I bought a Gewurztraminer I think will hold up to the spice."

Her stomach rumbled as she considered. "One glass should be okay. How was your day?"

"Relaxed. I ran some errands, spent some time with my family, did a little reading. Helped David get settled in, and dodged all his attempts to engage my sympathy and pull me into taking sides. I heard he called you, by the way."

"That he did. Good times."

He laughed. "How was your day?"

She sighed. "Intense. And worrying."

"I'm not surprised." He grabbed the bottle opener from the drawer of the credenza and stabbed it into the cork. "First an ADA, then a judge."

"But it's not just that." She summarized the day for him as she ate, holding off on her wine until she had several forkfuls of food in her stomach.

"I remember reading about Ossokov. You think what he painted to the press was all for show?"

"Maybe." She rolled the stem of the wine glass between her thumb and forefinger. "Or maybe seeing Bob was a sort of PTSD flashback for him. I've been in situations where a person or a place I didn't expect to see pulled me into a whole different state of mind."

"Absolutely possible, it happens all the time." Matt refilled his empty glass. "But you don't sound very convinced."

She drew in a long, slow breath, carefully considering how deep she wanted to go with her thoughts on it all. Bob Arnett had been her work partner for two decades; Matt had only been her romantic partner for a few months. Talking behind Arnett's back felt like a betrayal of trust—but wasn't that exactly what she'd been trying to build with Matt, a foundation of trust?

She took the plunge. "Something about Ossokov's response to Bob is bothering me—I think because the way Bob is responding to all of it is bothering me, too."

"How so?" Matt sipped his wine.

She took a deep breath. "I'll start with Ossokov. The way he stared at Bob, even when I was the one asking the questions, was... I don't know. Almost like he was *offended* Arnett would show up at his door. If he was just feeling harassed by the unit he'd have been offended by me, too, but he wasn't. Like Arnett's presence in particular was some act of aggression."

"Did you ask Bob about it?"

"I did. He swears nothing particular happened between them during the investigation."

Matt shifted in his chair. "You think he's not being straight with you?"

She raked her bottom lip. "I trust Bob more than anybody in the world, and I can't imagine why he'd lie. And Bob has always preferred to be the backup eyes and ears, he's not the one out front. I engage, he observes. I've always been able to draw people out, and he watches and analyzes. So if a suspect had honed in on someone, it wouldn't have been him, it would have been the other detective."

"Who was the other detective?"

"I started to ask him, but Marzillo called and I forgot. I'll ask him tomorrow."

"Maybe something happened that Bob just doesn't remember," Matt said. "You investigate hundreds of crimes a year. It's like asking me if I remember all the conversations I had with a random patient I saw fifteen years ago. No way that's going to happen, even after I consult my contemporaneous notes."

"Exactly like that," she said.

Matt took a long sip of his wine and leaned back in his chair. "Well. I don't know what's going on, but I know you well enough to know if something about this is bothering you, it's bothering you for a reason."

She put on a teasing love-struck expression and reached over to stroke his hand. "Aw, you always know the right thing to say."

He scrunched his face at her playfully. "I mean it. But you also said Bob's reaction was worrying you?"

Her face dropped again. "That's even harder to pin down. He just feels... off. Distant and closed. I can't help but feel like there's something he's not telling me. You know how when you come back onto land after being on a boat all day and you feel wobbly like the ocean's still moving under you? That's how this feels. Like the ground under me is moving, ever so slightly."

Matt squeezed her hand. "Maybe he's just upset because he knows the people involved? You worked with Ashville fairly closely, didn't you?"

Jo nodded. "That's another thing, actually. I thought I had a reasonably accurate sense of her character, but the more we learn about all this, the more clear it becomes that she plays fast and loose with boundaries. Nothing illegal, but the way she chased off Hauptmann crossed a line in my opinion. And as much as I don't want to, I tend to believe the Hauptmanns that she asked the officer who responded to the nuisance call to find a reason to take him in."

Matt connected the dots she didn't want to speak out loud. "You think Bob knows more than he's saying about Ashville and Ossokov?"

Jo tapped the tines of her fork on her plate. "I really don't want to believe that. Holding back the truth isn't like him."

Matt looked down at the table. "No, not from what I've seen."

"Anyway." Jo set her fork onto the plate and pushed it away. "Maybe it's just because I've had next to no sleep for two nights, and I'm not likely to get any tonight, either, with a killer out there waiting to murder someone in the small hours."

DAY THREE

CHAPTER TWENTY-NINE

Just after midnight, she emerged, changed in her gym clothes.

An hour a day she should be spending with her partner, who was most likely in bed now without her. I had no sympathy for people who didn't appreciate what they had.

My heart thudded in my chest like a dog's tail on a carpet. She was right on time. I didn't feel ready. When I'd planned it all out, I'd decided fast was better. Less time for the police to figure anything out, less time for me to get too lost in my head over-thinking everything. But twenty-four hours flew far faster that I'd imagined once everything was in motion, and I felt like I was on a carnival ride that couldn't be stopped.

I checked the time. It took her ten minutes to get to the gym, and she normally worked out for fifty minutes. She didn't shower until she was back home. Since I was fifteen minutes away, that gave me forty-five minutes to watch and mentally prepare.

The parking lot was nearly empty thanks to the late hour. I parked as close to her car as I could while both avoiding the single security camera that hovered over the front and staying in sight of the front window. The entire storefront was conveniently made of glass, from sidewalk to ceiling, so anyone outside could watch everyone working out.

She stood talking to the guy behind the counter. They always chatted for a minute or two, and he always said something that made her shake her head and laugh for a moment. I decided weeks ago he must be some connoisseur of dad jokes, the kind that make you wince and moan. Most of the people who went in swiped their cards and hurried past. He'd look after them for a moment as they headed in, like he was casing them. Maybe he was.

The instant she walked away from him, her taut expression returned. Then she made her way to the treadmill, a tight bundle of tension, all scowling face and stiff muscles. She warmed herself up slowly over the first two minutes, then in an almost desperate burst accelerated into a full run, as though trying to escape herself. Within a few minutes she hit her stride, legs moving rhythmically while her mind slipped elsewhere. Then the muscles in her face relaxed—she even closed her eyes like she'd fallen asleep. 'The zone,' I've heard athletes call it: a place where endorphins kick in and peace swells from the center out.

I stared, fixated by the transformation. She smiled and wiped the sweat from her brow. How could a few minutes of physical exertion allow her to put it all aside? To put everything on her mind into a box, from the difficult decisions to the guilt from her failures?

A crack startled me, followed by a slash of pain. The plastic lid on the coffee I'd been sipping had popped off, and the hot liquid seared into my clutching hand. Swearing, I set the cup in the holder and retrieved the lid from the floor.

Just as well. She was on to the Nautilus machines now, and she'd be finished soon anyway. I needed to get into place.

The rocks of the asphalt dug into my jeans as I sat behind my car, cold air biting into my cheeks. I focused on my physical discomfort, contrasting it with the warm post-workout glow she'd be feeling, surrounded by the smell of sweat and cleaning products rather than the tang of car oil and garbage from the nearby dumpster.

She appeared, gamboling toward the car, face rosy.

I crouched—I had to time my emergence perfectly—and held my breath as she rounded the row of cars.

Her trunk popped and I sprang up, keeping my steps silent, hurrying up behind her.

"Excuse me," I said.

She jumped, the placid expression on her face replaced by fear before she even saw my face. "I don't have any money."

"I don't want your money," I said, and pulled back my hoodie so she could get a clear view of my face.

Her right hand snaked slowly toward the workout bag still hung over her shoulder.

I planted my feet and swung the crowbar behind my back in a wide arc toward her head. She crumpled like a puppet whose strings had been snapped, and landed at the foot of her car. I hit her again, twice more. Then I checked her pulse to be sure she was dead.

I shook my head as I walked away. Unforgivably stupid—to be caught out alone past midnight, with all the things she saw in her job every day?

But then, nobody ever really thought it would happen to them.

CHAPTER THIRTY

Jo tossed and turned, alternating between being too hot and too cold, hovering in a state halfway between full wakefulness and full sleep, constantly waiting for her phone to shriek her awake.

Half an hour before her scheduled alarm, she woke fully and snatched up her phone.

No texts. No calls. No murder—everything was okay.

She snuggled into Matt, allowing his body heat to thaw her face. His chest rose and fell in time with his breathing, and her own breath began to follow his, pulling her back into the peaceful solitude of sleep.

But the corner of her brain that had been obsessing all night whispered to her. *Something isn't right*, it told her. *Something doesn't fit.*

She pushed it aside and breathed in Matt's woodsy, musky smell. *This* was the beauty of living together, she told herself. How the comforting feel and smell of a person became as much a part of *home* as the walls and roof around you—if you let it.

The cross contamination. It doesn't make any sense.

Her shoulders tensed but she burrowed deeper into Matt's

chest, using him as an anodyne for the confusion and ugliness she wasn't ready to face.

Then her phone alarm sounded. A tinkling, child-like song that would get louder and more insistent if she didn't respond to its first gentle tones—she moaned, rolled over, and turned it off.

"Come back," Matt croaked, voice thick with sleep.

She turned to do just that, but her phone pealed again—this time with the shrill blare of a call.

She scrambled to hit the call button.

"Detective Fournier?" Laccy Bernard's voice crackled over the line.

Jo bolted up. "What's wrong? Did you get another text?"

"Yes, about another murder. Deena Scott—she was Ossokov's defense attorney."

CHAPTER THIRTY-ONE

Jo screeched into the peach-stucco-and-brick Granton strip mall and flew to the crime-scene tape. Once out of the car, she and Arnett strode as quickly as possible over to Bernard, who was pacing near the marked-off area. As soon as she saw Jo, she marched toward them, phone held out in their direction.

Despite already having seen a screenshot, a chill settled over Jo as she glanced down at the phone. This text was more specific, including Deena Scott's name and the address of the gym, followed by "three down." Again sent from a new number, this time just before eight in the morning.

Jo stared back up at Bernard's face. Despite ashen skin and wide eyes, her expression was grimly determined.

Bernard gestured toward the crime scene. "Your dispatch sent some other detectives. I don't think they realized it was connected to the other murders."

"Detective Goran figured it out when he saw the blindfold. He called me on the way." Jo searched past the crime-scene tape for Eli Goran's close-clipped brown hair, and found him standing next to his partner, Charles Coyne. Coyne jutted his chin in her direction; Goran turned and waved her over. "We need to go talk with them. If anything else happens in the meantime, text me right away."

Bernard nodded and went back to surveying the crime scene.

Jo and Arnett checked in with the officer securing the perimeter; once they'd outfitted themselves in PPE, he logged them in and let them past. They hurried over to the detectives.

"This is turning into a habit. The second time in as many months you show up to take a case from us," Goran joked.

Coyne nodded his head toward a pair of feet sticking out from behind a car. "Vic's right over there."

Jo followed his nod. "Marzillo's here already?"

"She lives just outside Granton," Arnett said.

"Right, of course." Jo chastised herself for lack of focus and turned back to Goran and Coyne. "What are we looking at?"

"Pretty clear-cut," Goran answered. "Beaten to death with a crowbar. Perp left that behind, by the way, so I'm guessing he used gloves and we'll find nothing. And put a blindfold on her, like the others."

"Who found her?"

"Homeless guy who uses behind that dumpster as his pied-à-terre. Mickey Millward. Claims he didn't touch anything and just went into the grocery store to have them call us," Goran said.

Jo glanced around the strip mall, taking in the layout. The gym sat on the innermost corner of two building complexes that formed an L. The long side of the L also contained a sandwich shop and a Thai restaurant, both currently closed; the smaller section held a twenty-four-hour mini-supermarket and a Starbucks. The parking lot filled the square between the two, and also extended between the two sides of the complex into the back side, where a series of dumpsters lined the property's fence. "Hopefully someone's got security footage," she said.

"We have uniforms canvassing as we speak," Coyne said, then pointed up toward the mini-mart. "But I'm not optimistic, 'cause of the angles."

She followed the gesture, and nodded. The security camera fronting the market pointed outward, away from the gym and the part of the parking lot that poked back between and behind the buildings. The gym's camera did the same, facing straight out away from the far end of the lot.

"Is there a back way out of the lot?" she asked.

Goran nodded. "Yep, out of sight of all cameras. And there's a break in the fence behind the dumpster you can access on foot. Millward uses it, and told us everyone from the apartment complex on the other side does, too."

Jo rubbed her brow. "So we'll need to canvas that complex."

"Happy as I am to turn this over to you," Coyne said, expression somber, "we're already here, so we might as well help. We can take the apartments."

"We appreciate it," Jo said, not fooled. SPDU detectives always had full plates; their offer to help reflected how disturbed they were by the series of killings. "The faster we can identify anyone who might have seen anything, the better."

"We'll alert you as soon as we have even a hint of anything." They strode off toward the perimeter tape.

"Have you informed Hayes about this yet?" Jo called out to them.

"We didn't want to rob you of the opportunity. We know how much you love your gabfests with her," Goran called back over his shoulder.

Jo gave him a sarcastic smile and wave. "If they hadn't offered to help us, I'd flip him off."

"Not to mention the gathering crowd." Arnett tilted his head toward the onlookers standing outside the outer perimeter, some with cameras out and recording.

Jo swiveled and crossed the pavement to Marzillo. As she

rounded the edge of the car, the rest of Deena Scott came into view. She was short, not much more than five-two. Slender. Early fifties. Dark brown skin, short natural hair streaked with gray. Her simple gold wedding band brought a lump to Jo's throat—she had a spouse, maybe even children, waiting somewhere for her to come home. Her eyes were covered by the blindfold, but her mouth lay open in a slack gasp. She lay on her back, dressed in tight-fitting workout clothes, arms posed in the same position as Ashville's and Sakurai's had been. But while the other two women's blood had been relatively contained, Scott's head, and the pavement around it, was drenched.

Marzillo launched in without preamble, voice weary. "Bludgeoned to death, most likely with that crowbar." She pointed to where it lay, not two feet from Deena's head. "ME will have to confirm officially, but I'll risk it."

Also not in the mood to mince words, Jo squatted down to peer at the brown-stained blindfold. "Added after, same as the other two?"

Marzillo's eyes flicked down. "Much harder to tell in this case. I'll know once I remove it, because if the blindfold was on before the blows, the cloth will have been pushed into the lacerations."

"Time of death?" Arnett asked from Jo's side.

Marzillo grimaced. "I can't be precise until I calculate ambient temperature, et cetera. Best I can guess right now, less than eight hours based on incomplete rigor mortis, but probably closer to the longer tail of that."

"So earlier than our other two? Before dawn?" Arnett asked.

"Almost certainly. Look at the state of the blood around the edges of the blindfold. It's dried out considerably, more than I'd expect in just a couple of hours."

Jo stared down at the gym bag lying next to Scott, and the small towel resting just next to that. "She must have just finished working out. If so, the gym should have footage of her coming and going, or at least some form of check-in tracking."

Peterson appeared at their side. "Goran said she was Ossokov's defense attorney?"

"Yep," Arnett said.

"Narrows down the suspect list considerably, I'd say," Peterson said.

Jo stood, and her hand flew to her necklace. "Possibly."

Peterson cocked his head. "Possibly? Three blindfolded victims killed in three days, all closely related to Ossokov's case."

"Why would Ossokov want to kill his defense attorney?" Jo asked. "He was released because the lab made a mistake that somehow contaminated the DNA results. How could she possibly be responsible for that?"

Arnett kicked his legs out as he straightened up. "General rage she didn't win the case? Or in retrospect he figures she should have thought to challenge the DNA evidence?"

"That's possible." Jo's phone rang, interrupting her. "It's Lieutenant Hayes. Guess Goran and Coyne decided to call her after all." She tapped on the call. "Josette Fournier."

"Are you on your way to HQ?" Hayes asked.

"Arnett and I are at the crime scene," she answered.

Hayes paused. "What crime scene?"

"Deena Scott." She flashed Arnett a confused glance, which he returned.

"Goran and Coyne are on that," Hayes said.

"They called us because she's blindfolded like our other victims," Jo said.

"And nobody thought to inform me of this?" Hayes said, tone clipped.

Jo winced. "We just got here ourselves."

Hayes hesitated again, then continued. "Then you won't

mind leaving Goran and Coyne to it and turning right around. I need you in my office ASAP. Cooper Ossokov's attorney just filed a civil suit against the state that claims malfeasance on the part of the DA's office and the SPDU specifically."

CHAPTER THIRTY-TWO

Jo pulled up the copy of the filed complaint as a too-pale Arnett hurried back to HQ. "You want me to read it aloud?" Jo asked.

"Hard pass on the mind-numbing legalese. Give me the highlights." The tires squealed as he sped around a turn a little too quickly onto the highway.

Jo grabbed the travel mug Matt had prepped while she'd raced to get ready. With her notepad balanced on her thigh, she scrolled through the documents as quickly as she could without losing details—the suit ended any doubt that Ossokov was at the heart of the murders, and she had to sort out how everything fit together as quickly as possible.

An all-consuming chill settled over her as she skimmed the list of named parties. "The suit calls out the DA's office, specifically Sandra Ashville, and both you and Steve Murphy of the SPDU." She glanced over at him to gauge his reaction, and to guide her own.

"Ossokov lists me specifically." It wasn't a question.

"You okay?" she asked.

He shrugged stiffly. "This isn't the first bullshit lawsuit filed against the unit and it won't be the last."

Except, as far as Jo knew, it was the first one that had ever named him. She wasn't buying his reaction—but now, with Hayes looming, wasn't the time to push it. "And Steve Murphy? He was your partner for the case?"

"Yep." His eyes swept across the road.

Jo called up what she knew about Steve Murphy. He'd retired about five years before, when he turned sixty-five. He was a good enough guy, but as old-school as they came. His father had been a detective, and his grandfather before that. He was the sort who believed in baptism by fire for trainees, and if you didn't live up to his expectations, he had no problem letting you know. He held the standard for everyone; as long as you got the job done, he didn't care what you looked like or what you did with your private time. But if he did decide you weren't of the right caliber, his mind was made up. Jo had frankly been surprised when he retired—she'd assumed he'd have to be pried out with the jaws of life.

She winced as she added him into her understanding of the Ossokov case. Sandra Ashville's willingness to bend the rules. Steve Murphy's single-minded doggedness. Bob's strange reactions about the case. Whatever it all added up to, it wasn't good.

As she tried to coalesce it, the half-formed thought she'd had in bed that morning came back to her. Something about the cross-contamination of the blood samples was tugging at her. Why?

She shook her head in frustration and continued to the allegations, spitting out her translation for Arnett as she went. Wrongful conviction due to misconduct at both levels. Specifically, that the blood sample was not accidentally contaminated by the lab analyses, but had been purposefully tampered with. There was no reason for any other sample of Zara Richards' bodily fluids to be present at the time the target blood sample was analyzed since a comparison profile was already available. Law enforcement had been harassing him for years, the suit argued, and when all else failed, Sandra Ashville had directed the detectives to manufacture evidence.

Jo's head spun. She flipped back through the timeline she'd put together in her notes. Zara Richards' car and her cup had been found first. That evidence would have been collected before her body was found a week later. Any of the DNA collected from the body would then have been gathered with other evidence from the body. Ossokov and his car hadn't been brought in until at least a day later than that. But when exactly the samples were sent would have depended on how backed up the CSIs were—the tests might have been sent out at the same time, or they might have been sent out on different days. The only way to know how any of it had gone down for sure was to pull the evidence logs.

With shaking thumbs, she shot off a text to Marzillo and Lopez:

In the Zara Richards case, was Zara Richards' DNA evidence sent out at the same time as the blood sample from Cooper Ossokov's car? Wouldn't they have been sent out and tested at different times?

Three dancing dots indicated Lopez was replying.

We're looking into it.

"Everything okay?" Arnett asked.

"Yeah, just trying to make sense of the timings involved in everything."

She pretended to return to skimming the documents, fingers gripping her necklace as she read. What the hell was going on? One possibility, the one she hoped was true, was that Ossokov was flat-out fabricating the accusations, likely because his whole I'm-not-holding-a grudge schtick had been a ploy for him to buy time while his attorney figured out what to do to help sell his book.

But she herself had been picking up strange vibes from Arnett, and she wasn't comfortable with what they'd learned about Sandra Ashville's methods. So it wasn't a stretch that Ossokov really did believe there had been malfeasance, and he or one of his attorneys had noticed the same oddities in the timeline Jo had.

And maybe he was right: maybe Ashville and the detectives, including Arnett, *had* fabricated evidence somehow.

Every cell in her body screamed out against the very thought. She knew beyond a shadow of a doubt that Arnett would *never* be involved with something like that. His unfailing integrity and unfailing loyalty to the justice system was the biggest reason she'd come to trust him the way she did.

But what if those two things came into conflict—his integrity, and flaws in the legal system? Which would win out?

No—she squeezed her eyes shut against the thought. That would never happen because Arnett believed deeply in *the integrity* of the justice system. He believed the rules were there for a reason, and exemplified the principle that there was nothing a good cop hated more than a bad cop. No way on earth would he *ever* manufacture evidence.

Which left her with one last, desperate option: that Ashville and Murphy had cooked something up between them that Arnett knew nothing about.

She wanted to believe that more than she'd wanted anything in her life. But Arnett wasn't stupid. Yes, she was the one of their pair who picked up on the subtlest signals people sent out, but he was no fool. Was it really possible something like that could have gone down without him realizing it?

She shook her head to clear it and swiped back to the beginning of the document. As she did, her eyes landed again on the specific parties named in the suit—Sandra Ashville, Steve Murphy, and Robert Arnett.

"Why didn't he name Winnie Sakurai?" she blurted out.

Arnett looked up at her. "Why would he? Any misconduct he's alleging would have happened long before the evidence went before a grand jury, let alone before a judge was assigned."

"Right. But with regard to the current killings, if our theory is Ossokov is killing people he's angry with because of his incarceration—if he didn't blame Sakurai enough to name her in the lawsuit, why kill her?"

CHAPTER THIRTY-THREE

Arnett's brow creased as he pulled into the parking lot of HQ, and some of the color came back into his face. "You're looking for rationality in irrational behavior. He doesn't give a shit about the suit, the suit is a distraction."

Jo snapped off her seat belt and hurried out of the car. "So why not throw everything at the wall?"

"I'm sure the lawyer thinks the lawsuit is real, and told him naming Sakurai wouldn't fly. A jury found him guilty, not the judge." He pushed through the building's door.

Jo watched the tiles fly past as they hurried down the hall, her mind churning away, digesting the implications and lining up the details.

ADA Hanson was already there when they reached Lieutenant Hayes' office, posture stiff and face tight. Hayes' shoulders were hunched toward her ears.

"Fournier, Arnett, have a seat." She turned to Hanson. "They're just coming from the Deena Scott crime scene. Apparently she was Ossokov's defense attorney—which means at least now we know who our suspect is. He appears to be killing anyone and everyone who played a role in his incarceration."

Jo addressed Hanson. "How well do you remember his case?"

"I spent the weekend studying most of Sandra's cases, including his," he said.

"Can you see any reason why Ossokov would have an issue with Deena Scott's defense?" Jo asked.

He shrugged. "It's hard to battle a DNA match. It's the gold standard as far as juries are concerned."

"And, ultimately, she took on his appeals and got him freed," Jo said. "So I'm having a hard time connecting the dots as to why he'd want to kill her."

Hayes waved her off. "He's obviously lashing out at everyone involved. Just because she eventually got him off doesn't mean he doesn't blame her for not being able to prevent his incarceration in the first place.

"Or she became disenchanted with him," Hanson said. "If she refused to take this suit on, that could have been enough to anger him."

Jo needed to get ahead of what she knew was coming. "Another possibility is the suit was a defensive tactic to kneecap the investigation and clear the way for him to keep killing."

Hayes cleared her throat, annoyed at having been anticipated. "That brings us to our next point. Since we now know Ossokov is our perpetrator, obviously our next step is getting a search warrant for his home and car as soon as possible. But equally obviously, there's no way Arnett will be able to execute that warrant since he's named in the suit." Hayes turned to him pointedly. "I don't want you anywhere near Ossokov, and that means you can't be anywhere near the case."

Jo held her breath—this was the excuse Hayes had been looking for to pull her off the case. But nobody knew the case like she and Arnett did, and she needed to stop them before they killed another member of law enforcement.

Hayes' face shifted like she'd just bit into something disgusting. "Fournier, you'll be taking over."

Relief and confusion washed over Jo. "I'm still on the case?"

Hayes shot a quick glare at Hanson. "We agreed on that before you got here. We all know this lawsuit is a crock, and I'm not going to allow this little shit to interfere with our ability to investigate the murder of our colleagues by filing a spurious lawsuit. Without Arnett you'll need more hands, so since Goran and Coyne are already helping you work Deena Scott's scene, they'll continue to assist you."

Jo glanced surreptitiously at Hanson, who nodded. DA Barbieri had made the call.

Hayes spotted the exchange. "That is, at least until word comes down otherwise. In the meantime, three detectives should be more than enough considering we know who the killer is. I've already had press inquiries asking if Deena Scott's killing is related to the other two, and I expect to have very good news to give them within the next few hours. That's all for now."

"One more issue, if I may," Jo said.

Hayes looked annoyed, but nodded.

"If Ossokov is taking out the people that put him behind bars—then Steve Murphy and Bob Arnett are next."

"All the more reason to get Ossokov's house searched so we can bring him into custody before he kills again." She nodded toward the door. "Why are you still standing here?"

CHAPTER THIRTY-FOUR

Arnett strode down the hall at top speed. "No chance in hell I'm gonna step aside while this asshole kills members of our own. If it gets me fired, so be it."

"It won't be hard to keep you out of sight but still involved. I'm more worried that the possibility that Ossokov is our killer—"

"*Possibility?* Come on, Jo. What connection do Flynn or Hauptmann or Bruce Ashville have with Deena Scott? The only reason you're resisting the obvious conclusion is because you don't want to face that Murphy and I are next on his hit list."

"That's not what I was going to say. *Of course* Ossokov is at the center of this, there's no denying that. Nothing else makes sense. But there are details that don't fit, and understanding those details is crucial to predicting what his plan is and what his next move is. Who knows, maybe he joined forces with Mitch Hauptmann and *that's* why they took out Winnie Sakurai, because she knew about Hauptmann's witness tampering. Maybe he's manipulating us. But yes, you're absolutely right— the idea that he's coming for you next terrifies me."

He didn't meet her eyes. "Let him come. Then we'll have him dead to rights."

Jo stared at his profile, for once completely unable to guess his thoughts. Suddenly she felt like a pit had opened up under her and she was falling through infinite space. Her work life—for good or bad, the majority of her world—depended vitally on her connection with this man. Without warning, that connection had disappeared.

She grabbed his arm and propelled him into a conference room. Once the door clicked firmly behind her, she turned to him. "There's nobody in this world I trust more than you. You know that, right? Even more than my own mother and sister."

His face went blank. "I appreciate that. I feel the same way."

"I haven't pushed you on this because that's not what we do. Lord knows you've shown me infinite patience when I've needed it, and always had my back without me having to ask for it."

A muscle in his jaw twitched. "True."

"But you've also always called me out on my BS when I needed *that*. So now it's my turn." She locked her hands firmly onto her hips. "I need to know what the hell is going on."

He studied her face. "And if I tell you I don't know anything, you'll believe me?"

"You've been strange and cryptic since this all began, back even to Sandra's crime scene. So if you say you don't *know* anything, sure, I believe you. But then I want to know what it is you *suspect*."

He gave a wry smile and shook his head. "We've spent way too much time together."

"Probably true." She mirrored his smile. "Out with it."

His face tightened again. "I don't *know* a damned thing. But the way it all went down was strange."

She pointed to one of the conference table chairs. "Start at the beginning."

He dropped into the chair. "As far as I can guess, the beginning was the clash between Sandra Ashville and Grace Bandara, the ADA who was prosecuting the two prior Ossokov rape victims, Tasha Quintana and Jennifer Woods. Bandara's evidence had holes. One of the women could describe Ossokov and recognized his voice, but couldn't pick him out of the lineup before he spoke. The other picked him out just fine and provided a DNA match to Ossokov with her rape kit, but he claimed the sex in that case was consensual. Ashville was worried the jury wouldn't believe her, and it would taint the Richards case."

Jo nodded. Juries, especially predominantly male juries, were still too willing to claim reasonable doubt in accord with a man's testimony over a woman's when it came to sexual assault. "Right. That's why everybody decided to let Ashville move forward with the Zara Richards' case, and set the other two aside."

"Not everybody. Bandara fought tooth and nail to keep moving forward with all the prosecutions, and things got ugly."

"Ugly how?"

Arnett leaned forward, his elbows on his knees, one hand rubbing his temple. "That's where it gets difficult, because I never fully knew. I only know that Ashville kept at the DA until he agreed to let her try the Richards case without the others."

"And you don't know what moved the needle?" Jo asked.

"Not for certain. But I think what finally put it over the top was when the DNA results came back that put Zara Richards' blood in Ossokov's car," Arnett said.

"The DNA results we now know are, at best, contaminated," Jo said.

"Yes."

Jo whistled. "Very convenient timing for Ashville. So you think either she or Murphy planted that evidence?"

"I've been trying very hard *not* to think that," Arnett said. "At the time it all felt strange, and like you say, convenient. But it wasn't until Ossokov's conviction was overturned that I really questioned it all."

"Who collected that sample? Was it a tech or Murphy?"

He shook his head. "I don't know. I assumed a tech at the time."

Jo took in a slow breath, screwing up her courage. "Here's the issue I have with all of that. Sure, we all get fuzzy on the details of what happened fifteen years ago. But I know you, and I know your detecting style. Nothing happens on a case you're associated with that you don't know about."

He nodded, eyes fixated somewhere on the wall behind her. "It takes time to build up trust between partners, you know that. Murphy and I only worked together for a couple of months while you were on desk duty. Our communication was very different."

Jo watched him carefully. "So you had no idea anything strange was going on?"

He turned to her, gaze steely. "I still don't. Accusations of misconduct are nothing to screw around with—you can't put 'em back in the bottle. If a cop does something dirty, I damn well want them held to account because bad cops put us all at risk. But I also need to be damned sure what really happened before I condemn someone. Steve Murphy and I weren't hanging out watching football, but I didn't have any reason to believe he wasn't a good cop. To this very moment, I have no evidence that either he or Ashville did anything wrong, and I'm holding out hope that there's some explanation for all this." His eyes swung over to meet hers. "Just like I hope *you're* doing for *me*."

She held his gaze for a long moment, then nodded. "If we

want to know what Ossokov's motives really are and who he's going after next, we need to find out the truth about what happened with that DNA evidence."

Arnett slowly nodded back, then pulled his phone out of his pocket. He tapped, then waited.

The voice that answered was grizzled and bombastic. "Well, well, well, Bob Arnett. Had a feeling I'd get a call from you today."

"Good to talk to you again, Steve. If you knew I was gonna call, you must know why I'm calling."

"Heard from my lawyer not half an hour ago," Murphy said. "Helluva way to start the day."

"Better than waking up dead. Like Sandra Ashville, Judge Sakurai, and Deena Scott," Arnett said.

Murphy hesitated. "He's gotta be stopped."

"Agreed. So we need to come have a chat with you," Arnett said.

"Who's *we*?" Murphy asked.

"Jo Fournier," Arnett answered.

"Oh, right, right, right. You were partnered with her before I retired. She's a pistol."

Arnett grimaced. "You at home?"

"Nope. Just sat down to an early lunch at The Wooden Leg."

"We'll be there as soon as we can." Arnett hung up the phone without waiting for a response.

———

Jo and Arnett worked up the paperwork for the warrant on Ossokov's residence and vehicle as quickly as they were able, then headed out to see Murphy. As they walked out to the Crown Vic, Jo's phone rang. "It's Marzillo. You mind if I take shotgun?"

Arnett shook his head and headed toward the driver's side. Jo tapped to connect the call. "Janet."

"I'm here with Christine." Marzillo's voice was hushed, and grim. "She and I have made some discoveries regarding the lab work done in Zara Richards' case. Can you talk?"

"I'm here with Bob. I'll put you on speakerphone," Jo said.

"Before you do—the news isn't good," Marzillo said.

"We know." Jo's stomach roiled as she tapped the speaker-phone button. "Go ahead."

Marzillo cleared her throat, and Jo heard papers rustling in the background. "I dug back until I found the analysis that identified the sample taken from Ossokov's car as Zara Richards' blood. It was sent to DNA CompCorp."

Jo nodded. DNA CompCorp was one of the backups they used when the department's own analysis lab had a longer-than-usual turnaround time. "So they outsourced it."

Marzillo shook her head. "That's just it. I checked into similar tests we ordered on other cases at the same time. They all went to our standard lab. In fact, I couldn't find a single other test we sent out to DNA CompCorp for a three-week window around that time. There was no reason I could find for this one to be outsourced, especially given the extra expense involved to the department for an out-of-system analysis."

Lopez jumped in. "And all the other analyses associated with the case were done through our internal lab."

"So someone made a purposeful choice to send it to an outside lab," Jo said. "And it sounds like that rules out contamination?"

Marzillo spoke as if the words were choking her. "I can't see any way contamination is possible. By the time the blood smear was collected from Ossokov's car, the tests of Zara's Starbucks cup, and the duct tape on her hands had already been analyzed. They sent her DNA sample at the same time to be analyzed for exclusion purposes. So her DNA profile was already on record when they analyzed the blood from Ossokov's car. I don't see anything that shows it was sent in a second time, so I can't see how any mistake could have been made."

The blood drained from Arnett's face. "You're sure?"

"Positive."

Jo sorted through the implications at light speed. "So let me be sure I have this right. That means the sample supposedly taken from Ossokov's car was actually Zara's blood."

"Yes. And since we know that isn't possible, that means someone either swabbed Zara's blood into the car for the techs to find, or swapped whatever blood was taken from the dash with a sample of Zara's blood."

Jo's eyes searched the skyline for an alternative. "Wait. Do we even know if there really was blood found in Ossokov's car at all?"

"We do," Lopez said. "There are photographs of a blood smear on the dash."

"Do we know who took that photo and collected the sample?" Jo asked.

Marzillo cleared her throat. "The photograph was supposedly taken by Zach Lavendera, who also supposedly collected the sample and sent it out for analysis."

Jo tensed. "Supposedly?"

Lopez jumped in. "I figured it would be a good idea to double-check the signatures, so I just got back from The Dungeon. I dumpster-dived not only these records, but several other sets of analyses Lavendera ordered around the same time. I took pics of the signatures and overlaid them, and while I'm far from a handwriting expert, I can safely say his signature was forged. There's a high degree of consistency between the signatures from the other cases, but the two from the Ossokov case are very different—and match each other."

A chill settled over Jo. "And that's why it was sent to an

outside lab. To make it less likely the strange signature would catch someone's eye. Someone did tamper with the evidence."

"Correct," Marzillo said. "The only problem is we have no way of knowing who."

Jo glanced over at Arnett, who nodded. "We may have an answer to that."

CHAPTER THIRTY-FIVE

The Wooden Leg was the sort of old-school tavern made up of stained wood, brick walls, and sports ephemera. The tang of hops smacked Jo as she entered, making up for the low-light sensory deprivation that forced her to stop short inside the entrance until her pupils adjusted. Patsy Cline belted out heartbreak from the jukebox, serenading the smattering of established regulars resignedly hunched over their alcohol of choice. The throw-back-dive-bar vibe was so strong it called up the taste of cigarettes in the back of Jo's throat despite the decades-old ban—but then, the smoke residue was probably still seeping out of the ancient fixtures.

Murphy sat at a table in the back, directly under a framed Tom Brady jersey, with a half-full pint of Guinness cradled in one hand. He spotted them before they spotted him—probably one reason the bar kept the light level low—and greeted them with a broad smirk.

Jo studied him as he stood and gave Arnett a forearm-clench-fist-pat-on-the-back hug. In the five years since he'd retired, he'd aged more than ten; his hair had gone completely white, and the wrinkles in his pale skin had shifted from creases to folds. His nose and cheeks were shot with broken capillaries. He looked at least an inch shorter than she remembered, hovering just under six foot, and his starter paunch had evolved into a full-on beer belly.

He turned to shake Jo's hand. "Good to see you again, even if the circumstances are shit."

"Thanks for talking with us. I'm sure the last thing you want during retirement is to revisit issues like this." Jo slid into the chair diagonal to Murphy while Arnett dropped into the one opposite him.

"What are you gonna do? Ossokov is a poster boy for the type of asshole that never goes away. He was trouble from the day he was born, and he'll be trouble 'til the day he dies." He raised his hand to signal the bartender. "You on duty?"

Arnett nodded and turned to the bartender. "Coffees'll do."

The bartender wiped his hands on a towel, then turned to grab mugs.

"You said your lawyer talked to you already, so you don't need me to go over it all?" Arnett asked.

Murphy's expression tightened. "He's suing the common-wealth because we're all indemnified, but the reality is he's going after you, me, and Sandra. Hard for her to defend her reputation when she's dead." He raised his glass to her. "She'll be missed."

Since they had no glasses to raise, Jo and Arnett nodded their agreement.

The bartender appeared and slid two black coffees across to Jo and Arnett, along with another pint of Guinness for Murphy. Which he hadn't ordered—he must have had a standing keep-'em-coming order in place.

"What it boils down to," Arnett said, "is Ossokov makes the interesting point that since he wasn't the killer, there's no way Zara Richards' blood was in his car."

"I don't believe for a second he wasn't the killer," Murphy said, expression still tight.

"The girlfriend came forward to recant her testimony and confirm his alibi, and Dale Kranst is adamant he had no accomplice," Arnett said.

Murphy held his gaze. "They're all liars. That's what they do."

Arnett's tone softened a notch. "Why would the girlfriend suddenly come out of the woodwork and recant?"

Murphy raised his palm. "Maybe he threatened her from prison."

"After so many years? That doesn't fit, but there's plenty of evidence she went through rehab and is now a born-again Christian intent on repenting for her past." He paused as Murphy rolled his eyes. "And why wouldn't Dale Kranst tell the truth about a partner? It would only benefit him to assist the ADA. He never used an accomplice for his other kills. It's just too many stretches to make fit."

Murphy waved him off. "So there was a lab mix-up. Not the first time, won't be the last."

"He spent fifteen years of his life behind bars because of that mix-up." Jo sipped her coffee.

Murphy's laugh was bitter. "Exactly where he fucking deserves to be." He wagged his index finger between Arnett and Jo. "You tell her about his background? He was already going down for raping multiple women. Fits the profile for every psychopath ever. Loved starting fires, wet the bed, never had many friends. Yeah, I know the shrinks are saying now that doesn't always hold up, but the local uniforms spent more time with him than with their own kids when he was growing up. He's a menace. The only tragedy here is that he's out on the street again." He drained the remainder of his beer, then pulled over the new one, eyes now glassy.

"But we still have to deal with this lawsuit." Arnett sipped his coffee, made a face, and set it back down. "They've pulled the lab records. The blood from the car was the only blood tested at the time. There's no possibility that Zara Richards' blood somehow contaminated the sample."

Murphy waved away the suggestion with a smirk. "Who knows what the lab did or didn't do?"

"We do," Arnett said. "Because it was sent to DNA Comp-Corp, while none of the other tests from the case were."

"So, talk to the tech that sent it out." He shrugged, and drank.

"He's retired, but it doesn't matter." Arnett dumped a packet of sugar into his coffee, stirred it, then looked up at Murphy. "Because his signature was forged."

Jo caught the flash of fear before Murphy pasted on a skeptical expression. "They can't know that."

"I trust the tech who did the comparison." Arnett's eyes stayed on Murphy's face.

Murphy turned pugnacious. "More than you trust me."

"I trust that you want bad men off the street, and innocent men free," Arnett said. "I trust that when you were on the force you showed up every day with the best of intentions. But I need to know what happened and why, because Ossokov is coming after you and me next."

Murphy grimaced at him. "You know what happened, Bob."

"I don't know what happened with the blood," Arnett said. "This is your chance to tell me your side of the story so I can help you."

Murphy laughed, and his words slurred slightly. "How many suspects have I said that to?"

Arnett leaned forward. "We're not in an interrogation room here. It's just us, talking about old times over drinks. But if I have to, I'll have our tech compare the forged signatures with your handwriting."

Murphy's eyes slid off Arnett's, up to a spot above his head.

His thumb ran up and down the condensation on the beer while he stared. "You won't do that, Bob. Because you know what happened."

"Refresh my memory."

He turned to Jo, his eyes pleading with her. "Grace Bandara, from the Domestic and Sexual Violence Unit. She wanted to hold on to Ossokov like a steel trap, even if it meant he went free. Made a huge stink about it, and the DA was so concerned with how it would look if he favored one unit over another. Complete bullshit, because that's the damned job. But Grace whined at the top of her lungs about how her evidence was stronger because she had the DNA match, and DNA was always better. Argued the jury would never believe the vic had consented to sex behind a bar dumpster. Like we don't all know juries are just *aching* to victim-blame when it comes to rape, especially when the woman's been drinking."

Jo forced herself not to let her disgust show through—if he felt judged by her, he'd slam shut. She kept her face soft and nodded.

Encouraged, he continued. "And even if she did get a conviction, he wouldn't have served more than a few years and then he'd've been *right back out there* raping other women. But a homicide conviction, that meant mandatory life with no possibility of parole. We couldn't risk her fucking that up."

Jo nodded again. "Very frustrating."

"Frustrating isn't the word. Agonizing. Infuriating. Because we *knew* he did it. The third rape in the same one-mile radius in just over two years? Similar MO, except he'd escalated to murder? *Come on.*" He jutted his head toward her as he spat out the last two words, sending a wave of alcohol-laden breath toward her. Her stomach flipped; she'd seen countless decaying bodies, but she'd never been so close to vomiting.

"The DA told us Grace's evidence was the safest bet. That if we got better evidence, he'd reconsider. And that pissed me off, but I'll tell you, not as much as it pissed off Sandra. So, she told me to do whatever I had to do to find whatever would put him away for life."

Jo put on a purposefully exaggerated expression. "But I'm confused. If you didn't have the evidence—"

Murphy looked around and lowered his voice. "You want the real deal? Here it is. Sandra had been on a losing streak. Watched a string of scum just walk on off into the sunset due to technicalities or lack of evidence. She wanted the win and wasn't going to let it go."

"And you wanted to make sure he was off the streets for good," Jo said. "Only now he's back on the streets and he's killing the people who put him there. One every morning for the last three days like clockwork, and you're most likely next."

"Let him come. Look at me—he'd be doing me a favor." Murphy signaled the bartender for another beer. "I know what you're thinking, I can see it in your face. You think it was an easy choice? It wasn't. But I had a chance to put the fucker away for life, and I wasn't gonna scratch on the eight. And I wouldn't take that choice back, not for a second. But every time I look in the mirror, I see that damned forged evidence bag staring back at me. And no amount of these"—he pointed to the beer—"gets rid of it. And you're no better, Bob, so don't you dare fucking judge me."

Arnett shook his head. "You never told me you were going to plant Zara's blood."

Murphy narrowed his eyes at Arnett. "Don't fucking start that. You knew. Of course I didn't say it outright, just like Sandra didn't tell *me* outright what to do. Plausible deniability. But it was all clear."

Arnett shook his head again. "I wasn't in that conversation with Sandra. You had it when I wasn't there."

Murphy's glass froze in midair. "You didn't have to be. You knew what the issues were. You knew she and I talked things over. And you fucking for sure knew when everything suddenly turned on *that particular dime*."

Arnett opened his mouth to respond, but Murphy cut him off. "No. If I'm putting my cards on the table, you're putting *your* cards on the table." He punctuated his final words by pointing the glass at Arnett, causing beer to slop over the side: "*You. Knew*."

CHAPTER THIRTY-SIX

Arnett wouldn't meet Jo's eyes as they walked silently back to the car.

Once Jo slid into the driver's seat, she checked her phone. "Search warrant hasn't come through yet. Hopefully it will by the time we get back to HQ. God only knows how long it'll take us to search, and I want Ossokov off the streets and unable to kill again well before the sun sets tonight."

Arnett nodded.

She started texting. "How likely do you think it is Murphy will remember that conversation even by tonight? No matter what, this changes everything. Murphy and Ashville *did* plant evidence, and that means Ossokov has a legitimate foundation fueling his rage. I'm going to request a surveillance team for him."

"Hopefully you won't need it. You'll have the warrant in hand momentarily."

"I wouldn't put it past him to disappear while we're waiting."

Once she finished up the text, she fired up the car and pulled out, grappling with what just happened. In all her years at the SPDU, she'd never had a case of police misconduct dumped directly in her lap, let alone one that potentially implicated her partner.

Arnett stared out of the windshield. "I need you to know I'd never have been party to that."

"I do know." She paused, taking a deep breath before continuing. "But I have to report what he said to Hayes and Barbieri."

He nodded again. "Without a doubt. You want to go alone?"

She knew what he was asking. If they went to report Murphy's confession together, she'd be showing support for Arnett, passively declaring she believed he did nothing wrong; if some disciplinary action came down on him, part of the stink would indelibly stick to her. If she went in alone, it would be her way of distancing herself from Arnett, of effectively saying she wasn't willing to take the chance that he'd behaved inappropriately.

She kept her eye steady on the road. "I say we stop off and talk to Hayes now, while we're waiting on the warrant."

In her periphery, she saw Arnett's acknowledgment.

They drove the rest of the way in silence, with Jo trying to banish the insistent nagging of Murphy's accusation.

———

Hayes waved them in as soon as they reached her door. "I just got off the phone with Barbieri. He agrees with you that surveillance for Ossokov is a good measure. And I just got word that the warrant came through. Hopefully in a few hours' time, you'll have him in custody and have inculpatory evidence safely logged in the locker."

"Hopefully." Jo's stomach clenched at the thought of what

she was about to do. "There's another issue we need to talk to you about."

An oddly hostile curiosity flickered on Hayes' face as she glanced from Jo's face to Arnett's. "What's that?"

Jo turned to Arnett. He cleared his throat and summarized what Murphy had just told them.

Hayes sank back against her chair, her face slack with shock. "Son of a bitch. You have to be kidding me. And you knew nothing about this?"

"Nothing," he said.

"Because I can't have this happening among my people." Hayes pointed at Arnett. "So say it again, for the record."

"I knew nothing," Arnett said.

"Murphy himself admitted he never told Arnett what he was doing," Jo added.

Hayes pulled over a pad and started jotting notes. "Right. Okay. Shit. Well. In terms of fires to put out, I already have you staying away from Ossokov, so that's good. With that statement and Fournier as a witness you weren't involved, I think we can keep you active. I'll need to talk to the state lawyers about Murphy, and they'll want a statement from you about it. And Ashville's dead, so there's no point in bringing in the BBO on it."

"Should I be the one executing the warrant, or should Goran and Coyne do it?" Jo asked. "Ossokov now has me associated with Arnett, so given this information and the lawsuit, it may be better to keep me away from the search."

"You're worried you'll come under suspicion." Hayes' eyes narrowed into a calculating grimace. She took a long moment before responding, then her mouth curved into a smile. "If we pulled detectives off investigations every time a suspect claimed they weren't being treated right, we'd have nobody left to investigate. If anything, you came straight to me with the information about Murphy, so I don't see how anyone could try to claim you're covering anything up. And you're the one who knows all the background on this case. Unless the problem is you balk at handling difficult situations when the unit needs you?"

Jo held her gaze. "No, ma'am. I only want what's in the unit's best interest."

Hayes made another note on the pad and waved toward the door. "Good. Then let's get on this. Update me when you arrive, and once you're finished."

Jo rose. "Will do."

Once around the corner and out of earshot, Jo pulled out her phone and began texting. "Did you see that? She's hoping this is going to pull me into accusations of a cover-up, or some sort of harassment. I'll be damned if I'm going to let her put me in jeopardy."

Arnett glanced back toward the office. "You're not going to execute the warrant?"

"Of course I'll execute it, but"—her usually buried New Orleans accent reared up—"my mama didn't raise no fool. I'll be making sure I have plenty of help. Meaning, witnesses."

CHAPTER THIRTY-SEVEN

Ossokov was waiting with his lawyer, Don Kent, when Jo, accompanied by Goran, Marzillo, Peterson, and Lopez arrived at his mother's house half an hour later. An attorney out of Boston, Kent had a reputation for fighting for underdogs that had been wronged by the justice system, and an intimidatingly successful series of civil suits. Over six feet tall, he was a lean, raven-haired white man with deep lines etching his tanned forehead but none creasing his expensive suit. Jo glanced around for the candy-apple red convertible his image called up in her mind, but discovered she was wrong—the convertible was lime-green metallic.

Jo pulled out the warrant paperwork. "First things first. I need your client to account for his whereabouts last night through this morning."

Kent had a whispered conversation with Ossokov behind turned heads and raised hands. "Yesterday was his day off. He did yard work, then watched the Bruins game. After that he read until he fell asleep at about three in the morning. He got up at ten thirty this morning. His mother fell asleep before he did, and was gone to her own job when he woke up."

"Is there anyone who can confirm that? Did his mother happen to look in on him, anything like that?"

"We'll check with her when she gets home, but not that we're aware of." Kent pointed to a device over the front door. "After your visit yesterday, he purchased a security camera. That will show him doing the yard work, but doesn't account for the rest of his time. His phone location will show him at home, but I'm sure you'll say he could have left his phone behind," Kent said.

"Excellent mind-reading skills." She handed him the paperwork.

He glanced over the warrant with experienced flicks. "Burner phones, firearms—what's muslin?"

"A type of material found at the crime scene," Jo answered.

"The blindfold." He turned back to the paperwork, and his skeptical expression turned to a glare. "My client needs his phone. You can't leave him without it."

Jo gestured to Lopez. "My tech expert has a universal forensic extraction device that'll transfer the contents in seconds."

Lopez held up a black case, wiggled it back and forth, and smiled. "I never leave home without my Touch2 Ultimate."

Kent's jaw clenched. "It says here you're removing his mother's car for on-site analysis? How are either of them supposed to get to work?"

Jo crinkled her brow sarcastically and turned to Lopez. "What's that company called? The one you pull up on your phone that drives you places?"

"You're thinking of Uber or Lyft." Lopez shot a finger at her, then crinkled her own brow. "But I also remember hearing about these big vehicles that carry lots of people around town and make regular stops places?"

"Buses." Jo's face cleared as she turned back to Kent.

"Rideshares and public transportation. What amazing times we live in."

A red flush crept up Kent's neck. "I don't appreciate the attitude, Detective. This isn't a joke."

Jo's face returned to professionally impassive. "I agree, the murder of three members of the justice system in three days is absolutely *not* a joke, and *I* don't appreciate the manufactured righteous indignation at what you know are very basic aspects of us doing our jobs."

Kent's eyes narrowed. "This is harassment."

"The judge says it isn't. You're welcome to watch. Your client is welcome to watch, too." Jo shrugged.

But Kent knew, as did she, that it would only upset Ossokov to watch law enforcement go through the house, and make him more likely to do or say something incriminating. He instructed Ossokov to stay back with one of the uniformed backup policemen, then followed along with Goran as Jo motioned Marzillo and Peterson inside to carry out the physical search.

They started with Ossokov's bedroom. Neat and tidy, it contained very few personal possessions. When they found nothing, they continued on systematically through the house. As Jo rifled through an accordion file of documents lying out on the kitchen table, Marzillo's voice, tense and staccato, called out from Rebecca Ossokov's bedroom. "Jo. I need you to come look at this."

Lopez looked up sharply from the laptop she was processing, then followed Jo into the room.

Jo noted the room's aggressively 1990s decorating theme—the maroon-flowered wallpaper border over light-pink walls cocooned a light-wood bedroom set complete with two-cabinet headboard. She'd heard it said that women favored the hairstyle they wore at the height of their youth; she wondered if the same was true of bedroom decor, and made a note to reevaluate her own. She turned the corner to find Marzillo standing next to a tall bureau, eyes wide. Marzillo lifted a gloved hand and precisely pointed one finger at something settled in amid the perfume bottles and figurines. Jo peered closely, trying to make out what it was.

A large, eviscerated eyeball. With toothpicks sticking into it.

Behind her, Lopez sucked in a deep breath. "Oh, *hell* no. My *abuela* was deadly serious about three things: her rice and beans, her *pitorro*, and her *Santería*. Take my advice and stay far, far away from that. Like, pick-it-up-with-tongs kinda far away."

Marzillo glared at her. "You don't really believe in that, do you?"

Lopez stuck her hands up and took two steps back. "It's not a question of believing, it's a question of don't-be-stupid. I don't believe zombies and vampires really exist, but I damn well know how to take 'em out if one day it turns out I'm wrong."

"Not a bad philosophy," Jo said, stepping in to examine the eyeball more closely. "Did you learn anything from your grandmother that might help us here?"

Rooted in place, Lopez craned her neck toward the bureau. "Looks like a cow's eyeball with that oval pupil. My guess is it's to ward off the Evil Eye? I remember something similar with a pig's tongue when my abuela wanted to stop some gossip. I can ask my mom if you want, maybe she'll know." Lopez shuddered. "No matter what, I can tell you right now, I wouldn't want to meet Ossokov's mama in a dark alley."

Jo gave a fair-enough head wag. "The good news is, neither severed eyeballs nor Santería paraphernalia fit into any of the categories covered by the warrant, so we can't remove it, anyway. But we definitely want pictures of it."

"If nothing else, it'll make fun banners for the unit Christmas party," Peterson said.

When they emerged three and a half hours later, they'd found nothing other than the disturbing cow's eye. Kent's smug expression failed to hide an inkling of relief as he and Ossokov watched the car being taken away and the police pack up to leave

Once out of earshot next to their cars in the street, Jo called Arnett and put him on speakerphone and caught him up.

"Shit, shit, shit," he said.

"He must have hidden it all somewhere," Goran said. "Maybe in the janitor's closet at the dentist where he works? Or at a friend's house? Somewhere close by in the neighborhood?"

"Maybe. I'll stop by and see if the dentist will let me search without a warrant. If not, we'll get one." Jo jutted her chin at Lopez. "You're going over his cell phone records and emails with a fine-toothed comb, so hopefully there's something in there. Someone he hangs out with, or some place he spends his time, at this point we want to consider everything."

"I'll check his location tracking too. Maybe there's some shed in some run-down park we can trace him to," Lopez said.

"But if he's smart enough to use burner phones to communicate with Lacey Bernard, he's smart enough to keep anything incriminating off his official records," Marzillo said.

"We have to hope he isn't," Jo said. "He wouldn't be the first criminal to make a stupid mistake. And even if he hasn't done anything stupid, if we dig deep enough, we'll find *something*. Friends, friends of friends, all of it."

Goran gestured to his phone. "Coyne just blew up our inboxes. He got the gym footage. Deena Scott drove up in her car just past midnight last night, and finished her workout at just before one in the morning. Unless she hung around the parking lot for an extended period of time, she was likely killed shortly after leaving."

Jo tapped at her phone. "Thanks. Any luck with the rest of the canvassing?"

"Several people at the gym recognized her, but didn't pay attention to what happened after she left. Nobody at the apartment complex heard or saw anything out of the ordinary, but most were asleep by then."

Arnett's voice crackled over the speakerphone. "I'll get a start on listing out all the other cars shown on the video in case our killer wasn't smart enough to use the back entrance."

Jo turned to Marzillo. "I know we pulled you off your analyses to come do this, so I'm guessing you don't have an update for us yet on Deena Scott's crime scene?"

"The ME's initial report should be waiting for me when I get back to the lab. My next priority is to get the samples sent out, and to match up the blindfold on Deena to the fabric we already have."

"Thank you." She glanced back over at Ossokov and Kent, who were still watching from Ossokov's front door. "Normally I'd bring him in and see if I could charm some sort of information out of him. But with Kent stuck to his side like fly paper, there's no way we're going to get away with that, especially when they're screaming harassment with every other breath. We'll have to wait until we have something we can use to apply pressure."

"Hopefully he'll do something stupid while we have surveillance on him tonight," Goran said.

Jo shifted to be sure neither Ossokov nor Kent could read her lips. "You're splitting the surveillance with another team?"

"Yep. Coyne and I will be on him until he goes into his job tonight, when the backup will take over. The dental office has two exits, but there's a spot one block over from it where they can keep watch over both at the same time. We'll sleep and be back at his place by four in the morning. Seems like that's his preferred time to take people out, so we'll be bright-eyed and bushy-tailed for it."

"Make plenty of strong coffee. I'd like to believe all our

attention will convince him to back off the murders, but I doubt it. And if he's this good at covering his tracks, we're not going to be able to take him into custody any time soon. So if he does try again tomorrow morning, we need to be there to catch him in the act."

CHAPTER THIRTY-EIGHT

I'm not sure when I last enjoyed myself as much as I did watching the police execute the search warrant, knowing they wouldn't find anything. The frustration on Fournier's face when she came out of the house was absolutely priceless. The only thing that would have been better is if I'd been able to watch her inside.

I let myself relish the feeling for a short while, but not for too long—I had work to do, and there would be plenty of time, enforced or otherwise, to sit back and enjoy the release of closure once I was finished.

Closure. An elusive concept, and a future promise you can't ever be sure of until it arrives. That had been the one worry nagging at me through all of it—that after all of the planning and execution, after taking all of these significant steps, I'd walk away just as tormented as I was when I started. I deserved—needed—peace.

But in the short term, the amusement helped energize me for the next steps.

This time, I couldn't keep watch on my next target. Without that security blanket my anxiety skyrocketed—each phase had its difficult aspects, and for this one, I was running blind. But I had a few very important tasks to complete, and the block of free time allowed me to devote my full attention to them.

Through the course of my life, I've learned so many things from books. Nowadays, of course, there's YouTube as well—so many things you can learn by watching, from waterproofing your house to picking locks. I had several devices I needed to make and with very little research and a few innocent-looking objects, I was on my way. I spent the rest of my afternoon finalizing them and making sure they were functional.

When I was satisfied, I double-checked everything. Then, once I was sure I'd done everything I needed to do, I grabbed my coat, headed out, and allowed myself to enjoy the next phase.

CHAPTER THIRTY-NINE

Jo grabbed a healthy dose of Starbucks on her way back to HQ, and handed a venti drip to Arnett when she arrived. He thanked her effusively, but barely looked up from the security footage he was poring over.

"How's it going?" she asked.

He paused the recording. "Slow but steady. The gym's external camera is pointed directly toward the main aisle, so I get a nice, clear, head-on shot of the license plates that come from that direction. But if they come from the perpendicular direction, here"—he gestured to the screen—"it's hit or miss."

She slid into her chair. "While you do that, I'm going to pull up the two rape cases Ossokov was indicted for before Zara Richards' murder and see if I can find anything relevant there."

"The system wasn't as fully computerized back then, so I pulled the physical files." He jutted his chin toward two folders, then restarted the video.

"Thanks." She pulled the files over, then flipped open the one for Tasha Quintana.

From nearly the first page, Jo could see why everyone had been so sure the Zara Richards assault was related to Tasha's. A twenty-four-year-old white administrative assistant with brown hair and eyes, she bore more than a passing resemblance to Zara Richards. She'd been assaulted close to midnight outside a pub in Oakhurst; according to the report, she'd met two friends for drinks, but had switched to water halfway through the evening because she had to work the next day. She left before they did, alone, for the same reason. Her assailant appeared out of the dark and forced her by gunpoint into a dead-end alley behind the bar. When he was done, he told her to count to a hundred before turning around, and that he'd shoot her if she moved before that. During the assault, he attempted to control where she looked, but when he forced her behind a dumpster enclosure, she managed to get a full look at his face illuminated by the light next to the enclosure. He wore a condom and gloves, so her identification was crucial.

Jo's phone buzzed, interrupting her with a text from Goran.

Some guy came over to pick up Ossokov. Ran the plates, it turned out to be his uncle. Ossokov drove uncle back home, is now on way to work.

Jo sent back an acknowledgment.

Guess he really doesn't like public transportation.

She finished up the file on Tasha and switched to Jennifer Woods. Jennifer was twenty-six, white with brown hair and brown eyes, very much the same physical type as both the other women. The rape was almost identical to Tasha's; Jennifer was a flight attendant originally from Chicopee, living in Boston, back for the weekend visiting family and friends. She'd gone to a pub in Northampton to meet a blind date set up by her mother for an after-dinner drink. The man never showed up, and while she waited, sipping a glass of wine for over an hour, another man struck up a conversation with her and bought her another glass of wine. He came on strong so she made her excuses and left. As she searched her purse to call a cab, a man appeared out of the darkness, forced her at gunpoint into the alley behind the bar, and raped her behind a utility shed. He'd apparently learned his lesson from the previous rape and was careful to make sure Jennifer never saw his face, but this time the condom he wore broke, leaving DNA evidence behind. When he realized this, he cursed at her, and told her if she went to the police, they'd never believe her because he'd tell them the sex had been consensual. He used the same count-to-one-hundred technique to buy time to get away.

The no-show blind date sounded pretty darn suspicious, and Jo latched on to it as she scoured the file. As it turned out, Bandara's suspicions had also been aroused by the missing man, but it turned out he had an iron-clad alibi—he'd been in a car accident on the way to the date that broke one of his legs, and had been taken directly to the hospital via ambulance. Jo swore under her breath and returned to the rest of the file.

The possibility that the man who stood her up was her rapist had occurred to Jennifer, too. Once she calmed down enough to call the cab company as originally intended, she went back to her mother's house, where she was spending the night. She didn't tell her mother at first, worried that she'd blame herself for having fixed Jennifer up with the man. But when her mother heard her crying inside the bathroom, the truth came out. She insisted Jennifer go to the emergency room.

Jo pushed the files away as she finished, frustrated she hadn't learned much. The evidence was strong that Ossokov had committed the rapes; Arnett was right when he said Ossokov would have been smart to take his overturned conviction and slip away into the night. He wouldn't be the first egomaniacal narcissist who wasn't able to let go of a slight even when it was in his best interest, but there was nothing in the files that got her any closer to proving he'd committed the current murders. Thank goodness the surveillance teams were watching him—hopefully they'd be able to prevent him killing anyone else.

Jo's phone buzzed with another text. Before she could answer it, Arnett spoke. "Marzillo's summoning us to the lab."

"Let's go," she said.

As she grabbed her coffee and followed him, she threw another frustrated glance back at the files. So much could go wrong with waiting and hoping to catch Ossokov in the act—she said a prayer that Marzillo had found something—anything—that would help them.

CHAPTER FORTY

There are many things about law enforcement I'll never understand. But the one I find the most amusing is that undercover cops actually think we don't know they're undercover, like the absence of a light bar and zebra paint is some Cloak of Suburban Camo that renders them invisible. Maybe for some people the sight of two fiercely serious men driving a neutral-colored sedan is completely ordinary. Maybe most people don't bother to track the vehicles around them, never worried about who might be following them. I suppose it's just one more way I'll never again be like other people.

I wasn't a bit surprised when I spotted them. I knew it was only a matter of time before they tried to surreptitiously watch their primary suspect, and I had a plan for dealing with it. One that not only would undermine them but enable me to use the situation to my advantage.

Still, I watched for a while to be sure. Watched them hang several cars back, change lanes after judicious delays, sip their coffee with unending patience.

Once I was certain, I picked up the phone.

CHAPTER FORTY-ONE

When they reached the lab, Marzillo stood over a table with the swatch of bloody fabric they'd found blindfolding Deena Scott. As they entered, she pulled off her gloves and shifted over to her computer. Jo was struck by how tired she looked, with bags under her brown eyes and a flock of black curls straying from her bun.

"You look like hell," Arnett said to her.

"Such a charmer." Lopez glared at him. "Those without mirrors should not throw stones."

"I'm just concerned," Arnett objected.

"Three crime scenes in three days." Marzillo shook her head and gulped her coffee, eyes closed to savor it, then reluctantly set it back down. "I just forwarded you the ME's report for Deena Scott. We're waiting for the tox screen, of course, but otherwise, no surprises. The blows to the head killed her."

"Got it," Jo said.

"We put extra techs on the trash we picked up at the scene, along with other bits of detritus around the parking lot. Nothing seems directly related to the attack. We also checked the car but didn't find any fingerprints that don't belong to Scott or her husband."

"Damn." Jo sagged against the corner of Lopez's desk. "But we knew that was a long shot. Everybody in the lab must be working around the clock getting all this done—please let them know we appreciate it."

Marzillo waved her off. "Hayes helped by authorizing as much overtime as we need and rushes on the analyses. And in that vein, I have both some good news and some bad news. Bad: ballistics comparisons came back inconclusive; the bullet was too damaged to determine much of anything. Good: your idea to swab the trees outside Sandra Ashville's house, the one you thought our killer might have leaned against? The blood turned out to be human."

Jo perked back up. "Were they able to get a DNA profile?"

"Not yet, but it's out on a rush. I know I don't have to tell you still not to get your hopes up. Who knows what neighborhood child was playing in the woods." Marzillo turned back toward the table with the fabric, and pulled out another pair of gloves. "Now that the ME is finished with the autopsy, I have the fabric used for Deena's blindfold. I'm about to see if it matches the other blindfolds if you want to watch."

"Should we suit up?" Jo asked.

"I've already separated and labeled the hairs and other matter that was attached to it, but yes, that would be best."

Once in their PPE, they peered over as Marzillo carefully pulled out the scrunched fabric. A chill tugged at the base of Jo's spine at the percentage covered in blood, long since dried into variegated pools of brown streaking the length. "I hope she didn't suffer."

Marzillo shook her head. "The ME said he was fairly certain the first blow was substantial enough to knock her unconscious. The angle of the others suggest she was already on the ground when they were administered, lying face down. The killer most likely wanted to be sure he'd finished the job."

Small consolation, but it was something, at least.

With skilled, precise movements, Marzillo flattened the stiff fabric atop a large sheet of what looked like white butcher paper. Tiny spots of blood flaked onto it, waiting to be collected. When she had it as flat as she could manage, she shifted the paper toward the waiting pieces of fabric, stopping several inches short of allowing the pieces to touch. "I don't think we need Lopez's software for this one."

The killer had sliced though this section of the cloth with quick, irregular cuts that fit easily together with one of the others.

"It matches up with Sakurai's blindfold." Marzillo pointed to the matching piece.

Jo mentally rotated the pieces. "There's a missing rectangle of fabric that's been cut away from between them."

"Confirms there's likely at least one more target," Arnett said.

Jo glanced at the clock on the wall. Just past seven—Ossokov would be at work. She shot off a text to Goran and Coyne to confirm they'd tailed him successfully. "Christine, I know you just got it all, but have you made any progress on Ossokov's personal records?"

"I'm still working on it, but it's not promising." Lopez stepped back, stripped off her PPE, and returned to her desk. "Based on his registered cell phone and email accounts, he doesn't seem to have many friends and he doesn't go out much. Work, the library, a sandwich shop, and that's it."

"I'm not surprised," Arnett said. "Other than the girlfriend, he was a loner back when we originally investigated him."

"He does go for a walk around the neighborhood every afternoon, but according to the location tracker, his movement is continuous. No stops for any period long enough to register."

"Is the tracker sensitive enough to pick it up if he just drops something off or picks it up?"

Lopez pursed her lips skeptically. "Depends on how quickly he did it. When I walk my mom's dog and she makes a deposit in the bank of life, that doesn't take long enough for Google to mark it as a destination. So it'd have to take longer than that."

"Can you map it out for us? It might be worth at least driving by and looking for anything obvious. I'll also check around the sandwich shop," Jo said.

"Could be he's leaving his real phone at home when he does whatever he does with the burner phones," Arnett said.

Jo nodded. "I don't suppose we can pull out any cell-tower magic like we did to catch Diana— No." Jo cut herself off. "That only worked because her phone was at the target locations only on specific days and times that we already knew about, and not there at others."

Lopez touched her finger to her nose. "But I'll keep digging, and I'll stop by the dental office tomorrow during the day, see if anybody there has anything to say about him."

"Thanks." Jo's phone shrilled a call. She grabbed it out of her pocket and checked the number. "It's Hayes, calling instead of texting."

Lopez's face froze. "That's never good."

Jo shook her head as she tapped on the call. "Fournier."

Hayes' voice shot out high and sharp. "The bastard spotted Goran and Coyne. He figured out we were tailing him."

Jo's brain kicked into gear, calculating the repercussions. "Not a problem. It would have been better if he hadn't realized, but it doesn't really matter. The other team is about to go out and relieve them, we can just make sure—"

"No," Hayes cut her off. "We can't. Because he called his lawyer and his lawyer called the DA's office. He said the tail constitutes clear retaliation for the lawsuit Ossokov filed. Barbieri told me to pull it back immediately."

CHAPTER FORTY-TWO

"Son of a bitch." Arnett slammed a fist on Lopez's desk. "How the hell did he spot them?"

Jo paced the room, thinking. "We need to warn Murphy."

"There's no point. You heard what he said, he doesn't give two shits if Ossokov shows up to kill him." Arnett threw a hand out dismissively. "Hell, it sounded like he'd welcome it."

"Doesn't matter, we have to try," Jo said.

"He's not going to answer." Arnett pulled out his phone and tapped to put through the call. They waited as it went through, and the line rang over speakerphone. He slapped the call off. "We're the last people he wants to talk to after what he told us today."

"Give me the number," Lopez said. Arnett gave it to her, and she put through the call. They waited again as it rang, then went to voice mail.

"Dammit." Jo punched her thigh as she paced. "How about his wife? Will she pick up your call?"

"She might, but since she left him about a year ago, I'm not sure how useful that'll be," Arnett said.

She changed direction toward the door. "Then we need to go to his house in person."

———

Arnett followed her. "You want me to go with, or steer clear?"

"I'm pretty sure I didn't lay down the foundation of a lasting friendship with him earlier today," she said. "He's more likely to listen to you, and I can't see why it would be a problem for the lawsuit."

They pulled up to Murphy's salt-box colonial just outside of Oakhurst fifteen minutes later. Jo's stomach dropped at the sight of the dark windows. "I'm guessing he's not the sort to go to bed at eight?"

"Your guess is as good as mine these days." Arnett strode up the driveway and rapped on the front door. "Steve, open up."

Jo leaned close to the door, but couldn't hear any movement inside. "Try calling him again? Maybe we'll hear his phone ringing."

Arnett pulled out his phone and tapped. "It's ringing. And now it went to voice mail again." He stabbed at the phone to disconnect.

"I didn't hear any ringing inside. Do you think he'd still be over at The Wooden Leg?" Jo asked.

"After this long? I'm not sure whether to hope he is or he isn't." He shot off toward the car.

"I'll drive," Jo said. "You try his ex-wife."

He nodded, slid into the car, and dialed. After two rings, she picked up. "Hello?"

Arnett jumped in, explaining what was going on.

Once he got out the gist, she interrupted. "No, sorry. I can't get sucked back in. That's why I left, the wondering where he was at all hours, if he was drunk or dead somewhere. I'm sorry, but I just can't." She hung up.

Arnett slammed the phone against his leg. "Mother. Fuck."

Jo glanced from the flow of traffic to examine his clenched jaw—she needed to pull him out of his head. "What else do you know about him? Where else could he be headed on a Monday night?"

Arnett's mouth narrowed into a tight line. "No idea. Maybe somebody who worked with him longer'll know." He tapped into the phone.

Jo braked and turned into The Wooden Leg's parking lot. Before the car came to a full stop, Arnett had his seat belt off and the door open.

The dim light inside the pub was far less noticeable after the dark of night, and Jo's eyes adjusted almost immediately. They both scanned the room but didn't see Murphy.

"I'll check the men's room," Arnett said.

Jo crossed to the bar, still scanning occupants as she went. The bartender, in the middle of pulling a beer, noticed her immediately. "Weren't you two here earlier?"

She shifted her blazer to reveal her badge. "We were. You remember the guy we were talking to?"

His eyes bounced back up, face tight. "Murphy. Comes in once or twice a week. He's a cop, too, isn't he? Or was?"

She nodded. "He still around?"

"Nope." Worry sprung onto his face. "Why?"

"When did he leave?" she asked.

He shot a quick glance at the two regulars avidly pretending not to listen, and lowered his voice. "Not too long after you left. Said he had some errands to run and he'd catch me later."

She also lowered her voice. "Is that usual?"

He wagged his head. "Depends. Sometime he has a couple of beers, more often he sticks around for four or five. Always seems to know when I'm about to cut him off, though."

"Does he come in his own car?"

The man's posture tensed—he wasn't interested in being

held responsible for letting a patron drive drunk. He swept a hand around the perimeter of the room. "How exactly would I know? We got one window and it's painted black."

"No external cameras, then?"

He pointed to a small camera pointing down from the corner. "I got one pointed right at the register, and I say a prayer of thanks on the days it doesn't go on the fritz."

She gave a sympathetic half-smile. "Right. Got it. I don't suppose you know where he goes when he leaves here?"

He looked like he was about to shut her down, but after another furtive glance around lowered his voice again. "You want my opinion? I've listened to a lot of bullshit, and people start to fall into types. The way he relives the glory days like he's still in the middle of 'em, I'd bet my signed Cal Ripken Jr. rookie card he has exactly nothing going on in his life. My guess is he goes somewhere else to drink where they don't know how much he's already had, either home or to another bar."

Arnett materialized from the dark hall. "Not in there."

Jo thanked the bartender, then, once outside, recapped for Arnett. "My guess is he's at some other watering hole. We need to check as many as we can as quickly as we can."

"Go. I'll pull up what kind of car he drives."

CHAPTER FORTY-THREE

After ensuring the police surveillance was gone, I was able to turn my full attention to the most serious work of the day.

Steve Murphy was different from the rest of them. One of the most guilty, for a start—I didn't know exactly what they'd done to tamper with the blood evidence, but it didn't take a genius to know the detectives were the ones most directly able to manipulate it. But the real difference was the way he'd utterly failed to find a salve for his guilt. The others found ways to embrace life, to capture moments of peace, to put foundations under themselves that rooted them and gave them balance they had no right to have. But for Murphy, peace was non-existent. Like me, even if for different reasons, it was the Holy Grail he searched constantly for, the shining beacon he could never quite grasp. And because of that, I understood his struggle in a visceral way.

Also because of that, as I'd followed all of them over the past months, my time with him was most fascinating. No—that's not the right word. Compelling? That's nearer to capturing it. I had to watch the rest mostly from longer distances—strategically placed cameras, public parks I could navigate with relative ease. But with Murphy, I had to get up-close and personal, because there are only two things he did to pass his miserable days: shoot, and drink. Since shooting ranges are extremely careful about security, I had zero chance of observing him there. That left drinking. Copious amounts of drinking.

He had several haunts he frequented, which confused the issue at first. But after a few days of observation, I realized the variety was a blessing for remaining unnoticed, and that it signaled something important about him. When you drink constantly but, like Steve Murphy, retired detective and super-human protector of Oakhurst County, have pride and a reputation to protect, you couldn't be seen sitting in the same lurid hole night after night, drinking yourself to oblivion. So he rotated his appearances in establishments both in Oakhurst and in neighboring towns; sometimes at The Wooden Leg, sometimes at O'Connor's, sometimes at The Rusty Nail, sometimes at The Tap Club. Sometimes he went to more than one of them in a day. All dank, depressing places without windows because the people who came to them didn't want to see or be seen; they wanted to hide in a corner, unidentified and unbothered and unjudged. Where nobody knew their sins, and they could pretend to themselves they were something better than they truly were.

So my next task was to identify which of those dens of despair he'd burrowed himself into, sucking down his liquid Prozac, blissfully unaware of what was coming for him.

CHAPTER FORTY-FOUR

Jo and Arnett slipped through Oakhurst's deepening darkness for nearly two hours, searching every pub and bar in town. When they came up empty-handed, they returned to Murphy's house, hoping he'd returned home while they were away. He hadn't. They called his ex-wife again, but she refused to answer their call. They went directly to her house, but she wasn't at home.

Jo rubbed her brow with her fingertips. "I guess we can try nearby towns? But with no other idea where he might be, I'm at a loss."

"At this point we're wasting time and energy we need for other things," Arnett said. "Just as likely he met a woman and is back at her place right now."

It was a valid point. "And I guess that means if we can't find him, Ossokov can't find him."

"Here's hoping." He glanced sideways at her. "I have an idea, but I don't think you're gonna like it."

Her stomach flopped. "Let's hear it."

"We can't stake out Ossokov, but we can stake out Murphy.

You need to go get some sleep, but I'm gonna be up all night worrying about this anyway, so I might as well come back with my own car and keep watch. Goran and Coyne were planning on relieving the other team at four in the morning, I'll see if they can come here instead. That'll give me time to grab a few hours' sleep before heading in, and that way whenever Murphy comes home, we'll have eyes on him."

Jo started to speak, but couldn't find a tactful way to say what needed to be said.

"Just spit it out," Arnett said.

She sighed. "What if Ossokov is just as happy to run into you here as he would be to find Murphy? We have no way of knowing you're not his next target. You go home and I'll stay to keep an eye out."

Arnett pointed in the general direction of her house. "Nope. You need a full night's sleep so we can get some evidence on this bastard. And I don't think he'd hesitate to kill you any faster than he'd kill me." He threw up a palm to preempt her objection. "Sorry, but this is my fight."

Jo scrunched up her face. "Oh, cut the let-him-come-get-me-macho-BS or I'll call Laura right now and tell her what your plan is."

He stared at her, unbelieving. "You're seriously threatening to rat me out to my wife?"

"If you insist on being completely careless."

His face flinched like it couldn't pick an emotion. Finally a wily smile cracked his face. "Then I'll go to the station and pick up an undercover vehicle with tinted windows. If Ossokov spots it, he'll know it's a cop, but have no reason to think it's me."

Jo sighed a frustrated burst of air. She'd rather he stay far away from the situation, but those were her personal feelings, not her professional ones. Danger was a part of law enforcement, and if it were her, would she skulk off and hide under her bed? No way in hell.

"Okay," she said. "I'll allow it."

But as she drove home after dropping him off, the unsettled feeling nagging at her stomach intensified. Damn Goran and Coyne for allowing themselves to be spotted, and damn Ossokov for spotting them—

Something about that clanked with her but she had no idea why. Ossokov had made it clear he thought he was being targeted by the police, so it was reasonable that he'd have been on the lookout for a tail—

So reasonable in fact, it was almost predictable. Like maybe he'd even purposefully provoked it...

But why would he want the police to try to tail him, only to pull them off? To buttress his harassment claim? But surely it ran the risk of interfering with his real primary motive, the murders?

There was something here she couldn't put her finger on. She couldn't shake the feeling that Ossokov was playing them, that he had them right where he wanted them instead of the other way around. The little inconsistencies, they were trying to tell her something—there was some layer to Ossokov's plan she hadn't figured out yet. And with Arnett hanging around like a sitting goose, it was vital she figured out what he was up to.

She rubbed her temples. She was thinking about it all too hard. When her brain got like this, she needed to give it space to untie its own knots. To let all the little pieces of information she'd been accumulating bounce around and come together. A long shower, or a snifter of Calvados in a dark room with jazz playing, something to point her mind in another direction and let her subconscious take over.

Frustrated, she smacked her palms against the steering wheel. Maybe the team was right and the problem was there was no problem. Maybe she was overthinking this, looking for complications where there weren't any, trying to impose rationality onto someone who wasn't rational. Ossokov was angry—

enraged—about the misconduct that had put him behind bars. Fueled by that sort of rage, was he really playing the sort of manipulative mental chess game she was crediting him with? He was killing the people he felt were responsible, any and all of them, even tangentially. That was all that mattered.

That, and the fact that he wasn't going to stop until they stopped him.

———

As she turned in to her driveway just before midnight, Matt's car loomed up in front of her.

Damn, damn, damn—she pounded the steering wheel again as she said the words. Both because she really, really needed some alone time to process everything that was going on, but also, how could she have completely forgotten him again? She hadn't called or texted him all day, something she'd rarely failed to do when they *weren't* living together. How had moving in with him sent him to some black-box purgatory in her head like the mental equivalent of socks missing from the laundry?

Her mind flitted back to the question Lopez had posed over dinner. Was she destined to end up like Sandra Ashville, putting all of her passion into a job that would one day either kill or abandon her? Why couldn't she find the balance between being a dedicated detective and a reliable partner?

Because, a voice in her head answered back, *the situation with Matt isn't about workaholism. It's about your screwed-up defense mechanisms.*

She scanned the house as she got out of the car. No lights on —he'd gone to bed. Relief that she'd get the alone time she desperately needed was quickly followed by a wave of guilt— she shouldn't *want* that time alone, she should want to spend it with her partner.

She opened and closed the door as quietly as she was able,

then tiptoed through the house, waiting for the light to flood onto her like an escaping prisoner. But she made her way to the bedroom without incident, and the lump on Matt's side of the bed remained reassuringly still.

Her phone buzzed in her pocket. She pulled it out to check —a text from Sophie, asking if she were awake. She tiptoed back out of the room and across the house to the kitchen.

As she reached for the switch, something pushed against her leg. She froze, instantly on alert, then flooded the room with light.

"Brrooowrr," Cleopatra trilled.

Air gushed from her lungs, and she reached down to stroke the cat. Apparently her mental block wasn't just for Matt—she also kept forgetting she had a cat now, too. She scooped her up and carried her to the kitchen table, tucking her into her lap as she put through a Duo call to her sister.

Sophie picked up immediately. She also was sitting at her kitchen table, hair piled up into a messy bun, dark smudges under her eyes. "I hope I didn't wake you. I couldn't sleep and I needed someone to talk to."

Jo kept her voice low. "You're fine. I actually just got home. Matt's asleep though, so I'm trying not to wake him."

Sophie paused a moment. "I miss that. Having someone to come home to. Or to come home to you. The house feels cold without David here." She lifted a martini glass to her lips.

The fatigue on Sophie's face made Jo wish she could reach through the phone and hug her. "I'm so sorry, Soph. I know how much that hurts."

"I know you do. That's why I called, because you're the only person who really knows. So you can tell me how even though I'm in pain now, the sun will come up again and I'll be stronger and better off than I was before."

Jo reached for the diamond at her throat—the stone from her former engagement ring—as she measured her words against what she'd gone through when her fiancé Jack died in her arms. "The sun *will* come up again. And whatever you decide, it *will* be for the best."

Sophie laughed dryly, and scrunched her face skeptically. "Hmm, that's not quite what I said. And I know you far too well to pretend you don't pick your words carefully."

Jo let out a slow puff of air. "Yeah, sorry. You just caught me at a bad moment, and I'm having a hard time putting on an *Annie* impersonation. But don't read too much into it. I do believe the pain will pass and you'll find yourself unexpectedly happy again before you know it. It's just—well, it's just not quite as straightforward as the way you put it."

"How so?" Anxiety joined the fatigue in Sophie's eyes.

"Like I said, don't read too much into it. My situation with Jack was very different from yours, so the course of the heartache will probably also be different. The pain did ease, and things did get better. But there's a small core that's always there, like a peach pit stuck in my stomach that never goes away." She sighed. "And going through these things—death, betrayal, any kind of loss—it changes you. I'm still dealing with the repercussions of that, even as we speak."

Sophie's expression shifted to concern. "Is everything okay? Is it Matt?"

Jo sighed again. "No, I'm the jerk. My brain just seems determined to sabotage me. I can't seem to uninstall the firewall erected by my previous relationships. Just when I think it's disabled, it pops up again."

Sophie's eyes narrowed. "Oh, no. What did you do?"

Jo winced defensively. "I've been working late on a case, and I keep forgetting to text him and let him know I'll be late, so he's waiting at home for me with no word."

Sophie's face cleared. "That's not so bad. It's not ideal, of course, but you only just moved in together. It takes a while to get used to that sort of change. Give yourself some grace."

Jo paused, trying to cover her surprise. It wasn't like Sophie to cut Jo slack; throughout their lives, she'd been the one most likely to point out Jo's flaws. "No, you're right. I guess I just want to be sure it's that, just a question of getting used to it, and not that I'm fundamentally unable to hold down a decent relationship."

"You love him, right? You want to be with him?" Sophie asked.

"I do. Or at least, I think I do. But when I saw his moving boxes in my garage, I had a low-grade panic attack. So am I just lying to myself because I *want* to love him?"

Sophie was quiet a moment. "Funny, I've been asking myself a very similar question lately. Humans are so good at lying to ourselves, aren't we?"

The words sent a chill through Jo. "God, I hope not."

Sophie's brow creased. "That was an odd response."

Suddenly Jo felt like she was being pushed down into the chair by a thousand lead blankets. She clutched Cleopatra into her chest with her free hand. "Sorry. That wasn't about you, or about me. That was about Bob."

Sophie's concern returned. "Tell me."

She walked Sophie through the case, ending with the Steve Murphy conversation. When she was done, Sophie chewed her lip. "This Murphy may just *want* to believe Bob knew. Diffusion of responsibility is a powerful drive. If he wasn't the only person to condone the action, he doesn't have to bear the burden alone."

Jo rubbed Cleopatra's ear. "But the way he said it—it left me with a different feel. Not like he was grasping for someone to share the blame with, but more like—I don't know how to describe it—more like scorn. Like—the way you'd look at someone who was embarrassing themselves."

Sophie stared down into the half-depleted martini. "Or the way people look at a wife who's trying desperately to pretend her husband hasn't *really* fallen out of love with her."

Jo's mind flew back to the conversation she'd had with David the day before—had it really only been a day ago? "He called me yesterday, I was going to tell you the next time we talked. He wants me to convince you he just made a stupid mistake, and he'll make it right if you take him back."

Sophie gave a strange snort-snuffle-hiccup sound. "Did you believe him?"

Jo weighed out what he'd said. There had been a sincerity to his pleas that rang true, but also an accompanying cluelessness that rankled. "Here's my opinion, which is probably worth what you paid for it. I don't think David has fallen out of love with you. And I certainly don't think he loves *her* more than he loves you. I just think David will always love himself more than anyone else."

Sophie stared off-screen for a moment, up toward the second floor of her house. "Even than the girls, you think?"

Jo squeezed her eyes shut against the pain of the truth. "Unfortunately, yes. Not to say he doesn't love them, and you, dearly. But he's never been the sort of man who can put his own needs aside. At least up until now. Maybe this whole disaster has jolted him out of that."

"How likely do you think that is?" Somehow Sophie's eyes were both resigned and hopeful.

Jo shook her head and heaved another large sigh. "I'm just as torn on that as I am on whether Bob's lying to himself about how much he knew."

"Hey, is everything okay?" Matt appeared at the kitchen doorway, voice thick with sleep.

Jo straightened up. "Sorry, I didn't mean to wake you. I'm talking to Sophie. Go back to bed."

"I should let you go," Sophie said.

"No, it's okay, I'm always here for you, night or day." Jo

glanced between her sister on the screen and Matt in the doorway, trying to read their reactions simultaneously.

"I know. And you've given me enough to think about for one night. Now go. Love you." Sophie hung up without waiting for a response.

Matt crossed over to Jo, kissed her cheek, and sat down in the chair next to her. "Don't worry about having woken me. I've been worried because you weren't home yet, so I've been in and out of sleep."

She studied his face—concern, but with an undeniable undercurrent of emotion. Her jaw clenched. With everything she was dealing with right now, she wasn't sure she had the energy to take responsibility for someone else's emotions. She needed to refuel for Ossokov, not deflect guilt trips and cater to yet another person's needs—

She instantly chastised herself—she was being petty and selfish. "I'm sorry, I should have texted. And I know this is the third night in a row I'm apologizing for the same thing, and this is a bad start to us living together, but—"

"But what?" he asked, watching her closely.

She sagged back in the chair. "But nothing. No excuses. I don't know what's wrong with me."

He nodded slowly. "Did we move in together too quickly? I can ask David to find another place and move back to my house."

She reached over and grabbed his hand, gazing straight into his eyes. "No, the timing isn't the problem. I want you here, and I want to make this work. It all boils down to my fears, and the only way to get past the fear is to go through the process of dealing with it. But that's not really fair to ask of you, so if you want to leave I completely understand."

He smiled softly. "I have no problem learning how to be together with you. I just need to know that's all this is."

That's precisely what Jo needed to know, too. And while

she believed in the power of honest communication, she'd learned the hard way that spouting doubts when you weren't sure they reflected reality was the fastest way to destroy trust in a relationship.

She returned the half-smile and squeezed his hand. "That's all this is."

DAY FOUR

CHAPTER FORTY-FIVE

Finding Murphy wasn't hard—just a question of driving town to town to each of his regular hangouts until I spotted his car. He always parked in the back, most likely to keep anyone from spotting his car if they casually drove by. But my driving wasn't casual, and I finally found him at The Tap Club in Philby.

I had to go inside to watch him. Not a huge problem; these weren't the sort of venues that had extensive security set-ups, and the low-light conditions wouldn't yield detailed footage. And I'd developed a few appropriate disguises—hats, nondescript clothes and big sunglasses that, even in the dark, fit right in.

I settled in to watch him one last time. There was a ritual to his drinking, predictable and sad. He sat, agitated and tense, like a man late for an appointment hoping the bartender will hurry his drink. Drinks plural, actually, because he usually ordered the first two as a pair. He threw back the first like a man who'd just escaped the Mojave Desert, each bob of his Adam's apple also dropping his shoulders a fraction of an inch, until he set down the glass with nothing but a ring of foam slipping down the side. Then, after a moment's pause, he'd reach for the second, more slowly this time, and drink off a third of it. This time he'd savor the beer, his eyes closing as the liquid eased down his throat and the alcohol infused his bloodstream. By the third drink, the tension in his face would go slack, and something that approached a smile would play at his lips. He'd get chatty with any fellow patron within easy talking distance, and tap the bar along with songs he liked. Sometimes he even put money into the jukebox and picked a song or two.

When he reached that point I honed in, physically hovering over the beer I'd ordered but hadn't touched, an invisible filament pulling me to absorb what passed for peace in Steve Murphy's world.

His illusory peace. The others—the ADA and the judge and the defense attorney—their peace, even if fleeting, was real. It sent out soothing tendrils that rooted their psyche in sanity. But the alcohol Murphy poured into the gaping chasm of his soul was a symptom, not a solution. Underneath the patina of song singing and guffawing, the maw of his pain waited.

That's how he was like me: no amount of yoga or bird-watching or treadmill running could touch the snarling beast eating away at me. Everything I'd tried was akin to putting a Band-Aid over the gushing blood of a severed limb. I almost felt sorry for him because I understood the pain so well: it never stopped, not during the loud times and certainly not during the quiet times, not even in your sleep—it gave you nightmares or caused you to wake in the middle of the night, suffocated by darkness, terrified to move, your heart thrumming like the wings of a hummingbird.

But two things made me different from Murphy. First, that I was smart enough to realize that alcohol, or drugs or gambling or shopping or any other potential 'ism,' would only make the problem worse. I knew when the alcohol left his system the pain would be worse than when he started, that he was chasing his tail in a circle he'd never be fast enough to escape. Second, that Murphy had created his own hell by committing despicable acts, while my pain was created not by me; those same acts had ripped away any chance I ever had of having a normal, peaceful life. His daily struggle was the very least he deserved—in fact, his slow erosion was a blessing compared to the stark, dramatic shredding my own psyche had undergone.

I timed how long he smiled and sang. Because, sure enough, right on schedule, his momentary relief slipped away. The smile slackened into stupor, the singing into slurring. His pain roared back in the form of anger, small at first, little snipes at the guy next to him who spilled a beer. Then the gripes magnified, until the bartender leaned in close and threatened to cut him off. He pulled out some cash, threw it down onto the bar, and stormed out with the slow purposefulness the drunk use to keep the stumble out of their step.

I slipped out after him as the bartender turned to help a new customer, quickening my step once the creaky ballast of a door swung in place behind me. He wasn't far in front of me. He'd barely made it around the corner into the back lot before stopping to relieve himself against the wall.

Revulsion pulsed through me and I considered killing him right then, smiling at the thought of the self-important former detective being found with his dick out, lying in a puddle of his own piss.

He finished, zipped up, and headed toward his car.

I did a quick double-check to be sure nobody was around.

"Steve Murphy?" I called out.

He turned, swaying, and almost fell over. He caught himself—barely—against the back of his car. "Who are you? Do I know you?"

With one hand, I pulled off my glasses and hat so he could see my face. That was the benefit of catching him drunk—I'd have no chance against a sober cop, even an older, retired one who likely still carried. The downside was I had to hope he was *aware enough to process what I was saying. So I reminded him who I was and what he'd done to me.*

Then, as I watched the beautiful, terrified realization break through his alcohol haze, I triggered my telescopic truncheon and smashed it into his skull.

CHAPTER FORTY-SIX

The sky over Philby was still ink black as Jo, forcing her anger down into the pit of her stomach, hurried up to the crime-scene tape blocking off the back half of The Tap Club's parking area. The call had wrenched her out of a dreamless sleep, and for one confused moment she hoped she was having a nightmare that a fourth member of law enforcement had been murdered on her watch—but no, it was horrifyingly real.

How had Ossokov outsmarted her? She'd done everything she could to protect Murphy—warned him, tried to get surveillance on him, searched every dive in Oakhurst for him. But she couldn't help but feel she should have been able to prevent it.

She shook her head and forced herself to focus. She couldn't afford the luxury of either guilt or anger right now, she needed to remain clear-headed and on target. Arnett was the next victim in line, and she was no closer to catching Ossokov than she'd been four days ago.

As if on cue, Arnett's blue Cadillac CT4 pulled up as she checked in with the responding officer. Arnett crossed to her side, his gait fast but stilted, a dead giveaway that he was suppressing an anxiety he'd never admit to.

"Don't worry," he said. "I don't have any intention of going behind the tape. But I need to know for myself."

Jo grimaced. It wasn't ideal, but as long as he didn't enter the crime scene, he couldn't be accused of tampering with anything or anyone. "Are you here? I hadn't noticed."

She turned back to the RO, a stocky, buzz-cutted barrel of an officer whose nameplate read M. Severn. "Catch me up."

Severn looked down at his notes. "Owner, Ryan Preston, said he came out to dump the evening's trash after closing up shop. Found Murphy dead on the asphalt by his car in the back. I saw the BOLO for him when I logged into my MCT this morning, so I recognized the name and contacted you all directly. Your CSI team is with him now."

Jo stepped to the left so she could see around the corner of the building. Marzillo and Peterson were vaguely recognizable in their PPE, blocking her view of what they were processing.

"Did Preston recognize Murphy?" Jo asked.

"He did. Said he comes here once, maybe twice, a week. He'd been here for a couple of hours, had several beers, and left about an hour before last call, around twelve ten. He said he didn't notice anything out of the ordinary about Murphy's demeanor, and that he left alone."

Jo was impressed—Severn was thorough and succinct, both qualities she appreciated in the current moment. "What time did Preston find him?"

"Just after two thirty in the morning. He says it takes him about an hour to close up after the last customer leaves, and then he tosses out the trash as he heads home."

Jo reached for her PPE. "Good work."

Once she'd kitted up she beelined for Marzillo and Peterson, trying to ignore the astringent scent of urine. She stopped short as the two turned toward her, silent faces grim, revealing the figure lying on the asphalt. They parted as she moved closer, still without a word.

Fighting back the anger and desperation, Jo stepped carefully around him, forcing herself to analytically take in and sort the details. The left side of his blindfold showed patches of blood, and matted hair stuck out above and below it. His mouth was now twisted unnaturally into an open slash that caricatured his grimace when he'd accused the man she trusted most in the world of misconduct.

"Another crowbar?" she asked.

Marzillo didn't blink. "We don't know. We haven't located the weapon yet."

Jo tilted forward, calculating the concentration of blood. "Looks like the blow came from the front, above the ear?"

"That's my guess, but I can't say until we remove the blindfold."

Jo scanned the area. Far enough away from the corner of the building that nobody would have seen accidentally. Farther away from the car than Deena Scott had been, and at the back rather than the side, due to the layout of the parking lot. But, otherwise, the scene was largely the same as Scott's, complete with posed arms.

But different from Ashville's and Sakurai's in important ways. They'd been killed in a backyard and a park respectively. What was the significance of those differences? Was it purely a matter of convenience, of where the killer was able to catch the victim alone and out of the eyes of security cameras? And why was the first murder done with a gun but the others weren't? Winnie had been killed by a weapon of opportunity, a rock taken from the site, but the killer had brought the crowbar to kill Deena Scott. In those two cases, they'd left the weapon right on scene, but not in this case, or Ashville's.

Her hands clenched into fists. And why the blindfolds? Why the posing? Everybody already knew he'd been the victim of a miscarriage of justice. Was this just his way of playing with them, just his above-and-beyond 'fuck you'? Was he really that egotistical that he'd risk covering himself in his victims' blood just to thumb his nose at them?

She shook her head to clear it. None of it mattered. She was overthinking again.

She turned and strode back to the perimeter, stripped and bagged her PPE, and then crossed to where Arnett was waiting in his car. He rolled down his window as she tapped in a phone call.

"I want Ossokov in interrogation, now."

CHAPTER FORTY-SEVEN

Half an hour later, as Arnett, Goran, and Coyne all watched from behind two-way glass, Jo strode into the spartan interrogation room, started the recording, then slid into the plastic chair across the table from Kent and Ossokov. Kent sipped casually from a venti Starbucks cup he'd apparently taken the time to pick up on the way, telegraphing nonchalance. Ossokov, his matching cup untouched, sat straight and tense, one leg bouncing continually.

"Use this time wisely, Detective," Kent said over the lid of his coffee. "It's the last time you'll be talking to my client."

Jo was well aware she was walking a fine line. She had nothing close to the type of evidence needed for a grand jury indictment, and if she arrested Ossokov at this point Kent would hold that up as further harassment. Her only hope was to provoke Ossokov into revealing something, or making some other mistake. So she chose her words carefully and kept her expression inscrutable. "That's not a very helpful attitude."

Kent laced his fingers together and set his hands on the table. "I don't feel the need to advise my client to assist in a witch-hunt. You already searched his home and took a court-ordered DNA sample that we know will exonerate him, especially since, in light of the harassment suit, we'll be making sure the analysis is carefully supervised to ensure no more 'mistakes' are made."

"A witch-hunt. Huh." Jo tilted her head. "That's an interesting take on it. Here's my take, a perspective shared by the Oakhurst County SPDU. Four people are dead, all killed by the same person." She paused, weighing whether Kent's and Ossokov's surprised expressions were genuine. "That's right, four. Early this morning we found former Detective Steve Murphy murdered in a parking lot."

Kent's expression morphed into undertaker-greeting-bereaved-family, and he shook his head. "I'm very sorry to hear that. But it has nothing to do with my client."

Jo was more interested in the fear that flashed across Ossokov's face. "You don't have an alibi for the previous murders. Since you made quite a show of making sure our surveillance unit was pulled off you last night, I'm hoping for your sake you have a solid alibi for the early hours of this morning."

Ossokov's eyes widened and flicked to Kent; they whispered a quick conversation before Ossokov responded. "I was at work until just before midnight. Then I went home, watched TV, and went to bed."

"Which your mother again can't verify because she was already asleep."

"That's correct," Ossokov said, eyes flicking between her and Kent.

Jo bought herself a moment by sipping her coffee. Something here wasn't right—Ossokov's reactions were off. The shift in his demeanor didn't match any of the options she'd anticipated. Despite what pop culture tried to claim, there was no telltale signal, like avoiding eye contact, that let you know when someone was lying; the very same behaviors that signaled deception in one person signaled veracity in the next. What mattered was a *shift* in behavior, a shift in communication and body language from their norm when engaged in casual conversation with no reason to lie. Ossokov's demeanor should have remained unchanged from the interview at his house, or should have doubled-down in terms of passive aggression. But he was tense and anxious in a way he hadn't been before. Why? Surely he must have known they'd pull him into interrogation once they found Murphy?

She probed more directly. "Four people intimately involved in your conviction—the prosecutor, the judge, the senior detective on the case, and your own defense attorney—have all turned up dead. That's far past any possibility of coincidence, and there's no avoiding the conclusion this has something to do with you."

"Was there a question in there?" Kent asked. "My client has nothing to do with these murders, so I'm not sure what you expect him to say."

As Kent spoke, Ossokov's gaze glanced from Kent's profile to the far wall, off to Ossokov's right.

Jo's radar honed in—he'd never done anything remotely like that during their previous conversations. People often stared at the ceiling when they were thinking, or at the door when they wanted to leave, but quick furtive glances at a far wall was either something a person did habitually or didn't do at all.

Jo kept her expression neutral and sipped her coffee again as she followed his glance, careful not to tip him off to her attention. There was nothing on the wall to capture his attention: no artwork, no window, nothing but plain, aged white paint. She mentally followed the direction of the gaze through to the outside world—it was in the general direction of his house.

A possibility glimmered in the back of her mind. She decided to run with it.

She held up her empty palm. "If you have nothing to do with this, Cooper, help us understand why it's happening."

"We're not going to do your job for you, Detective," Kent said.

Jo continued to speak directly to Ossokov. "My job is to talk to whoever might know why these murders are happening. The only connection between these people is you, Cooper. So if you're not responsible, you must have an idea who is. Tell me where I should be looking."

"My client isn't interested in your head games, Detective. He's not responsible for these deaths, and he's not responsible for the actions of whoever is. That's all he can tell you."

Ossokov glanced at Kent, then quickly at the wall again. "You're insinuating that someone's doing this on my behalf?"

Fear flashed in his eyes—but her attempt to blame someone else should have inspired relief, or smugness.

"I'm not insinuating, Cooper, I'm saying it outright. After you were released from prison, you claimed you were at peace with the wrongful incarceration. I found those articles compelling." Jo shifted her eyes subtly to Kent and back. "But now you've decided to file this lawsuit. What, or who, changed your mind?"

Red crept up Kent's neck. "This is your last warning, Detective. The lawsuit is out of bounds."

But Ossokov had gone rigid—she'd hit some sort of nerve.

She sipped again—with Kent ready to walk, this was her final shot to either provoke a reaction or plant a seed, depending on where the truth lay.

She shifted forward toward Ossokov. "The killer left a distinct message referencing the justice system on each of the victims. If you didn't do this, someone else who's angry about your miscarriage of justice did. I can understand why people who love you—or people who want to take advantage of the situation—would want to take action." She threw up a single finger to let Kent know she was almost done. "But what they don't realize is they're putting you at risk of going right back to prison in the process, as well as endangering themselves."

Ossokov glanced between her and Kent again, uncertain how to respond.

She leaned still closer and drove the dagger home. "I can't help but remember how angry your mother was when we showed up at your house."

Kent pushed back his chair and stood. "That's enough. Either arrest my client or let him go. It's disgusting and unconscionable to threaten the lives of people he loves when he's already suffered so much at the hands of your department." He grabbed Ossokov's arm and marched him out the door.

But Kent hadn't acted quickly enough. She'd seen the panic on Ossokov's face when she mentioned his mother.

She pulled out her phone as Arnett, Goran, and Coyne pushed into the room.

"Interesting tactic," Coyne said. "You can't really think threatening his mother will make him jump to confess?"

Arnett stared directly at Jo as he shook his head. "That's not what she's doing. There's more to it."

Jo tapped a call through to Lopez, who answered immediately. "Jo. How did it go?"

"I need you to do a couple of things, as quickly as possible. Ossokov is going to call or text someone, maybe more than one person, as soon as he's out of this building. I need to know who. Also, we need to access all of Rebecca Ossokov's phone and email records, including location information."

"Wait. You think she might be the killer?"

"Ossokov is at the center of this, that's undeniable. If he's not our killer, it has to be someone deeply angry on his behalf, and she fits that description best. She should be off work by now, so I'll head over there as quickly as possible, but I'd bet anything Kent is breaking every traffic law on the books to get there before I do."

"On it," Lopez said.

"We also need to go back and double-check for anyone else who might be close to Ossokov, or for any crossover with our other suspects. Anyone on the outside who knew him in prison or was close to him before he went in. Friends, relatives, anybody obsessed with him or his case, even that seventy-year-old uncle who lent him the car. I'm going to put Lacey Bernard on this, too, and between the two of you, we should be able to come up with a decent list quickly. Very quickly, because whether it's Ossokov, his mother, or someone obsessed with him, they've shown remarkable skill at outwitting us. And since Arnett is the last person alive who was directly hands-on with Ossokov's case, he's the next target."

———

As Jo predicted, Kent was waiting at Ossokov's house when she arrived, and had advised Rebecca Ossokov not to speak with her. He made a statement on her behalf, telling Jo she'd come home from work at just after six the night before, had made herself dinner, then had read until she went to bed at ten thirty. He also warned Jo that since putting Rebecca Ossokov under surveillance would necessarily mean putting surveillance on the house where Cooper Ossokov lived, he'd waste no time reporting it as further intimidation and have the surveillance removed immediately.

"He didn't call or text anyone," Lopez said over the speaker as Jo raced back to HQ, Goran and Coyne in their car behind her.

"Damn," she said. "So I was either wrong, or he had another burner with him."

"Ballsy. What if we would've searched his borrowed car?"

Lopez said. "In other news, I secured Rebecca Ossokov's phone and email records, and scoured Cooper's again. Didn't take much time because she's just as much of a hermit as he is. And I got hold of his visitor list while he was in prison. Began and ended with one person: his mother. No groupies that he allowed to write to him, nada."

An electric buzz ran up and down Jo's limbs as she navigated a turn. "If he's in on this with his mother, they wouldn't need to talk to anybody else. Thanks, Christine."

After hanging up, she put word out to her confidential informants that she needed information about who Ossokov might have been friends with in prison, who he might be hanging out with now, or who he might have reconnected with. Then she called in to check with Lacey Bernard.

"Hang on. Steve Murphy's dead?" Bernard said, after Jo jumped straight in.

Jo froze. "You didn't get a text about this one?"

"Nothing. I've been checking obsessively since I woke up at four this morning," Bernard said, voice fatigued.

Jo's mind raced. Not only had they come directly after each of the other murders, they'd threatened Lacey when she hadn't reported everything quickly enough. So why not now?

Lacey spoke again. "Maybe you made it too hot for him."

"I hope that's it." Jo transitioned back to why she was calling. "Lopez is looking at everything we can get a handle on, and I've pulled in some of my CIs. But you have a different set of sources and contacts. Can you dig in and see what you can pull up?"

"Trust and believe if he's hanging with someone on the down-low I'll find them. You may not be able to put him under surveillance, but I sure as hell can."

Jo tensed. "No, Lacey, that's not what I'm asking. Don't tail him. We're dealing with someone dangerous and they already have you in their sights."

"But you think digging into his life is gonna make me *less* of a target?"

"I do. He spotted our tail in no time flat, and our guys are very good at what they do. He's watching, actively."

Lacey didn't respond.

Jo's tires screeched as she cut the corner into the HQ parking lot. "I need to hear you say you're not going to tail him."

"I won't," Lacey said grudgingly.

"Thank you. Call me if you find anything and I'll do the same." Jo hung up, slammed to a stop in the parking lot, and jumped out of the car with Goran and Coyne following. She stopped by Arnett's desk to grab him, then led everyone to Hayes' office, feeling like a demented Pied Piper.

Everyone remained standing as she caught Hayes up.

"So because Ossokov didn't react the way you expected him to, you now think his mother's the killer?" Hayes asked.

"I haven't ruled out Ossokov as the killer, and they may be working together. Because yes, I do think there are things that fit better this way. It never made sense to me why he'd bother to file the lawsuit if he was intent on killing everyone involved anyway, and—"

"For this very reason." Hayes made a sweeping gesture. "Because any move we make against him, he can scream harassment from the rooftops."

"And I agree, that may well be right. I'm just saying we need to cover our bases. We need surveillance on both Ossokov and his mother."

Hayes shook her head like she couldn't believe what she was hearing. "You know we can't do that. The instant we do, he'll have us for harassment."

Jo bit back her frustration—she'd hoped given the circumstances Hayes would drop the antagonism and listen, just for once. "If we go to the judge and make clear what's at stake here, one of our detective's lives, we should at least be able to get another agency to—"

"What exactly is that argument supposed to look like, Fournier? Am I supposed to tell him or her that I want to practically guarantee Ossokov will win hundreds of thousands of dollars because one of my detectives can't take care of himself?" Arnett, Goran, and Coyne all bristled, but Hayes didn't seem to notice. "Money that the state could be using to patrol dangerous neighborhoods or protect at-risk children? He or she will tell you the same thing I'm telling you—if you're worried about Arnett's safety, then put the surveillance on *him*."

Jo tightened her stance and lifted her chin. "Excellent, put surveillance on Arnett. But what if he isn't the only target left on the killer's list? The only way we can cover our bases is by watching *Ossokov and his mother*."

Hayes' face screwed up into an angry grimace and she started to say something, then caught herself. Her face relaxed into a firm smile. "Detective Fournier. Neither you nor I have time to stand here arguing in circles over circumstances we can't change. The best solution is for you to go out there and find something ironclad that'll let you arrest them without any possible stain. So get out there and do it."

Jo clenched her fists, and her jaw. "Yes, ma'am." She turned to go.

"One last thing," Hayes said.

Jo turned back.

"If I find out that for some reason you decide to ignore my direct, clear instruction on this and put any form of surveillance on Ossokov or his mother, I won't just bust you down to traffic cop. I'll remove you completely." She glanced around pointedly at the other detectives. "And I'll hold you personally responsible if anybody else does, too."

CHAPTER FORTY-EIGHT

The feeling of freedom after killing Murphy was the shortest yet —which worried me. But I was closing in on the end, and that's what I had to focus on now. Once it was all behind me, I'd be able to sleep at night again. And knowing that—well, as I drove out to my destination, I found myself singing along with the radio again.

I parked a block away from my target, in front of a group of houses I knew didn't have security cameras. Not hard in that particular neighborhood; it wasn't a ghetto but it wasn't fancy either. The house I was headed for did, but only one, angled to capture the stretch from the door out to the driveway—leaving the back and the sides of the house completely blind. I'd placed my own tiny camera in a tree in the neighbor's yard so I could be certain the house was currently empty.

After parking in a safe spot, I cinched my hoodie around my face, and, with my head down in apparent concentration, jogged away from my car. Two houses on the path had cameras I couldn't avoid, but nobody would know when to look for me on the footage, and even if they did, my hood would make it impossible to recognize me. But safe is better than sorry, so I was careful not to break stride when I jogged past those two cameras, and kept my head down.

When I reached the blind side of the target house, I quickly ducked into the yard and crouched down behind a row of bushes. The sound of a passing car sent my heart racing, and I stayed down a long minute just to be sure I was safe. Then I carefully scanned the bottom edge of the house and the underside of the bushes, searching for what I needed. When I found the right spots, guided by the internet's infinite wisdom, I finished my task as quickly as possible, covered my tracks, and left no trace. Then I jogged back out of the yard.

Just as I came off the property, another car rounded the corner, heading right toward me. Adrenaline burst through me like I'd been hit by the darts of a taser. Had they only seen me running again on the pavement—or had they seen me near the side of the house?

I forced myself to keep my pace steady and my head down as the car approached me. I glanced up from under the edge of the hood. The driver and her passenger, a teenaged girl, seemed to be engaged in some sort of argument, paying no attention to me. They passed without slowing, and turned again at the next corner.

I slowed my pace slightly and tried to recapture my breath. That was exactly the sort of unpredictable situation I couldn't plan for, and that would take me down if I wasn't careful—if the mother and daughter hadn't been fighting, they'd have seen me, and remembered me. They might have even stopped to ask what I was doing.

Far too close for comfort.

I picked up the pace again, giving myself a pep talk. Everything I'd accomplished would be for nothing if I screwed it up now. I had to put the fear aside, dig down deep, and stay steady for just a while longer.

On to my next target.

CHAPTER FORTY-NINE

Jo exploded through the door into Marzillo and Lopez's section of the lab. "How am I supposed to do my job if she's throwing up walls every time I turn around?"

"Whoa, pony." Lopez jumped up from her chair. "Catch me up. Walk me through it."

Jo paced as she explained. "I realize she wants me gone, but is she really willing to put someone's life on the line to get that?"

"She's not wrong, though. We can't risk putting surveillance on Ossokov and his mother." Lopez grabbed a can of Starbucks' Nitro Cold Brew out of her mini fridge and tossed it to Jo. "Drink this."

"Very smart to dump caffeine on top of that adrenaline," Arnett said, glancing at the can. "And what happened to your Rockstars?"

"Nothing." Lopez pointed at the open Rockstar on her desk. "A good hostess is always prepared for a variety of needs. And never, ever underestimate the power of caffeine, especially when some killer is trying to take members of the team out." She turned to Jo, who was glaring at her. "You know I'd rather stab myself in the eye with a whale harpoon than agree with

Upstate Ursula, but her number-one priority right now has to be making sure we don't hand Ossokov both a free-ride-for-life and get-away-with-multiple-murder card by the end of this."

"But—" Jo started.

"No buts." Lopez waved an index finger up and down in Jo's direction. "This here, it's not anger at Hayes. It's frustration and helplessness because some crazy dude and/or his mother want to unalive your partner, and you feel it's your responsibility to protect him. I'm right there with you. So push the panic aside and let's figure out what we can do within the boundaries that reality has inflicted upon us."

Jo's anger deflated. Lopez was right—during her own brief stint as lieutenant, what would she have done? Would she have thrown caution to the wind and endangered her unit by sending out a surveillance team in such a sensitive situation? No.

But the limitations set by the priorities of that leadership were a big part of why she'd resigned the position.

She snatched over an empty chair across from Lopez's desk, cracked open the Nitro Cold Brew, and took a long pull.

"Right," she said after she swallowed and winced at the cold coffee. "What's that quote you love, Christine? That the Mandarin word for 'crisis' is a combination of the symbols for 'danger' and 'opportunity' and how that means we should turn obstacles into possibilities?"

Lopez grimaced sheepishly. "Yeah, so, turns out that's not a thing. Tony called me on it and when I checked it out, 'crisis' is a combination of 'danger' and 'crucial point.' Not really the same message at all."

Jo squeezed her eyes shut and rubbed her brow. "So much for that particular pep talk. But the principle is still sound. We need to find a way to turn this situation to our advantage."

"Agreed. So how?" Lopez asked.

"Easy." Arnett pulled open the mini-fridge and grabbed his own can of Nitro Cold Brew. "We use me as bait. Because

Hayes was right about another thing, too. I'm an Oakhurst County SPDU detective, not a kindergartener. I'm paid to catch killers, not hide from them."

Jo took another sip of the coffee. "As much as I hate it, it makes sense."

"Neither Ossokov nor his mother are stupid. If you have surveillance on Arnett, they'll spot it a mile away and bail," Lopez said.

"So we'll have to be subtle." Arnett cracked open his can. "Or appear to create an opportunity for them. Do something that seems to leave me vulnerable."

Arnett's words pinballed around Jo's mind, pulling together something she'd been trying to make sense of. "No, that's exactly wrong."

"Why?" Arnett asked.

She held up an index finger asking for a moment to complete her thought, then pounded the rest of her Nitro Cold Brew to help it come together. "Sakurai loved birdwatching. Deena Scott was a gym rat. Murphy was—Murphy liked to drink. Our killer isn't hanging out waiting for random opportunities. They're watching, closely, for ways to exploit the victim's schedules."

"They killed Ashville at home," Lopez said.

"She had no life outside of work. And if your choices are the well-fortified and CCTV-monitored DA's office or courthouse versus her remote lake house, which would you pick?"

"Point taken," Arnett said. "But my schedule is tougher than Ashville's. I barely work out—don't roll your eyes—and when I do, I do it here at the HQ gym. I go shooting out at the range, also heavily secured. Laura and I have date night once a week, but we vary what we do, and there's no way I'm bringing her into this." He pulled out his phone. "In fact, I'm sending her to go visit her sister in Vermont immediately."

They waited while Arnett made the phone call, but Laura's

voice mail picked up. He left a message telling her to leave for her sister's house and call him back when she was on the way.

"That should completely freak her out," Lopez said, eyes wide.

Jo shook her head. "She's been married to a cop for decades. It'll scare her, but she'll be okay. And, our killer doesn't seem to be interested in collateral damage, so I don't think they'll go after her."

"Problem." Arnett typed out a text. "They could go the sniper route pretty much anywhere, even as I'm walking into the building here."

Lopez ran her hand along her ponytail. "They could've shot Ashville from the trees, but they didn't. They want their victims to know what's coming."

"They know Arnett knows what's coming, so that might change," Jo said. "I say we announce you're on administrative leave. That will force them into a box—they'll have to hit you at home, and that'll put us in control. Bernard needs something to print anyway, so I'll make sure she gets the news before the others."

Arnett scratched his chin. "I have a security camera at home —but then, so did Ashville."

"Hers weren't positioned to capture the road or the pier. Do yours cover your entire property?" Jo asked.

"The front entrance of the house, but there are blind spots."

"They've done their research, so they know about the blind spots. We can take advantage of that," Jo said.

"I don't run, don't go for walks, I don't even do yard work. Laura gardens and we have a neighbor kid who does the mowing and the big stuff. The only thing left is the ten-yard walk from my car to the front door, and that would be captured on camera."

"If I were the killer, I'd take the camera out," Lopez said. "Is your camera hooked up to Wi-Fi?"

"Yep. We access them through an app, but we've been careful to use secure passwords."

"Doesn't matter. Someone with skills can hack into them and take them offline whenever they like. If they don't have skills, a ski mask and a baseball bat'll accomplish the same thing. In that case you'd know there was a problem, but it'd take time to repair," Lopez said.

"Which is fine for our purposes," Jo said, "because we *want* them to think they can get past the security. So we leave it in place, but maybe put up some feeds in the neighbors' yards to cover the property. Then we place the team remotely, a few blocks away monitoring the cameras, so they'll be close but not visible."

Arnett nodded. "With me waiting inside."

"I think that gives us the best bet at controlling the situation, unless you guys can think of anything better?" Jo asked.

"What about you, Jo? Inside or out?" Lopez asked.

Jo raked her teeth across her lower lip. "I'll take the evening shift tonight in the van. Then when the teams change I'll go home, get a few hours of sleep, and return for the early-morning shift with Goran and Coyne so I'm there for the pre-dawn hours our killer seems to favor."

"I like it," Arnett said.

Lopez nodded.

"Anything else we're missing?" Jo glanced between them. When they both shook their heads, she pulled out her phone. "Okay, then. I'll call Goran and Coyne in here to set everything up."

CHAPTER FIFTY

Amid the stress of everything, I'd forgotten to eat again. I never used to forget to eat—I had an appetite the size of the Burj Khalifa. But now my stomach is a perpetual minefield of nausea. Even when I do remember to eat, I never know when it's going to come right back up at an inopportune moment.

As I sat down with a bag of something fast and cheap, I tapped and read over the report about Bob Arnett. They weren't calling it a suspension, but in essence, that's what it was. I'd been hoping for something akin to that; although I arranged my plans so I'd be fine either way, every variable I could limit or control was one less worry.

I brought up my cameras. The news report about Arnett was part of a mental chess game that was going to determine the rest of my life, and as such I couldn't afford to accept it at face value. Because the timing was strange—why would they put him on leave after Murphy's death? Why not the day before, when the lawsuit was announced in the press? That would have been the appropriate time if they were worried he'd compromise the lawsuit and the murder investigation. Possibly that was just how long these things took, but I couldn't afford to assume that was so.

I considered other possibilities. Had he upset his lieutenant? From what I'd experienced of Arnett, he was the sort who waited back at the edge of the shadows and let others take the attention, watching and waiting and planning his moves carefully. Upsetting his superior didn't seem to fit.

The other possibility was the news piece was a ploy. Detectives loved to release false information for their own purposes, and since they'd failed with the surveillance, this could be a strategy to regain control. No matter—from the start I'd known Arnett was going to be the hardest; not only was he smart and inscrutable, he had a broad range of allies and resources surrounding him. He, and they, knew I was coming for him.

If I were in that situation, I'd turn it into a trap.

In light of that, the complete lack of activity in his house took on a very particular significance. Some sort of prep was happening somewhere. They had to know I was watching—did the fact that my cameras were still functioning mean they hadn't found them, or that they wanted me to watch? The safer way was to assume they were well aware of the cameras, and that everything I saw through them was planned out for me.

I smiled into my food, enjoying the mental chess match.

I slipped my hand into my jacket and stroked the checkmate I had hidden there.

CHAPTER FIFTY-ONE

Jo crossed her legs in the back of the van, distracting herself from the impending attack by trying to decide which was worse: her thirst, or the need to urinate. She glanced resentfully at Goran and Coyne, both sipping coffee as they watched the two monitors in front of them. They could drink as much as they wanted to—when it came time to relieve themselves, a bottle would do the trick. She didn't have that option. She either had to strictly regulate what she drank, or pray for sturdy bladder control. Each set of headlights sped her pulse, and each intervening stretch of quiet sharpened her attention. The killer was out there. Watching, waiting, biding their time.

By ten, the neighborhood was silent; only intermittent porch lights triggered by cats and raccoons broke up the darkness.

Just before eleven thirty a teenager across the street from Arnett's house climbed down the trellis from her second-story window, dropped to the ground with a gentle thud, then jogged to the car she'd judiciously parked down the street. Jo beat back the urge to give chase and return the girl to her family by the scruff of her neck; while she knew that thousands of girls sneaked out each night and returned safely, she'd seen far too many of the ones who weren't so lucky, all for the sake of a few stolen kisses at some lurid lover's lane.

By the time their replacements rapped on the side of the van just before midnight, she was coiled like a cat ready to spring. She listened as Goran and Coyne gave their quick report, then headed home, steadfastly forcing herself not to drive down Arnett's street on the way out.

As she turned into her driveway and saw Matt's car, she had another moment of panic—but no, she'd called him before they'd started the shift in the van. Only four hours ago, but time on a stakeout stood still, and it felt like it'd been days since that conversation.

The house was dark; she slipped quietly inside. After hanging up her jacket, Jo picked up the cat, who settled into the crook of her shoulder as Jo crept through to the bedroom. For the sake of time and noise, she pulled off her shoes, socks, and pants, slipped her bra off through her sleeves, and slid into bed still wearing her shirt. Matt stirred slightly and slid his hand onto her hip, but didn't wake.

Despite the day's emotional rollercoaster and the evening's lack of caffeine, Jo couldn't sleep. Staring up at the shadowed ceiling, she listened to Matt's snores. She shifted carefully, trying not to wake him further, and grabbed her phone. She fired off a text to Arnett, then stared at the phone, willing him to respond.

All quiet. Go to sleep.

She sighed, and tried not to obsess about Matt's hand on her hip. She'd never been a cuddly sleeper, even back with Jack, because she overheated easily. Now, as she lay with a thousand ugly scenarios involving Ossokov and Arnett playing out in her head, Matt's fingers felt like coils of an electric furnace against her skin.

Beads of sweat pooled behind her knees, then at the back of her neck.

Finally, unable to be still any longer, she rolled away, causing his hand to gently drop off. The relief was almost instant, like opening the refrigerator door on a smoldering summer's day. She'd most likely still not be able to sleep, but at least she wouldn't be caught in a swamp while she reckoned with her anxiety-induced insomnia.

Eventually, she managed to drift off to sleep—until her phone shrilled her back awake.

She bolted up onto her elbow, Arnett's face flashing in her mind, and stabbed at the phone. "Fournier. What's happening?"

Lieutenant Hayes' voice answered. "I need you here, now. Cooper Ossokov has been killed."

DAY FIVE

CHAPTER FIFTY-TWO

Jo threw up her portable siren and raced to the crime scene, trying to make sense of what was happening.

In the fog of sleep, she'd had to ask Hayes to repeat herself. But when she did, the words still refused to compute and time had frozen.

How was it possible Cooper Ossokov was dead? There had to be a mistake, Hayes must just have said it wrong—like the time they'd announced the wrong best-picture winner at the Oscars.

Then, with a whoosh that had felt like she'd been sucked through a vortex, her brain kicked in, time sped back up, and her logical circuits flared back to life. "He showed up to kill Arnett, and the team took him out?"

"What? No, this has nothing to do with Arnett. He's safe at home, still under the watch of his security team. Someone killed Ossokov in the alley behind the dentist office where he works. With the same signature as all the other victims."

That woke her the rest of the way up. "Even the posed arms and hands?"

"Even the posed arms and hands. I'm on my way now."
Hayes hung up.

Jo snatched up the clothes she'd left by the side of the bed as she explained to Matt. The posed arms were proprietary information—they'd kept it back from everyone, even Ossokov himself. Only the detectives and the killer knew about it—which meant this murder wasn't an accident and it wasn't a coincidence.

Now, as she flew toward Chicopee, she forced her mind to calmly catalogue the implications. At best she'd missed something, and she had to figure out what. At worst, she'd completely screwed up, and completely misunderstood what was happening.

No—the main logic still stood. The only connection between all the victims was Ossokov.

Had Ossokov been working with a partner, possibly Hauptmann or Flynn, but had some sort of falling out? Or had Jo's questions during the interrogation planted more of a seed than she'd hoped, and rather than just leading them to whoever was killing on his behalf, he'd confronted them? Maybe he'd contacted them via burner and asked him to come to his workplace to talk in person. Maybe the confrontation got heated, and ultimately ended with Ossokov dead, maybe by accident? If so, it would make sense for the person to try to confuse the situation by using the same signature as the other killings.

Jo voice-commanded her phone to call Goran and Coyne.

"We're en route," Goran stated without preamble. "We left Arnett at home."

"Good thinking." She made a sharp turn. "Because I need you to bring in Rebecca Ossokov as soon as possible."

"You think his *mother* killed him?"

"At this point I'm ruling out nothing. But no, I think it's more likely she's not involved but knows who is."

"Got it. We're on our way."

She hung up, then screeched to a halt next to the dental office's sidewalk. Set in an industrial area of Chicopee, Denton Dental was part of a complex of similar buildings that varied somewhat in shape, but not in style. All were modular squares and rectangles, primarily made of red brick with corrugated accents and some roll-up delivery bays. Most buildings had no signage and had to be identified by address—a task made harder because several buildings shared each lot and were differentiated only by lettered suites. Denton Dental was 525B, and was one of the few in the area to have a prominent sign.

The responding officer filled her in on the details of the scene, then directed her to where Marzillo and Peterson were suiting up. Marzillo acknowledged her with a curt jut of her chin.

"You should've let someone else take this," Jo said. "When was the last time you slept?"

"I got a good, solid four hours." Marzillo glanced over Jo's face. "How much did *you* get?"

"Point taken." Jo suited up at breakneck pace, then stepped under the crime-scene tape and over to Ossokov.

"Behind the building, just like Murphy, and similar to Scott." Jo glanced at the only car in the lot, about fifty feet away from the supine figure, and checked the license plate. "That's the vehicle he borrowed to get himself back and forth to work. He may have been leaving after work, or may have called someone to meet him."

Peterson moved closer to Ossokov, and visibly flinched. "Holy shit."

Jo stepped to his side, and instantly understood—what was left above his shoulders was barely recognizable as a head. The arms were posed the same way as the previous victims, but in this case, the blindfold was simply draped over a misshapen pile of pulp and hair, with blood flowing into a large pool. Jo's stomach clenched, and she willed her gag reflex not to kick in.

"Are we even sure this is Ossokov?" Peterson said.

Jo pointed to the poorly executed yin-yang symbol on Ossokov's forearm. "I recognize the tattoo."

Marzillo took a closer look. "Fairly distinctive shade of BIC pen."

Jo ran a practiced eye over the rest of his body, squatting for a closer look at Ossokov's right thigh. "What's happening here? This blood pool is running toward the head, not away from it."

Marzillo directed Peterson to photograph the body and blood pool. Once he'd finished, she bent down and carefully lifted the leg. "Gunshot wound. Based on the size of the entrance wound, I'm guessing we're looking at a twenty-two."

"No scorching around the hole," Jo said.

"Nope. This was done from farther away."

"So that's new." Jo carefully circled Ossokov. "I'm guessing there would have been no reason to shoot him after bashing his head in, so the gunshot came first?"

"Or maybe Ossokov broke away after an initial blow, and our killer shot him to stop him getting away?" Marzillo said.

Jo's hand flipped up to the diamond at her throat. "Then why not just shoot him in the head once he was down and have done with it? Bashing in someone's head this way is difficult and messy. They'd have been hit by a tremendous amount of back spatter."

"Maybe he pulled out a gun to stop his attacker and accidentally shot himself? Or there was a struggle and the gun went off?" Peterson said.

"Something similar occurred to me on the way here. Also that maybe he figured out who was responsible for the killings and confronted them." Jo motioned to what remained of Ossokov's head. "But I don't think so. Whatever happened, there was some rage behind it."

"Maybe the killer went berserk when he wasn't falling over himself with gratitude," Peterson said.

"I'd appreciate whatever estimation you can give me about time of death as soon as possible. The RO said the industrial baker in the next unit over arrived at one this morning to begin work and found him like this. She didn't see any cars or anything unusual, and claimed it was clear he'd been dead for some time. I see now why." Jo straightened and scanned the building. "Hopefully there's some sort of security camera inside the building, and that'll help set the time."

"As soon as I have something more conclusive than that I'll let you know, but for now I can't place it much more precisely than the baker's information."

"Thanks." Jo returned to the responding officer and asked him to send out local PD to canvas the area and check into the security footage. Then she followed Peterson as he photographed the surrounding scene segment by segment, searching for anything that could give more of a clue to what happened. They'd nearly finished the space when her phone buzzed an incoming call. "Goran. What's happening?"

"We tracked down Ossokov's mother. She spent last night at her sister's house. Sarah Billings."

"Why?" Jo asked.

"She slipped getting out of the bathtub last night and sprained her wrist. Sister Sarah took her to urgent care, then insisted Rebecca spend the night so Sarah could take care of her. Of course the hospital has security footage."

"What time?"

"She slipped around nine thirty, and checked in to urgent care around ten fifteen. There had been a multi-vehicle crash on the pike, so they were busy and she wasn't seen until almost one in the morning. All documented and verified. I requested security footage just to be certain."

"Damn. So fully accounted for during the time Ossokov was murdered."

"Yep, but from what you said I figured you still wanted to talk to her. We're bringing her into interrogation now."

"I'll be right there."

———

Rebecca Ossokov's head snapped up as Jo entered the interrogation room. Random tendrils stuck out from her messy bun, and her crystal-blue eyes were swollen and rimmed with red. Both hands, one wrist wrapped in a brace, clutched crumpled tissues, and a cup of something sat ignored in front of her.

Hope briefly flashed in her eyes as she searched Jo's face. "Is this some sort of ploy to mess with my head?"

"No ploy." Jo put a full box of tissues in front of her. "I'm so sorry for your loss."

Fresh tears poured down her face. "You're *sorry*? You did this to him! You wouldn't leave him alone! First you take his life from him, then just when he gets it back..." Her anger devolved into sobs, and both hands flew up to clutch at her eyes.

Jo waited quietly until the jag subsided and Rebecca's breathing calmed. In a gentle voice she asked, "What do you mean by that, that this is our fault?"

Rebecca's face screwed up into an angry red ball, and her finger thrust into Jo's face. "You all cover for each other no matter what. You never thought he'd get out of prison and when he did you had to cover up your mistakes. You expect me to believe it's a coincidence that he files a lawsuit against your department, then two days later he's dead?"

Jo took a deep breath before responding, careful to keep her tone calm and non-confrontational. "Whoever killed your son also killed Sandra Ashville and the others. Do you really think we'd kill three members of law enforcement and his defense attorney just to frame your son, only to then kill him?"

Rebecca's arm dropped to the table, and her gaze zig-zagged around the room as she struggled to find an answer.

Jo gave her a moment, then continued. "Whoever killed those people, including your son, I want to catch them—even if they're a member of law enforcement." Rebecca's eyes snapped back to her. "I need your help to do that."

As Rebecca searched her face, Jo tried to telegraph her sincerity. Rebecca finally nodded, sending twin tears down her cheeks.

"Do you know of anybody else angry enough on Cooper's behalf to kill for him?"

Rebecca's fingers grasped at the surface of the table. "Nobody."

"No friends or girlfriends?"

Rebecca looked down at the floor and swiped at her face as more tears came. "Cooper has always been an introvert. He never had many friends, and the very few he had disappeared when he went away to prison. Inside, he kept to himself."

"Maybe somebody he met at his new job?"

"They're all gone by the time he gets there each night."

"Family? Maybe the uncle who loaned him the car?"

She gave a strange hiccup-laugh and fresh tears rolled down her cheeks. "The little family we have has always been wary of him. Nobody was surprised when he got sent to prison—they were surprised when he was *released*." Her mouth clenched momentarily into a tight circle. "Even my sister and her husband. He only loaned us the car for my sake, not Cooper's. I can still see in their eyes they believe the release was a technicality."

"Why would they think that?"

Red spots appeared on her cheeks, and she glanced away defensively. "You know he was in trouble before the murder. It wasn't the first time. He was always—a different type of child." She collapsed forward into her hands and shook her head vigorously. "If there was anyone other than me who was upset about what Cooper went through, I have no idea who it was."

Jo's mind flew back to Murphy's justification for tampering with the evidence. *He's a menace, and the only tragedy here is that he's out on the street again.* She hadn't paid much attention to the claim—no matter what Ossokov's previous history, there was no justification for tampering with evidence. But something about it now pulled at her—

Her phone buzzed an incoming call. Lacey Bernard.

"Excuse me one moment," she said to Rebecca, and pushed the box of tissues still closer to her. Once out in the hall, she tapped to connect.

Lacey Bernard's voice tumbled out, high-pitched and trembling. "Jo? I got another text."

"Just now? What does it say?"

"It says, 'Your poster boy is dead. You're next.'"

CHAPTER FIFTY-THREE

As Jo escorted Rebecca Ossokov out of the building, her mind kicked into high gear. She hurried to Hayes' office, where Arnett, Coyne, and Goran waited to debrief the interrogation.

"She's either lying or clueless," Hayes said when Jo concluded. "Most likely lying."

"Why would she kill her own son and pose him the same way as the other victims?" Goran asked.

"To throw us off. The shot in the leg tells us everything. They argued when he confronted her, and there was some sort of accident. Or she knows who did this, and is protecting them." Hayes waved dismissively. "Either way, with Ossokov dead, I can assure Barbieri and the press that the killings will stop."

Jo held up a hand. "Lacey Bernard just received a text that said, 'Your poster boy is dead. You're next.'"

"Before or after Ossokov was killed?"

"After. She just got it, about four this morning."

Hayes nodded. "Then we know what their next step is. Tell her we'll assign a team to her, and when this maniac shows up, we'll nab them."

Jo shook her head. "It doesn't make sense that the killer would suddenly let us know what his next intentions were—"

"Ossokov's death obviously changed things," Hayes said.

"—and this doesn't match up with the motive we've seen up until now. Lacey Bernard was on Cooper Ossokov's side."

Hayes' eyes narrowed, and raked Jo's face. "I think I'm finally starting to understand what your problem is. All of this, law enforcement, investigating crimes? For you, it's all about your ego. You need to be the center of attention, the smart one, the golden child. You go off on your own without departmental permission searching out glory when we don't hand you enough here, and if a case resolves itself without making you the hero in the process, you have to overcomplicate it so you can come out looking better. Our killer just gave you a gift, Fournier. The phrase you're looking for is 'thank you.'"

Jo blessed the years of training and experience that allowed her to keep her expression professionally neutral while feeling as though she'd just been kicked in the chest. From the corner of her eye she saw Arnett shift forward as if he were about to object—she lifted her right hand just below Hayes' line of sight to let him know she was fine.

Goran, however, wasn't versed in her signals. "Because we all know how well that gifted horse turned out for the Trojans."

Hayes' head whipped toward Goran, her mouth open and searching for words.

Jo hurried to distract her. "Sounds like we have a plan, then. Arnett and I will swap shifts with Goran and Coyne to keep watch on Lacey Bernard." She stood, and crossed the room to the door.

"Not Arnett." Hayes pulled a file from the top of a stack in front of her. "He's hands off, remember?"

Jo repressed the desire to leap across the table and strangle her. "Why can't he be around Bernard?"

"I know you're smarter than that, Fournier. That lawyer is

convincing Ossokov's mother right now that one of us is responsible for her son's death. Arnett can't be a part of this investigation. He technically shouldn't even be sitting here right now."

"Even though we have good reason to believe the killer may be targeting him?"

Hayes leaned back and crossed her arms over her chest. "If the killer is targeting him, why would we want to serve them both up on the same platter?"

"Because we can keep an eye on both of them that way," Jo said.

"You'll be compromised. Whoever's watching Lacey Bernard needs to have their full focus on her." She gestured to Arnett. "But I will authorize a second surveillance team for Arnett."

———

"Well, we have that, at least," Jo said to the other detectives once they'd convened around her desk, purposefully deflecting attention from Hayes' personal attack on her. She pulled over two spare chairs for Goran and Coyne, and motioned to them to sit down as Arnett dropped into his. "I'm leery of us splitting our attention, but given the circumstances, it's the best we can do."

Coyne crossed one ankle over the other knee, and shook his head. "The way she was going, I'm stunned she authorized two teams."

"Before we go any further here, because we're walking a fine line with her, I need to hear everyone's thoughts about who our killer might be. I'm not going to push something you all aren't behind."

"Hayes is right this is centered around Ossokov," Arnett said. "But you're also right—we're missing something."

"Jo hit the nail on the head," Goran said. "Why would

someone angry on Ossokov's behalf also want Lacey Bernard dead? It makes no sense."

"They've been texting her from the start, right?" Coyne tugged at his tie. "Why enlist her help, then suddenly threaten her? It's hinkey."

Jo nodded. "Since the killer never tipped us off before, this feels like a tactic to make us think she's the next victim when she really isn't."

"So you think Arnett is the actual target?" Goran asked.

Jo tapped the arm of her chair. "He's the only hands-on person left from the original investigation, and he's named in the lawsuit." Jo's phone buzzed. "Hang on, guys. It's Lopez."

As soon as she connected the call, Lopez's voice, uncharacteristically manic, poured over the line. "Hey, I've got news. You know how you asked me to start monitoring Ossokov's phone for any contacts yesterday? I have been, but there was a brief time lapse between when I cloned the phone and when I started monitoring in real-time. I went back to check and a few hours after we finished executing the search warrant he got a text. It said, 'The police are tailing you. That's harassment.'"

Everyone leaned forward toward the phone, including Jo. "Wait. Someone *warned* Ossokov he was being watched? Who?"

"That's just it. It was a burner phone. He texted back asking *who dis*, but got no response. Of course I checked the number along with the one from Lacey's call this morning. Both burners, both purchased at New England Walmarts, both no longer pinging."

Jo's head spun, and she squeezed her eyes shut. "Anything else we should know?"

"Nope. I'll call you as soon as I have anything else." Lopez hung up.

Goran jumped up from his chair. "Somebody's playing us. If Ossokov had an accomplice they must have been using some established burners to communicate. There'd be no reason to contact him on his actual cell phone."

"And he wasn't expecting the contact, otherwise why text the person back asking who it was?" Arnett said.

"Somebody was watching *us* watch *him*." Jo's hand flew to her necklace. "How?"

"We were careful to stay off *his* radar, but we weren't watching to see if anybody was tailing *us*," Coyne said, fists clenched around his tie. "Son of a *bitch*."

"Why warn him and then kill him?" Goran asked.

"They couldn't very well kill him when we had him under surveillance," Jo said.

"But it makes no sense. Why kill Ossokov's enemies, then kill Ossokov?"

Goran shook his head and dropped back into his chair. Coyne's hands continued their clenching.

Jo pressed her fingers into her eyes. It *didn't* make sense. But if the explanation didn't make sense, that meant she wasn't thinking of it the right way. When she had the right theory, everything would click into place, so she had to start over again, think outside the assumptions they'd been making. Was there another explanation, one where all the victims, including Ossokov, made sense?

But the more she tried to find one, the more her mind snapped back to the undeniable unifying force—Ossokov. He was the thread that pulled everything together. He was the only one who'd been hurt by the wrongful conviction, other than justice for Zara Richards, of course, but that was an abstraction—

Jo gasped as the pieces clicked into place. "The rape victims."

"The rape victims?" Arnett asked as Goran and Coyne exchanged confused looks.

"We've been thinking that because Ossokov is at the center

of this, either he must be the killer or some person obsessed on his behalf was the killer. But what if Ossokov *is* at the center of it, but not the way we've been thinking? He's not the only person who was hurt by the wrongful conviction. Zara Richards and her family were also hurt by it, because the real killer got away—"

"But she's dead, and aren't her parents dead now, too?" Goran said.

"She has a sister who lives in Minneapolis or somewhere, right?" Arnett said.

"Right, but there are two other victims here that aren't dead." Jo reached over and rifled through a stack of files, and pulled two out. "When Ossokov became a suspect for Zara Richards' murder, he was already under investigation for the rapes of Tasha Quintana and Jennifer Woods. ADA Bandara had already gotten indictments from the grand jury to prosecute, but Sandra Ashville convinced the DA that allowing her to try Ossokov for the rape-homicide alone was the safer way to go. That's why there was so much pressure to get that conviction. And someone had to break it to Tasha and Jennifer that their cases wouldn't be prosecuted."

"But so what, as long as the bastard got put away?" Goran said.

"But he didn't, did he? He got back out. He was back on the street," Jo said.

Coyne's face screwed up. "Sure, but it wasn't like he got off scot-free. He served nearly fifteen years."

Jo tilted her head and narrowed her eyes. "And would you be satisfied with that if it had been your daughter he raped?"

Coyne's neck and face turned so intensely red Jo worried he might be having a stroke. "Okay, I see your point," he grunted.

"And," Jo continued, "think about that number for a minute. How long is the statute of limitations on the rape of an adult woman?"

"Fifteen years," Arnett answered, voice tight. "Which means time had just run out on their ability to bring him up on charges again."

"Everything makes sense from that perspective," Jo said. "They'd blame Sandra for pushing their case to the side, and of course they'd be angry with Deena Scott for getting him out of prison, and Winnie Sakurai is the judge who said Ossokov deserved a new trial—"

"And the overkill," Goran said. "You said it yourself, when someone smashes someone's skull beyond recognition, there's serious rage behind it."

Jo nodded. "We've felt from the beginning that whoever the killer was, they wanted to look their victims in the face. But Ossokov was a big man. She couldn't risk him overpowering her or getting away, so she shot him."

"Holy shit," Goran said.

Jo nodded grimly. "We need to find out where Tasha, Jennifer, and Zara Richards' sister are. *Now.*"

CHAPTER FIFTY-FOUR

Goran and Coyne immediately turned their attention to tracking down Zara Richards' sister Zoe, while Arnett hunted down Tasha, and Jo focused on Jennifer Woods.

Zoe Richards turned out to be easy to eliminate. She'd moved to Minneapolis for graduate school long before Zara was attacked, and remained there after. She was now a long-time HR manager for Target's corporate headquarters, and Goran verified that she'd overseen a team-building retreat exercise over the weekend. She was currently in a week-long training seminar.

"No way she's been able to get to Massachusetts for a day, let alone several," Coyne reported.

"One down, two to go," Arnett said. "I'm pretty sure I've found Tasha Quintana. She lives over in Quincy and works in an insurance office, both well within driving distance of all our crime scenes."

"If she had to get back for a nine-to-five, that would explain why the weekday murders have been in the middle of the night rather than at dawn."

"I'll keep following up," Arnett said.

Jo turned her attention back to her slow progress on Jennifer Woods, cursing the commonality of the name. Hoping more information could help her narrow down her results, she reached for the file on Woods' rape case again. The information didn't pull her out of her dead end until she found a final notation Bandara entered before packing up the case—after the trial, Woods decided to make a fresh start out in California, where a cousin of hers lived in a small central valley town. With that, Jo tracked down her most recent contact information, including a phone number.

"Hello?" a man's voice answered.

Jo identified herself. "I'm trying to reach Jennifer Woods. May I speak with her?"

"Wrong number, brah."

Brah? Had her voice deepened overnight? "Can I check the number with you?" She read off what she'd tried to call.

"That's the right number, but there's no Jennifer Woods here. She sounds hot, though. If you find her, tell her to hit me up. You have the number." Someone in the background laughed as he hung up.

Jo rolled her eyes and searched for a more recent number. When she couldn't find one, she called the service carrier. Once she made her way up the supervisor chain and explained why she was calling, the manager verified that Jennifer Woods *had* owned the account, but cancelled it five months previously.

Jo pushed her luck. "These days it's more common for people to keep their cell numbers even if they change providers, isn't it? I don't suppose it says why she closed it?"

"That's true, but no, there's no explanation here I can see. We do have special notations when the customer has died because that process is a bit complicated, but I'm not seeing that here."

After thanking him and ending the call, Jo researched her Atwater apartment in an online real-estate website.

"Tasha claims to have been on a romantic getaway in Maine this past weekend," Arnett announced.

"I wonder if she stayed at the same B&B as Lopez?" Jo jotted down the contact information for Jennifer's landlord while reaching for her coffee.

"Not unless Karnelian Kottage specializes in vampire weekends," Arnett said.

Jo coughed on the coffee she'd just sipped. "Nice pun. Lopez would be proud," she said when she caught her breath.

He gave her a blank look. "What?"

"*Vampire Weekend*," she said.

He blinked. "Yeah, so?"

She rubbed her brow and tapped the landlord's number into her phone. "Never mind."

A woman hovering somewhere above fifty answered, with a distracted edge to her gravelly voice that made Jo wonder if she was truly paying attention.

"Yeah, Jennifer took off, what, five months ago? I miss her. She was a good tenant." She somehow managed to sound bored and wistful at the same time.

"Do you have any idea where she moved, or why?"

"The where I can't tell you. The why was she had some sort of family emergency, and begged me to let her out of her lease." A sucking sound came over the line, like she was drinking from a straw and had hit the bottom of the glass.

Jo stretched to rap on Arnett's desk, and put the call on speaker. "She didn't say what it was that made her pack up and leave in a hurry?"

"Nah. I wasn't too surprised because she never really talked about herself that much. Even when I asked she'd just be all, 'Oh, you don't want to hear about that, I'm not very interesting.' I *can* tell you she put her belongings in storage, though, so I think she's gonna be back someday." Ice swirled in a cup. "Sorry I can't tell you more."

"You've been very helpful. And it was very kind of you to let her out of her lease."

"Eh, not really. Finding renters isn't really a problem. Finding renters who understand that normal people go to sleep before midnight is a whole 'nother story."

"I don't suppose you happened to have an emergency contact for her?"

"You know, I just might. Hang on."

After a three-minute wait filled with swearing and the clang of metal drawers, she came back on the line. "Her cousin, Peter Constantine."

Jo jotted down the number, thanked her, and hung up. "My Spidey senses are tingling on this one."

"That's good, because Tasha Quintana's alibi checks out. Unless she has a private jet or a portal, she's not our killer," Arnett said.

"Let's see if the cousin picks up." Jo entered his number and connected the call.

An authoritative middle-aged man answered. "Constantine Tax Prep."

"I'm Detective Josette Fournier of the Oakhurst County State Police Detective Unit. I'm calling about Jennifer Woods—"

"Oh my God, is she okay?"

Jo made pointed eye contact with Arnett as she repeated herself, and Goran and Coyne scooted closer to hear the call. "From your response, can I assume you haven't seen your cousin lately?"

"You can, and I've been worried sick. I woke up to a phone message one day saying she'd be gone for a few months because she had to deal with something urgent."

"Do you have any idea where she went?"

"None. The message was very abrupt, and when I called, her phone had been disconnected."

"Do you know of anything odd that happened before she left, or anything that had been bothering her?"

Constantine paused before answering. "Why did you say you're calling again? Has something happened to her?"

"We hope not. We're trying to locate her."

"Why?" His voice was guarded.

Arnett made a slashing motion against his neck, and she nodded. "I can't reveal that at the moment, other than to say it's urgent we find her."

"You can't reveal that." Computer keys clacked in the background. "I'm sorry, but I only have your word that you are who you say you are. If you want information about Jennifer, you're going to have to—"

Jo's stomach sank, and she hurried to interrupt. "Mr. Constantine?"

"I'm sorry, Detective, a client just came in, and I have to go. I'm sorry I couldn't be of more help." He hung up.

Jo glanced back up at Arnett. "Well. My Spidey senses are now radioactive."

"Too bad we have zero idea how to find her," Coyne said. "And only a few hours before she comes after Arnett."

CHAPTER FIFTY-FIVE

I've heard two justifications for why some crimes, like rape, have a statute of limitations while others, like murder, do not. The first is that evidence degrades over time, and it isn't 'fair' to put someone on trial years after a crime. If that's true, why does it apply only to some crimes and not others? The fact is, DNA doesn't degrade when stored correctly, and it doesn't lie—but the DNA collected in my case is considered irrelevant simply because an arbitrary amount of time has passed.

The answer I get to that objection is the second justification: that murder is an 'irreversible' crime, and other crimes are not.

The first time someone said that to me, I literally couldn't breathe. My chest tightened and my throat seized up, and I almost blacked out before I was able to draw oxygen again.

Reversible.

If someone crashes into your car, it can be repaired. If someone steals your wallet in the subway, they can return it, or make restitution for the money they stole. That's reversible.

The night Cooper Ossokov raped me, I called myself a cab, rode home, and went directly to the room my parents kept for me in their house. I sat on my bed alone, not moving, for how long I don't know. I've had people ask me since, including in my deposition, why I didn't go directly to the police or the hospital. It's not normal behavior, they claim, to just grab a cab and head home. That's the behavior of someone who just had consensual sex, they say. It supports Ossokov's claim. Even members of the DA's office said it—including Sandra Ashville, as a justification for why my case should be put to the side in favor of something more 'winnable.'

The answer is simple—I was in shock. My brain had shifted into a self-protective mode, and despite being a normally intelligent, self-contained person, I wasn't able to process anything in that moment. My behavior was on autopilot, latching on to familiar patterns I'd engaged in a thousand times before as my psyche attempted to flee and find safety. To get away, so I could pretend it never happened.

I've found out in the years since that this reaction is very normal for women who've been sexually assaulted. But I didn't know it then. At the time I was in such deep shock, I didn't even know I was crying until my mother came into the room. And thank God she did, because I was about to shower, another psychological defense rape victims often reach for in an effort to feel 'clean' again. And it's only after we shower so often and so long and scrub ourselves so raw that our skin starts to bleed that we finally understand we'll never, ever feel 'clean' again.

After going to the hospital and the police, and after the two weeks my mother insisted I take off of work, I tried to go back to my normal life. Bad things happen to everyone, right? You stand back up and you move on with your life, and I wasn't interested in being a victim. Yet, every night the attack replayed itself in my nightmares. Even during the day, when I saw someone that looked a little like him or I couldn't see around a corner in the T station or a man stared at me a moment too long, the images *would flash through my mind and I'd struggle to breathe and I'd have to get away, as far and as fast as possible. And then just the thought of returning to that place would set off a crippling fear response, too.*

My work became a nightmare—there's always one or two on every flight who've had too much to drink or are just assholes who stare at you like you're their own personal ice cream cone and who 'accidentally' brush against your hand when you pass them their pretzels. I started needing to carry Xanax for panic attacks to even force myself on my flights. I became a flight attendant because I loved seeing the world, but the idea of sightseeing alone on my layovers now terrified me. And the evenings out with my fellow flight attendants in whatever city we'd flown to that day? The thought of strange men in strange clubs on strange streets sent me into cold sweats and bouts of vomiting. I stayed in my 'safe' hotel room with the door locked, latched, and a chair under the knob.

And despite having had normal relationships before the attack, the thought of letting a man ever touch me that way again made me crawl into a fetal position and cry.

Then, almost three months after the attack, I realized I was pregnant.

Every bout of morning sickness, every pair of pants that no longer fit, every time my breasts hurt when I put on my bra was like he was reaching out and attacking me again. I couldn't get away—he was with me, inside my very biology, and he always would be.

If I had the baby, I'd have had to stop flying by, at best, week thirty-six—if my body held up to the stresses of air travel on pregnancy. And I'd only been a flight attendant for a few years—my vacation time and other benefits were limited. I wouldn't be able to support myself, let alone a baby.

So I had an abortion.

Even the exam confirming I was pregnant triggered a panic attack. I couldn't face the prospect of having a male doctor do it, but even with a woman gynecologist I lay there, legs up in the stirrups, sobbing quietly to myself, praying for it to be over. I was terrified of how I'd react during the abortion itself, and luckily—I thought—they fully sedated me so I didn't have to be conscious for it. But not remembering the procedure was worse; afterward I was swamped with new nightmares where Ossokov came into the operating room and raped me repeatedly again.

Through it all, I spent countless hours wishing Ossokov had killed me rather than leaving me trapped in eternal hell.

Of course I tried therapy. And it helped. With the aid of a PTSD specialist I was eventually able to get through my shifts without the panic attacks. I was able to run my errands, and even go out—to locations I checked out in advance—with colleagues. I even managed to go on a few dates with nice men. The nightmares and fear reactions never died out completely, and it was always easier to stay in with a good book than go out into the world. But I got to a place where I could manage my day-to-day existence without constant panic attacks.

Then they let him out of prison.

Suddenly I saw him everywhere. The back of every head of hair that might be his. I scoured flight manifests and faces. Each time I entered a store, restaurant, airport, I had to check every person, everywhere. I stopped going anywhere I didn't have to. The flashbacks became daily occurrences and I struggled to fall asleep at night because I was so terrified of the nightmares that always came.

Reversible. Reversible?

Supposedly 'reversible' crimes can be righted with restitution. So I asked myself—what restitution could reverse the impact on me? What would bring back my ability to sleep through the night or have an evening where I wasn't looking over my shoulder? To have an afternoon or a morning—even ten minutes—where I could sit and be at peace?

I still don't know. But I knew the first step was making sure Ossokov—and those who enabled him to walk the streets and harm women again—were held accountable for what they'd done.

CHAPTER FIFTY-SIX

After sending out a statewide BOLO, the team dove into finding any possible trace of Jennifer Woods.

"She's not using her credit cards or ATM," Lopez reported. "And, I can't find any recent hits on her license plates. She either left that car in California or got rid of the plates."

Jo bounced her palm on the tabletop. "If she swapped them, they could go undetected for months. Any luck with the personal contacts?"

"She doesn't have many friends or much family," Coyne said. "A few co-workers and her cousin seem to be it. I haven't heard back from everyone, and the ones I did reach seem genuinely surprised to hear she may be in the area. Of course, that all might be an act, but that'll take time to break down."

"Confidential informants? I put the word out among mine, but nobody has mentioned anything strange involving a woman matching her description," Jo said.

Lopez flicked an invisible dirt particle off her desk. "Hard to believe when we have the most excellent description of 'brown-haired, brown-eyed, average-height forty-five-year-old woman with no identifying features', along with an ancient California DMV photo."

Jo tapped her pen on her desk. "Then we only have two options. One, send an army of law enforcement to pound the pavement around all our crime scenes and related locations with her picture. We need to do that regardless. But as far as I can see, I think we're gonna have to let her come to us. The good news is we're forewarned and forearmed, and if we play it right, we'll have the upper hand."

"So a repeat of the plan from last night?" Goran asked. "But also at Lacey Bernard's house this time?"

"Yes for Arnett, no for Bernard," Jo said. "If we split our focus over two locations, it's easier for Woods to find a weakness. I say we very obviously escort Bernard to a hotel with a team of guards protecting her, that way Woods has no choice but to go for Arnett."

"What if Arnett was never on her target list to start with?" Coyne asked.

"If that's the case, Bernard will be safe and we'll have bought ourselves more time to track Woods down." She shook her head. "But I just don't see how that's possible. Why would she hold one detective responsible but not the other one?"

"What if she just decides to wait until we stop paying for a hotel room?" Coyne asked.

Jo grimaced. "She's killed someone every morning for five days now. I don't see her taking a day off if she can help it. And now that we know who she is, we'll have tracked her down long before that. Every cop in the county is looking for her."

Coyne nodded.

"And your wife made it up to Vermont?" Goran asked. "If we're gonna do this, we need to make sure she has no alternate ways of getting at you."

Arnett nodded. "My daughters went up to join her. My brother-in-law is a survivalist. Their farm is remote and protected. And, he's well armed. If Woods is stupid enough to try anything up there, it won't end well for her."

"Great." Jo leaned forward. "Goran, Coyne, let's have the two of you hidden in the same place as last night, and we'll send the second team to the hotel with Bernard."

"Where will you be?" Arnett asked.

Jo grinned. "I'll be inside your place, with you. I hear Laura puts together a lovely guest bedroom."

"Bad idea," Arnett said. "If Woods knows you're there, she'll just take you out too."

"She won't know. You'll sneak me into the garage in the back seat of your car, and I'll stay out of sight."

Coyne shook his head vigorously. "I don't like it. The thought of having you both in there makes my ass twitch."

Jo grimaced. "I can't thank you enough for that image. But the fact is, it's my responsibility to have my partner's back. And I'm not interested in arguing about it."

Arnett glared at her. She ignored it.

Goran gave a sharp nod. "Okay, then. We'll be in constant contact via text and phone, and both teams will have access to the cameras on Arnett's house. Anything I'm missing?"

They all exchanged grim glances and shook their heads.

Jo stood. "Then let's do this."

CHAPTER FIFTY-SEVEN

When Ossokov's mother drove back up her driveway, I couldn't decide whether I was relieved or annoyed.

All along I'd struggled with blaming her. She was his mother after all, and it was hard for me to believe that a man who could do the things Cooper Ossokov did had been brought up by a loving, moral woman. But I'd recognized the pain in her face when they took her son to prison. Whatever her role in his creation, she'd more than paid for her crimes. Everything she loved had been taken from her.

Still, it made everything more difficult for me. If they'd arrested her, I could have breathed easier; if they thought they'd caught their culprit, they wouldn't still be actively searching. But if they were still looking, the list of possible suspects was impossibly small. It was only a matter of when they'd stumble on the right answer. I couldn't afford to let my guard down for a second.

I spent most of the day putting the finishing touches in place. Living out of a suitcase was less than ideal, but at least it made clean-up fast and easy. After I checked out of the motel, I drove down to Connecticut to purchase the last items I'd need and to do a final plate swap. It wouldn't help for long—even cops in different states shared information these days. But they wouldn't be looking so far afield just yet, and the delay it caused might be crucial.

As I drove, I watched the cameras via my cell phone, perched in its holder on my dash. When the police showed up at Lacey's, I pulled over so I could watch closely. When they came back out with her she was carrying an overnight bag and had wrapped herself in a scarf and glasses like she was avoiding the paparazzi. I snorted—that's the difference between journalists and law enforcement. Not all journalists, of course—but the penny-ante wannabes like this one who trade in sensationalism—when push came to shove, they ran rather than put themselves in danger for a story. Because it's easy to be a champion of justice for a cause you know nothing about, to advocate for a man you've never met, to stand up for a 'truth' when you have no idea what the truth is. At least Arnett had the courage to refuse to be chased out of his house, and the nerve to face the danger head-on. I could respect him for that, at least.

As I pulled back on the road, I recalculated and adjusted my timings. Despite supposedly being on temporary leave, Arnett had gone in to work today, so I needed to take care of everything before he got home. They'd almost certainly be using him for bait again tonight. But I had some bait of my own, and it was time to skewer it onto the hook.

DAY SIX

CHAPTER FIFTY-EIGHT

Can't tell you how much better stakeouts are when you have a nice, clean bathroom within reach, Jo texted Arnett from the overstuffed chintz armchair in the Arnett's blue-and-yellow guest bedroom, where she sat in night-lighted darkness.

The central heating's nice, too, Bob replied from the master bedroom.

> *Before tonight, I would have mocked you mercilessly for having night lights in your house, but I'd have broken my neck without them.*

She checked the time—just past midnight. So far, so good.

Laura got 'em for future grandkids, he replied.

Something about that panged, like a floodlight suddenly shining into dusty corners. The threat they were facing was real —this killer had taken lives in brutal, direct ways, and something about Arnett's eagerness to throw himself in front of it unsettled her. He had a responsibility as a member of law enforcement, that was true, but he also had a responsibility as a husband and father—and hopefully, a future grandfather. They were both familiar with the struggle to balance professional and personal responsibilities, and she'd watched him strive, conflicted, for compromises and solutions. But now—it was like a soldier who was too willing to run into a fusillade of machine-gun fire.

Like he was a guilty man standing up ready to take his punishment.

She pushed the thought down and tried to come up with something light-hearted to text him back. But her mind couldn't, or wouldn't.

Have you heard from Laura and the girls?

Snug as bugs in rugs.

Jo's eyes skipped around the room, bouncing from the soothing blue bedspread and buffet of cozy pillows to the paintings of flower-filled fields and the white bookshelf interspersed with family pictures. The dim cast of the light took her back to childhood, to evenings spent at grandparents' and aunts' and uncles' houses, when the warmth of family juxtaposed with the disquiet of unfamiliar surroundings and homesickness that wouldn't let her sleep. She'd get up and creep into the kitchen for a glass of water, really an excuse to slip away from the thoughts spinning around her head; the soft glow felt different and otherworldly, like she was caught in some space-time rift where everyone else had disappeared and left her trapped alone.

Now the isolation came from the distance between her and her closest friend.

She dug the heels of her palms into her eyes and told herself to get a grip. She'd told him she believed him—why couldn't she just let it go?

Because this isn't about him. It's about you.

Of course it was about her. She'd spent years learning to trust herself when it came to her relationships, and now her gut and her best friend were telling her different things. How did she reconcile that?

Her phone chimed the arrival of another text.

You need another cup of coffee? I'm about to make more.

No, she texted back. *I need to pace myself.*

As she set the phone back down on the end table, a small motion caught her eye. A tiny crack of light on the ceiling. But not normal light—just as she noticed it, it disappeared, then reappeared. From the angle, it must've been coming through—

Her heart sank as she turned slowly around.

CHAPTER FIFTY-NINE

The longest part of the entire plan was getting to know her, so I could gain access to the house.

After a couple of weeks of watching, I spotted an entry point —her grocery deliveries. Thankfully, delivery people have a hard job, and they're more than willing to believe whatever you say if it means they don't have to carry heavy bags up a long driveway to their target house.

The first time, after setting the bags on the porch, I rang the doorbell before I stepped back. When she came to the door, angry at having been disturbed, I put on a confused, flustered face— even managed to tear up—and apologized profusely.

"I'm so sorry, I'm new, and I think I messed up. I think I may have mixed up the orders. I"—I made a point of looking at her and looking away before continuing—"I was going to ask if you could make sure this was yours because I didn't want to put my hands all over it. But never mind, I don't want to make you—"

She smiled empathetically at me. "Oh, that's fine, we all make mistakes. You go ahead and check for me."

I pulled open the first bag and listed off several of the items.

"Yes, those are mine. But since you're here, would you mind bringing them in? I know it's not your job, but—"

I'd expected to have to work harder than that, but was more than happy to take a shortcut when it presented itself. "Oh, sure, of course, I'd be happy to! That'll make up for disturbing you." I picked the bags back up and brought them through to her kitchen.

"Thank you so much, you're a dear," she said. "Is it too late to put an extra tip in the app for you?"

I insisted that wasn't necessary, of course, and again played up my 'mistake.' And sure enough, when I intercepted the groceries the following week, she was full of smiles to see me. Everything was a breeze from there: learning the layout of the house, stealing her spare keys when she wasn't looking, returning them the week after so she wouldn't notice they were gone.

When I thought of her helpless, drugged, and bound and gagged, I winced. She was a kind woman, and she had nothing to do with any of this.

But I didn't have any control over that. Only Detective Arnett did.

CHAPTER SIXTY

A sickeningly familiar glow flickered on and off the guest bedroom's curtain.

This must be the distraction they'd been waiting for. A heightened, sharp calm took over Jo as she shifted into action. Maintaining a low stance, she unholstered her Beretta and flattened herself against the wall. She lifted her gun, then pulled back the corner of the curtain.

The only thing visible was the exterior wall of the house extending away from her—but the red-orange glow flicked along it, as well. A reflection—but from where?

Her phone chimed again. She glanced at the table and read the text from Goran:

House on fire. Get out, now.

The first tang of smoke hit her nose as she bolted from the room. "Bob! The house is on fire!"

Arnett appeared in the hallway, weapon pointed at the ground. "Which direction?"

Jo pointed back toward the guestroom. "That side, for sure."

He started toward the staircase. "Front door then. I hope to hell Goran and Coyne have us covered."

"Me first." She stepped in front of him, not giving him a choice. With measured, steps, she hurried to the bottom of the staircase, trying to ignore the blood pounding in her ears. Ducking to check behind the large leather sofa, she surveyed the room. "Den clear."

As Arnett approached behind her, she swerved to check access from the kitchen. "Kitchen clear."

She continued into the downstairs hall, then approached the side of the doorway, leading with her weapon. "Clear. She must be waiting outside."

Heavy hands pounded the front door. "Jo! Bob!" Goran's heavy voice called.

"Coming out," Arnett called back. He unlocked the door, and swung it open.

Goran and Coyne stood on either side of the door, facing the street. Arnett's porch light had activated, flooding the front yard with light. "I'm not seeing any movement," Coyne said.

"She has to be here somewhere," Arnett said.

"Not out front." Goran strode back down the porch, scouring the yard as he went.

Coyne called out from the side of the house. "Bushes clear."

"Maybe she expected us to exit via the back," Jo said, turning around. "You two stay here and we'll go— Oh, God."

The men swerved to follow her gaze. A hundred yards away, the neighbor's house was also on fire—and the flames were far up the sides, already licking around the upper windows.

"What the fuck," Coyne said, and did a one-eighty to the neighbor on the other side. "That one, too. What did she do, set the whole damn neighborhood on fire?"

Arnett jutted his head at Goran and pointed to the south-most house. "Radio the fire department, then head over to that house and get the Parsons out. Jo and I will go take care of Mrs. Visniky."

"No fucking way," Coyne said. "You stay with us."

Arnett raised his hand to cut Coyne off. "The fire's spreading too fast. Mrs. Visniky uses a wheelchair and needs help in and out of bed. If I don't help her *now*, she's dead."

CHAPTER SIXTY-ONE

The moments between when I activated the devices and when the fires caught were some of the longest of my life.

I'd done test runs out in the woods, of course. But homemade incendiaries, let alone remote-activated ones, are fickle. The internet assured me that if I shoved the device in a dryer vent, the built-up lint inside would go up like a tinderbox. But there's only one dryer vent per house, so my secondaries were set amid piles of dry leaves and twigs at the base of walls. And since my cameras didn't cover all of them, I had no way of knowing if they'd been discovered or interfered with by rats or raccoons under cover of night. So I sat, hunched down in the dark, stomach churning while the seconds stretched like hours.

Then a flicker of the flame broke through the darkness. Adrenaline replaced the stomach-churning as I watched the light intensify and waited for the first shouts.

When they came, I took a deep breath and flashed my mini Maglite down at my gun. I'd removed the safety. It was loaded. I flashed the light through the space in front of me—I had a clear shot.

Now, if I'd gambled correctly, it was just a matter of moments.

CHAPTER SIXTY-TWO

Jo grabbed Arnett's arm and lowered her voice. "That's exactly what she wants, for you to rush in there. It's a trap!"

He yanked his arm away. "You think I don't know that? But Mrs. Visniky isn't gonna die because of *me*."

"So let *us* go get her," Goran said.

Arnett pointed at the flames. "The houses'll be fireballs in minutes, and you don't know the floor plan. Go help the Parsons, they'll just need to be guided, not carried. *Now!*" He turned and ran.

Despite the frustration clutching at her, Jo nodded to them. Once Goran and Coyne took off toward the other house, she raced after Arnett, pushing down her desire to strangle him. "We need to be smart about this."

He didn't slow. "Don't start with me."

She put on a burst of speed and circled around to block his path. "I don't have time to navigate your I-feel-guilty death wish right now." He tried to push past her, but she continued. "Listen to me for one damned moment and maybe *nobody* has to die. Including Woods, because I want her to pay for what she's done, but we need her alive. So stop acting like a *martyr* and start acting like a fucking *cop*."

He stopped, clenched his fists, and stared up at the flames. "Talk to me. *Quickly*."

CHAPTER SIXTY-THREE

I struggled to count the voices as they came closer. One was a woman—that would be Fournier. But were there more than two male voices? I couldn't tell. I stared blankly into the pitch black and tried to ignore the acrid smoke as I strained to hear. A man said something about floor plans, and yelled at someone to save the others.

Then I couldn't make out anything—they must have been running to the house, because when I heard the woman next, they were much closer.

"Your stubbornness is going to kill you one of these days. I'll take the front and you make sure she doesn't escape out the back."

I squinted into the darkness. Did she really think I was that stupid? That my plan was just to have him run inside while I ran out back? What would be the point of that? No, she was smarter than that. So what was she really up to?

I shrugged it off. I needed to focus on him, and it really didn't matter what she did. She was guilty enough by association—if I needed to kill her to get to him, so be it.

CHAPTER SIXTY-FOUR

Jo eased up to the porch and, body flat against the house, tested the doorknob. It turned, unhindered. Gun up and ready, she kicked the door to swing it open, then peered around the edge, wishing to high hell she had a flashlight. The flames consuming the far side of the room's exterior sent enough light flickering in to allow her to get her bearings, but not enough to feel confident about what might be hiding inside. But as nervous as it made her, she didn't have time to come up with anything else.

The floor plan was, as Arnett promised, a mirror image of his house. She flipped the hall and den in her mind and felt along the wall for the light switch. She swiped at it, but the room remained dark. Jennifer either cut the electricity or the fire had taken it out.

Ignoring the smoky burn at the back of her throat, she cleared the hall and the den as best she could. She strained to hear over the soft hissing and crackling of fire consuming wood, but could pick up nothing.

As she climbed the stairs, she scanned again from her elevated angle, praying she'd spot Jennifer and be able to end this quickly. But she found nothing—if Jennifer was inside, she must be upstairs.

A pane of glass from the far window exploded, sending a wave of blistering heat over her. Fire spewed through the opening, licking the wall and shooting toward the ceiling.

She hurried up the stairs, heart slamming in her chest, pulling her shirt over her mouth with her free hand.

As she reached the top, a beam of light burst directly into her eyes, blinding her.

"Son of a bitch!" a woman shouted. "Where the hell is Bob Arnett?"

"Where's Mrs. Visniky?" Jo said, squinting uselessly in the direction of the master bedroom. "We need to get her out of here, Jennifer."

"Drop your weapon and get Arnett in here, now," Jennifer said.

"I can't do that. We need get Mrs. Visniky to safety." Jo felt rather than saw Arnett, pressed into the staircase, slither up toward her feet.

"If you want Mrs. Visniky safe, you need to get me Arnett."

Every instinct in Jo's body screamed in response to the encroaching fire—but she had to delay, had to give Arnett time to cover her. "The fire has already broken through the wall, Jennifer. If we don't move now, we *all* die. I understand why you killed the others. They failed you, and they let a monster back out on the street. But Mrs. Visniky didn't do anything to you. Don't do to her what they did to you."

"If you want her to live, you better get him in here fast." Her voice was steely.

Arnett's hand brushed Jo's ankle, letting her know he'd reached the top and was easing into position below the highest stair. She prayed Jennifer wasn't looking down near Jo's feet.

A timber crashed in the den below. The beam of light

jumped at the sound—Jennifer wasn't as calm as she was pretending to be.

"I don't have a radio. Arnett's waiting at the back door in case you try to come out," Jo said.

"Call him in here, then."

"He can't hear me over the fire." Jo fought to keep the gun steady as her throat seized, forcing her to cough.

Arnett's hand left her ankle.

"Well then. If he can't hear you," Jennifer said, "he'll sure as hell hear this."

The sharp report of a gun rent the air, followed immediately by a searing burn in Jo's chest.

CHAPTER SIXTY-FIVE

As Jo fell back and toward the wall, she fired her own weapon blindly into the darkness. Almost simultaneously, a third shot exploded next to her, and the beam of light fell away.

Arnett jumped up as Jo collapsed onto the stairs, his gun raised high. Jo pushed as hard as she could to slide herself further down the stairs, out of Jennifer's line of sight.

Jo heard a low moan—was it coming from down the hall, or from her?

"Don't move," Arnett called. He must have kicked away Jennifer's gun, because a scraping sound flew toward Jo and a flash of something dark slid down the stairs. Then the beam of light reappeared, strafing above Jo's head, then disappeared again.

"Shots fired, Fournier down. Need ambulance and assistance," Arnett said into his radio.

Jo gasped for breath, smoke seizing her throat. She tried to push herself up—pain erupted through her chest. Billows of black-gray smoke raced across the ceiling above her, and waves of heat pulsed over her. She dropped back down and tried to remain still, eyes squeezed shut, fighting back the desperate need to cough.

The shriek of sirens broke through the crackling of the fire. After an eternity, boots pounded toward her.

Goran's voice suddenly materialized next to her ear. "This is gonna hurt like a sonuvabitch, Jo. Hang on."

She nodded, and reached an arm out to wrap around his shoulder. He jimmied himself under her armpit and around her back, then hefted her up as gently as he could.

"They have Mrs. Visniky?" she asked.

"Woods claims Visniky is out in the shed, safely away from the fire. Arnett's getting her now."

She nodded, grimacing against the pain. "Get a move on."

"Big talk from someone who just took a bullet to the chest." He shifted down the stairs.

Jo grimaced. "God bless body armor."

CHAPTER SIXTY-SIX

"Don't be a *martyr*, Fournier." Bob Arnett smirked at her from over the top of his phone. "Take the pain meds."

She glared up at him from the hospital release forms. "Don't you have paperwork to fill out for your officer-involved shooting?"

He held up his phone and wiggled it. "Already done. Ain't modern technology grand?"

"And the investigator?"

"Took care of business before I was allowed to leave the site. Bagged my gun, took my picture, the whole nine. They want me to get some rest, eat, and meet with the union attorney before I do the official interview. He'll want to talk to you as soon as you leave the building."

The door opened and Matt hurried in, face tight with concern. "Hey. How are you?"

"Hey." Jo smiled up, more pleased than she expected to see him. "I'm okay. I had a vest on."

He leaned down to give her a kiss. "I checked with your doctor on the way in. Two bruised ribs and a contusion the size of a tennis ball on your chest, but he says the only thing you'll agree to take for the pain is Advil?"

"It's not so bad. The only reason I'm here was so they could run all the tests to make sure nothing more serious was going on." But she winced in pain as she stretched up to meet him halfway, and his face shifted. "I'll take something once we get this all wrapped up, I promise."

"What's there left to wrap up?"

"Jennifer Woods is out of surgery, and she asked to talk to me."

His brows popped up. "Without an attorney present?"

Jo set down the forms and stood, careful to keep the pain off her face. "If she wants to waive her rights, that's fine by me. I'll have Goran in there with me. He'll record the conversation on his phone and her doctor will monitor."

Matt crossed his arms over his chest. "I don't suppose it would do any good if I told you that you need to rest and let the other detectives handle it?"

"No more good than it would do for me to tell you to abandon a patient who desperately needs a life-saving surgery just because your bad knee was flaring up."

He raised his hands in surrender. "Point taken. Should I wait to drive you home?"

She smiled. "If you want to, I'd really love that. But I'm not sure how long it will be, so if you want Goran or Arnett to bring me, that's fine, too."

"Not a problem. I have a few items I can knock off my to-do list while I'm here waiting." He stepped over to open the door, then gestured her through.

She squeezed his hand on her way out.

Goran, waiting in the hall, watched her gait as she approached. "I'll lead the way. You set the pace."

She nodded. "What happened once they bundled me into the ambulance?"

"Woods drugged Mrs. Visniky with something and wheeled her out into the shed, then locked her inside. She was gagged and bound but never knew it. She slept through everything—woke up in the hospital. The last thing she remembers is making tea in her kitchen for the 'lovely woman who delivers my groceries.'" He put finger quotes around the phrase.

Jo shot him a bemused look. "Well. That answers how Woods got access to her, at least."

"We also sent a team to check out Lacey Bernard's house before we allowed her to return. Found three incendiary devices, one in her dryer vent and the others on either side of her house amid stacks of leaves."

"Damn. I've been meaning to clean out my dryer vent." Jo sped up slightly, growing accustomed to the stabs of pain. "Is that how she lit up Arnett's and his neighbors' houses?"

"That's my guess. They're still analyzing the scene." Goran pointed around a corner.

"The room with the officer stationed outside?" Jo said.

"You just may make detective yet," Goran deadpanned.

CHAPTER SIXTY-SEVEN

Jo peered into the room as she pulled open the door, intrigued to see, in person for the first time, the woman who'd managed to wreak such havoc. Jennifer Woods was remarkably unremarkable: white, five-ten with a lean, muscular build. Medium brown eyes peered out from under disheveled medium-brown hair. She sat propped up on her bed, the leg shot by Arnett bulging higher under the blankets than her other, looking impossibly harmless.

She turned as Jo strode into the room. "Detective Fournier. I can't tell you how relieved I am you were wearing a bullet-proof vest. I wish shooting you hadn't been necessary, but I needed Detective Arnett to show himself before we ran out of time."

Jo bit back a sarcastic remark about her marksmanship. "I have a few questions I need to ask you."

Woods nodded.

Goran pulled out his cell phone. When he signaled he was ready, Jo recited the Miranda warning. "Do you understand the rights I've explained to you?"

"Yes," Woods said.

"With these rights in mind, do you wish to speak with me?"

"Yes." Woods nodded. "But I have something else I'd like to say before you ask your questions."

Jo hadn't been expecting that. "We'd love to hear whatever you'd like to tell us."

Woods took a deep breath. "You know that just over sixteen years ago Cooper Ossokov raped me, and another woman named Tasha Quintana. You also know that the district attorney's office decided to abandon our case to prosecute him for Zara Richards' murder."

Jo nodded.

"Here's what you don't know. As Grace Bandara escorted me out of the building the day she informed me of that decision, someone pulled her aside. She asked me to wait, and as I did, I overheard someone talking about Cooper Ossokov. I'm not ashamed to admit I put my ear to the door. Sandra Ashville's, according to the nameplate."

Jo tensed, and momentarily considered telling Goran to turn off the recording. But no—whatever Woods had to say, everyone needed to hear it.

"She was angry, and her voice rose, and I'll never forget what she said. 'We need a win on this. I'm sick of our hands being tied and I'm sick of these assholes slithering through technicalities and plea deals. Do whatever you have to do to make it airtight, Murphy. Whatever. You. Have. To. Do.' She stressed those last words, hard."

Jo nodded and kept her face neutral.

"I tried to tell myself it was a standard pep talk." She laughed, and it came out like an anemic hiccup. "And I knew I should tell someone in case it wasn't. But I couldn't bring myself to do it, because if somehow that caused some technicality that put him back out on the street, I couldn't be responsible for that."

Woods stopped abruptly and stared into space. Just as Jo was about to speak, she looked into Jo's eyes, searching.

"I couldn't be responsible for letting him do that to another woman. Because before they locked him up? I couldn't eat. I could barely sleep, and when I did, I woke up screaming. I'd have flashbacks, all the time, feeling him on me, pushing into me, his disgusting, wet breath burning into my skin."

"PTSD." Jo nodded.

"Even on my best days I felt like a water balloon filled so full I'd explode at the slightest contact." Twin tears overflowed her eyes, and slid slowly down her cheeks.

As Jo watched, Jennifer's hands clenched at the bedspread, and her face shifted, and suddenly she was a scared, lost little girl with no idea how to find her way home. "I'm so sorry you had to go through that," she said, and meant it.

"When they let him out, I called ADA Bandara, but they told me she'd passed away and they passed me to Sandra Ashville. I told her I wanted them to prosecute him for my rape, and that I was sure Tasha would, too. She told me there was nothing she could do, because the statute of limitations for the rape had run out *the month before his release*." Anger flashed in her eyes. "Because of *her* misconduct, I lost any chance of ever having a half-way normal life. That's why I killed them the way that I did."

Jo struggled to follow the logic. "I'm not sure I understand."

Jennifer glared at her. "*They* got to go home every day, to someone or something they loved. Some happy place where they could find peace, even if just for a few minutes. But because of what *they* did, I'll never get any of that. No matter how hard I try, even things I used to love, like fishing on a quiet lake. Now, the quieter it is, the louder the thoughts are in my head. The best I can do is distract myself for a while, but the demons are always there. The only way to get back my peace was to make sure none of them would ever harm anyone again."

Jo started to speak, but Jennifer cut her off. "Do you have any appreciation of what it took for me to do that? Of how terrifying it was for me to face him? To put myself at risk that he'd hurt me again? But I had to do it. If I hadn't, he'd torment me for the rest of my life, because I'd never know if he was around the next corner. It was the only way I could get my power back. And sure enough, the first time I've been able to fully relax and breathe in sixteen years is the moment I finished beating Ossokov's skull to a pulp."

"But the others—they weren't the ones who hurt you," Jo said gently.

"They most certainly *did*. The justice system is supposed to be *blind*, unflinchingly exacting in meting out consequences that match guilt. It's not supposed to prosecute some crimes and not others, or bow to pressure from the press, or manipulate evidence to get what it wants. But these members of law enforcement weren't blind, and so I needed to send a message to the others. *That's why I put on the blindfolds and posed them like Lady Justice, so everyone would know, and remember.* If Sandra Ashville hadn't pushed to prosecute Zara Richards' case over mine and Tasha's, Cooper Ossokov would be in prison today. If Judge Sakurai hadn't allowed her to do that and hadn't reversed his conviction when she knew full well he was a serial rapist, he'd be in prison today. If Deena Scott hadn't pushed to have a client exonerated when she knew full well he'd raped other women, he'd be in prison today. And if Detective Murphy and Detective Arnett hadn't tampered with evidence—"

Jo threw up a hand to stop her, and kept her expression steady. "Why were you so sure they tampered with the evidence? During the appeal, the determination was that there was a mix-up at the lab."

Jennifer's eyes narrowed. "Because I can add two plus two. Sandra Ashville tells Murphy to do whatever it takes, and voila, there's a 'mix-up' at the lab? Please. But you're focusing on the wrong thing."

"What should I be focused on?"

"The biggest violation of all—the statute of limitations." Her voice rose. *"That law has to be changed.* People like Lacey Bernard who are such vocal proponents of Cooper Ossokov's innocence, they need to understand, and turn their attention to where it should be. Bernard is supposedly an anti-sexual-assault advocate. So why isn't she working to *get the statute of limitations for rape removed?"*

Goran spoke, scornfully, from behind the camera. "So why don't *you* just work to get the law changed?"

Jennifer turned her gaze on Goran, eyes filled with raw hatred. "How do you hold rallies and get petitions signed and stage sit-ins when you have a panic attack every time you leave your house? And even if I *had* done all of those things, we all know nobody takes notice until they're forced to, when the pain becomes their own."

Jo didn't bother to hide her bewilderment. "How was Lacey Bernard going to do anything about that when she was dead?"

Woods' face scrunched up. "She advocated for a monster. She was part of the reason he was released, and part of the reason he felt empowered to sue."

"She believed he was innocent, and that her advocacy was ultimately helping sexual assault victims. But Arnett? What makes you think he was in on any of it?" Jo shook her head in frustration. "You said yourself Sandra Ashville said *Murphy's* name, not Arnett's."

Woods cocked her head to the side and gave Jo an appraising glance. "Is that what he's telling you, that he didn't know anything about it? Because if he didn't realize what was happening under his nose, it was *because he didn't want to know.* And that's just as bad—if not worse."

DAY NINE

CHAPTER SIXTY-EIGHT

Jo pushed through the door to The Wooden Leg and fought back an unsettling wave of déjà vu. As her eyes acclimated to the low light and her nose to the stale hops, a figure materialized in front of her. Arnett, sitting at the table where Steve Murphy had waited for them—and in the same chair.

She slid into the seat across from him and jutted her chin at his untouched Guinness. "You didn't have to wait for me."

Arnett motioned to the bartender. "Thanks for giving up part of your Sunday. I know you have dinner plans tonight."

"Not a problem. Matt's cooking the entrée and my mother and sister will bring over the rest. I tried to make pancakes this morning, but my ribs had other ideas."

He smiled grimly. "Bodies are inconvenient like that. Especially since none of us are getting any younger."

"True story."

The bartender materialized at her side. "What can I bring you?"

"I don't suppose you have apple brandy?" Jo asked.

"I got Liberty Tree if you want local, and a Massenez Calvados if you got money burning a hole in your pocket."

She tried to hide her surprise, but apparently wasn't fast enough. The bartender grinned. "My mother's people are Quebecois. I was weaned on the stuff."

She smiled back. "I'll have the Massenez, please."

"How's everything on your end? How are you feeling?" Arnett asked.

"Still sore, but the case is wrapping up. The rush came back on that DNA from Sandra's tree, and it matches the profile we have on file for Jennifer Woods. Apparently she cut her hand on the tree bark."

"So we would have caught her anyway," Arnett said.

Jo nodded, and didn't say what they were both thinking: that he might be dead if they hadn't put the pieces together earlier. "Bernard is back home, but shaken to discover how close her house came to being barbecued. When are you and Laura going to be able to move back in?"

"Not sure yet. Between the fire damage and the water damage, the guy said three weeks. But there was a twinkle in his eye I didn't like."

"Thank God for home insurance," Jo said.

"Another true story." Arnett paused to take a sip of his beer. "So. I heard that Woods is pleading guilty. That'll save time and taxpayer dollars," Arnett said. "I haven't seen the recording yet. Did she say why the different MOs for each kill?"

Jo tried to read Arnett's demeanor as she answered—she had a strong suspicion about why he'd asked her to join him for a drink, and was clinging to the hope she wasn't right. "She did. Like we guessed, she wanted them to see her before she killed them, but wasn't confident she'd be able to overpower some of them. Winnie Sakurai was older and frail, so she had no problem there. Deena Scott was fit, but still small, and Jennifer had the element of surprise in the parking lot of the gym. Steve Murphy was drunk, and wouldn't have been able to fight off a kitten. But Sandra Ashville was relatively strong and very fit, and Cooper Ossokov was, not only big and strong, but psychologically terrifying to her. So she shot them."

"So why not shoot everyone? And why not just shoot Ossokov in the head and have done with it?" Arnett asked. "Never mind, I know the answer to that. Far more psychologically satisfying to physically cave in his skull."

The bartender appeared with the Calvados, set it in front of her, and walked off without a word.

"I'm gonna tell myself the reason he didn't react is he didn't hear what I said, not that he hears ten times worse every day," Arnett said.

"Whatever works." Jo lifted the snifter and sipped. "She didn't shoot them all because gunfire at the park, the gym, or the bar would have instantly drawn attention before she could get away. As for Ossokov, she wanted to disable him, but be able to look him in the face when she beat him to death. To literally take back her power from him."

"Yeah, well. She's gonna need that power where she's going." Arnett took another sip of the Guinness.

Jo watched Arnett's expression carefully as he lifted the beer. They'd worked on more cases together than she could count, and she knew the range of his end-of-investigation emotions. Pride and relief when they handed a strong case to an ADA, frustration when they couldn't find the needed evidence to prove what they knew, stubborn disappointment when they had to consign something to the cold case files. The mix of anxiety and dread on his face was new.

"So," she said pointedly. "Not that I don't love the excuse to have a drink with you, but I'm getting the sense there's something more you want to say."

He took another a gulp of the beer, then pushed it away. "I want to thank you for staying by my side through all of this. Not everybody would have."

"You've been by mine through some ugly times," she said.

"And if you tell me you didn't know what Murphy did, I take that at face value."

He glanced away, then met her eyes again. "I didn't know. But I suspected."

She nodded, and waited.

"I'm not trying to make excuses, I just need you to know what exactly happened and why. You pretty much accused me of putting both of us at risk because of my unresolved guilt, and you were right. You deserve an explanation."

"The most important thing to me is that we're honest with each other," Jo said, careful to keep her face neutral.

"I didn't know Murphy well. I'd never worked with him before. From the start he liked to do his own investigating. That was frustrating, but working with him was temporary, so I didn't give much of a shit. But then, after the power struggle between Sandra and Grace, it got weird. He talked to Sandra without me present, then disappeared to 'follow up a couple of leads.' But when I asked him about them, he just said 'nothing panned out.' Then, all of a sudden, there was this question of blood in Ossokov's car."

Jo nodded.

"I asked him about it—he said the tech saw it and swabbed it but forgot to send it in. It smelled fishier than a dried-up swamp but I let it go. Told myself I didn't know him and his style well enough and I had no reason to doubt his integrity. I'd only ever known him to be a good, honest cop. But then, everybody's always honest until they're not, right?"

"I think it's natural to believe the best of fellow law enforcement in the absence of counter evidence," Jo said. "Especially when we have to trust them to protect our backs."

"Maybe. But at the end of the day, I fell into the big trap. I knew beyond a shadow of a doubt that Cooper Ossokov was guilty of the other rapes. I'd met his victims and saw the DNA match, and I watched the smug smirk on his face when he told us how the sex with Woods was consensual. So I did exactly what we're not supposed to do—I let that cloud my judgment. And when I had to choose whether or not to make an enemy of a fellow detective by questioning his motives when I had no evidence, I decided it wasn't a risk that made sense when we were talking about a low-life rapist that was better off behind bars."

Jo gripped the snifter's stem. "We all make choices we regret. But what you did isn't the same as what he did."

"Isn't it? Don't good cops have a responsibility to shine a light on bad cops?" he asked, face drawn and eyes searching.

"We do. But it's easy in hindsight to look back and tell yourself you should have done something different. It's one thing if you'd known for certain he'd engaged in misconduct, but you didn't. So you learn from the experience by trusting your gut from now on in those situations. You make sure it doesn't happen again."

"That's exactly what I've done. I've second- and triple-guessed every potentially questionable situation for the last fifteen years, and I've made clear to everyone I work with what will and won't wash. And it's one of the main reasons I've wanted to stay partnered with you over the years. I know I don't have to think twice about your priorities."

Jo's mind flew to a moment, just a few months before, when for a split second she almost let a killer walk free. How close had she been to making the wrong choice that day? Just considering the question made her break out into a sweat. "We're all human. We try every day to be better."

"I'm not sure I can get past it," Arnett said.

She looked Arnett dead in the eye. "Would you ever plant evidence, even if you truly believed a suspect was guilty?"

He sliced the air with his hand. "Never."

"Would you report me if I did?"

"So fast it'd make your eyes bleed."

She broke into a smile and turned up her palms. "So, what's the problem exactly?"

He stared down at the table for a long moment. Then he inhaled deeply, gave her a watery smile, and finished his beer. "Don't you have a boyfriend and a creepy cat to go home to?"

———

The heavenly melange of garlic, onion, and cheese from Matt's spinach and mushroom lasagna greeted Jo as she pushed through the front door of her house.

Twice-a-month Sunday family dinners had fallen into a comfy, predictable pattern, but this was the first with Matt as a live-in member of the family. As such, Jo was grateful she hadn't had much time the previous week to worry about how it would go. She was even more grateful to drop into a chair at the kitchen table and sip coffee until her family arrived.

Her worry would have been wasted, anyway. The dynamic at dinner was easy and peaceful, unchanged from any of the Sunday dinners that had come before. And while Jo braced herself for what her mother would say when she and Sophie adjourned to the kitchen to clean up, her mother turned out to have other issues on her mind.

"I didn't want to ask in front of the girls, but what have you decided about David?" Elisabeth asked.

Sophie flinched. "I haven't yet, Ma."

"You must be leaning one way or the other," Elisabeth said.

Sophie's expression turned simultaneously sheepish and defensive. "It's not that easy. I have a lot of factors to consider."

"And you've been considering them for almost two months now."

"There's no rush, Ma," Jo said, giving her mother a pointed glare. Sophie wasn't used to being at the receiving end of her mother's spotlight of criticism; she was used to being the golden child while Jo was the one who failed to live up to expectations.

"There most certainly is." Elisabeth tilted her head toward the living room. "Those two girls in there."

Sophie's jaw clenched. "You're not suggesting I take him back for the sake of the girls, are you?"

Elisabeth bent to stack dishes into the washer. "Don't be ridiculous. You know I support whatever decision you make. I'm just saying that everyone is in a holding pattern until you make it, and the only reason to put it off is because you're punishing him. Which, if it wasn't for the girls, I'd be fine with. But they need to know what their new reality is. So, if you're done with him, let him go. If you aren't, or even if you aren't sure you aren't, let him back into the house and begin counseling."

The growing red splotches on Sophie's cheeks suggested she was about to say something she'd regret, so Jo jumped in. "Matt's finished unpacking. I was so worried about how everything would fit together, but I think we did a pretty good job. What do you think of the new office, Ma?"

Sophie threw her a grateful look.

"It looks like you always intended it to look that way. You two have very similar taste in styles, even if you disagree on color palettes. I've never understood how you can surround yourself with such bold colors, Jo. His eye is so much more classic." Elisabeth switched to the top shelf of the dishwasher as she loaded in the glasses.

"It looks like you two are happy as can be," Sophie asked. "You must be feeling better."

Elisabeth's head whipped around. "Feeling better about what?"

Jo shot a narrowed-eyed glare at Sophie. Sophie scrunched up her face, genuinely annoyed at herself, and mouthed "Sorry."

"Nothing, Ma. Just, with the murders hitting right as Matt moved in, I got a little distracted and forgot he lived here now. I forgot to call him and let him know when I was going to be late."

Elisabeth tilted her head at Jo. "That's not what she meant. Why would you need to feel better about a tiny thing like that?"

Jo cursed mentally. That was the problem with her mother —she was smart as a whip and if you were going to lie to her, you'd better be damned good at it. Jo had never been good at it, so for years she'd survived most things in their relationship by just not telling her mother about them at all. But, as her therapist repeatedly reminded her, that wasn't how you built trust and intimacy in a relationship. She reminded herself her mother was just concerned, and there was no reason to be defensive.

Jo cleared her throat. "I was also feeling a little claustrophobic, and wondered if I'd made a mistake having him move in."

"Claustrophobic how?"

"I had a lot going on and needed some space to decompress. Usually when I come home I have the house to myself and can just process what I need to process. Have a glass of Calvados and play some jazz music, even if it's midnight." Jo braced for the scornful response.

Her mother laughed and resumed her stacking. "Welcome to the joys of cohabitation. If it weren't for Greg's afternoons at the golf course, you'd have been investigating *me* for murder years ago."

Jo's jaw dropped.

Elisabeth laughed again. "What? You know I play golf. Didn't you ever wonder why I don't go with him?"

Jo was embarrassed to admit she'd never thought much about it. She glanced at Sophie, who seemed just as surprised as she was. "I figured you just didn't want to."

"Don't you remember how I took second place in that ladies' tournament down in Brenneville?"

A vague memory flickered to life in the back of Jo's mind. "I'd completely forgotten about that. Why'd you stop?"

Elisabeth waved her hand like she was chasing a fly. "Tcha. I mostly did it to pass the time when your father was gone working so much. I liked it fine, but I can take it or leave it. So with Greg I leave it, that way he can have time for himself, I can have time for myself, and I don't have to suffocate him in his sleep because he's on my last nerve."

Jo laughed at her mother's unusual use of the slang, and felt her composure slowly returning. "That's all well and good, but I can't always plan out when I'm going to need time to myself."

Elisabeth straightened up and put her hands on her hips. "And that makes you different from everyone else on the planet how?"

Jo searched for words, but found none.

Elisabeth gestured to Sophie. "Ask your sister. Of course there are times when you wish he'd disappear for a few hours. There will even be times when you can't stand the sight of him."

"I'm not sure I'm the best person to ask just now," Sophie mumbled.

"Nonsense." Elisabeth gestured dismissively. "Relationships aren't perfect and love isn't easy. A relationship isn't strong because of its good days and weak because of its bad ones. What makes a relationship strong is that on those hard days you both make a choice to stay and do what needs to be done until you get to the next good day. It doesn't matter that he's underfoot when you wish you had time alone. What matters is that he's by your side when you need him."

An image of Matt driving her home from the hospital flashed through Jo's mind. She glanced at Sophie, who was trying to hide the tears forming in her eyes, and pushed down the lump in her own throat. This was the upside of letting her mother into her life—under the sharp edges, there were gems of wisdom and love.

"Thanks, Ma." She pulled her mother into a hug, and reached out behind to squeeze Sophie's arm.

Her mother hugged her intensely but quickly, then stepped back and cleared her throat. "So. We need two coffees and three herbal teas, right?" She turned to pull mugs from the cabinet.

Jo hid her smile as the three women worked together to make the beverages, then returned to the living room where they'd promised Isabelle and Emily they'd all play Jenga.

As Jo stroked a curled-up Cleopatra on her lap, she took in the scene around her. Her nieces, competing mercilessly for the best moves, but then coming together in peals of laughter when the blocks came tumbling down. Her mother and Greg, playfully teasing each other; despite sitting on opposite sides of the room, there was no distance between them. Sophie, who, with a carefully composed expression on her face, watched her girls as she sipped her tea. And Matt, playfully engaging the girls, cannily following the fastest route to acceptance in her family. Something inside her twinged, and she struggled to put a label on it. Whatever it was, it pulled up a memory of the same feeling tugging at her when her mother dropped her off to her first slumber party.

Lopez's words at the restaurant came rushing back to her. *Look at Sandra Ashville. Her whole life was work, and she ended up divorced, then dead before she could retire. Is that what we all have to look forward to?*

No, that wasn't all. She was always going to be devoted to her job, and that meant she was always going to work long hours and be gone at inconvenient times. But she was also surrounded by people who loved her, and she was learning how to make them a priority. Even if it was sometimes a struggle.

After three terrible tower crashes, Sophie announced it was time for the girls to get to bed. Her mother and Greg followed suit. Everyone gathered the mugs and deposited them in the sink before giving hugs and kisses and strolling out to their cars.

After a final wave goodbye, Jo turned to Matt. "I shouldn't have had that cup of coffee. There's no way I'll fall asleep anytime soon."

He glanced toward the living room. "You want to watch a movie? I think there's a new—"

"Actually," she interrupted, pulling him toward her. "I was thinking there might be a way to burn up some excess energy."

"Ahh." He kissed her, then grabbed her hand and led her up the stairs.

When they reached the bedroom door, he looked down at the cat following them. "Sorry, Cleo. You'll need to wait out here."

A LETTER FROM M.M. CHOUINARD

Thank you so, so much for reading *What They Saw*, I'm deeply grateful! If you enjoyed the book and have time to leave me a short, honest review on Amazon, Goodreads, or wherever you purchased the book, I'd very much appreciate it. Reviews help me reach new readers, and that means I get to bring you more books! Also, if you know of friends or family who would enjoy the book, I'd love your recommendation there, too—word of mouth means everything to authors. And if you have a moment to say hi on social media, please do—I love hearing from you!

If you'd like to keep up to date with any of my new releases, please click the link below to sign up for Bookouture's newsletter; your email will never be shared, and they'll only contact you when they have news about a new Bookouture release.

www.bookouture.com/mm-chouinard

You can also sign up for my personal newsletter at www.mmchouinard.com for news directly from me about all my activities, releases, and updates; I also will never share your email. And you can connect with me via my website, Facebook, Goodreads, and Twitter. I'd love to hear from you.

SPOILER ALERT: if you're reading this letter before you read the book, I'm about to give some important things away!

Sexual assault, particularly rape, is an important theme in *What They Saw*. The idea for this book began percolating in my mind during a seminar I attended about the Golden State Killer, Joseph James DeAngelo. During that seminar, I learned that the prosecutors struggled to find a way to bring DeAngelo to justice because his rapes were no longer prosecutable—the California statute of limitations had run out on them. I was absolutely appalled—I'd very wrongly assumed there was no statute of limitations on rape. Thankfully, that was already in the process of changing, and in California there is no longer a statute of limitations for most felony sex crimes. But there are still exceptions, and if you were raped before 2017, the previous statute of limitations still applies.

So what about other states? According to RAINN (Rape, Abuse, and Incest National Network): https://www.rainn.org/state-state-guide-statutes-limitations), there are only *seven states out of fifty* that currently have no statute of limitations for any felony sex crimes—Kentucky, Maryland, North Carolina, South Carolina, Virginia, West Virginia, and Wyoming. Twelve states (like California) have statutes of limitations in some or most cases, and *thirty-one* states and the District of Columbia have a statute of limitations *on all felony sex crimes, even when DNA has been collected*. That means if you and the prosecutors don't act quickly enough, time will run out on your ability to bring your rapist to justice, and they'll get away scot-free.

Massachusetts is one of those thirty-one states. When I found that out, I knew I had to bring Jo face-to-face with that reality.

I believe it's important that we're all aware of the existence of these statutes of limitations, and of the very real repercussions they have on victims. To be sure I'm clear: the killer's solution to these issues in this book is not acceptable. But the only way these statutes will be eliminated is if we make our voices heard in non-violent ways. If you find these statutes to be unacceptable, I encourage you to reach out to organizations like RAINN to find out what you can do about them, and to let your representatives know how you feel. You can find them here: https://openstates.org/find_your_legislator/

Stay safe!

Michelle

www.mmchouinard.com

facebook.com/mmchouinardauthor

twitter.com/m_m_chouinard

instagram.com/mmchouinard

goodreads.com/mishka824m

ACKNOWLEDGMENTS

My biggest thank you, now and always, goes to YOU—thank YOU, so much, for reading my books! You are the reason I do this, and your support means everything. Thank you also if you've reviewed them, blogged about them, requested them from your local library, or told a friend about them—your support means the world to me, and I couldn't do it without you.

My team at Bookouture takes my stories and puts them out in the world. Rhianna Louise guided the early stages of editing; Alexandra Holmes, Martina Arzu, Jane Eastgate, Nicky Gyopari, and Ramesh Kumar all helped edit and produce it from there, and their help was invaluable. Kim Nash, Noelle Holten, and Sarah Hardy tirelessly promoted it; Hannah Deuce and Alex Crow helped market it; Alba Proko made the audiobook a reality; and Jenny Geras, Laura Deacon, and Natalie Butlin oversaw it all. So many amazing hands making it all happen!

I couldn't do what I do without the help of experts to guide me along the way. Thank you to the NWDA Hampshire County Detective Unit, to Leonard Von Flatern, and to Detective Adam Hill for their invaluable expertise and patience answering questions about police procedure and strange scenarios. Thanks also to Gary P. Merwede, Fire Chief, who answered my questions about incendiary devices and fires, and to both Jim Leydon of the Hampden District Attorney's Office and Cindy Von Flatern of the NWDA Office, who helped me understand how the district attorney's offices in Massachusetts work. I can't express how grateful I am to all of them for taking their very valuable time to help me! Any errors/inaccuracies that exist are my fault entirely.

Thanks to my agent, Lynnette Novak, and Nicole Resciniti both for your advice, guidance, and support.

Thanks also to my writing tribe, who encourage me, educate me, write with me, critique me, lift me up, and make me laugh. This includes my fellow SinC brothers and sisters (especially the drop-ins), my fellow MWA members (especially the Monday & Wednesday write-in crew), D.K. Dailey, Karen McCoy, Sharon Alva, Katy Corbeil, and my fellow Bookouture authors. Writing can be so solitary, I am truly thankful to have friends like you.

Thanks also to my furbabies, who keep my lap warm and remind me of good things while I'm spinning tales of murder, and who periodically force me up from my computer because they have to eat, be walked, and take potty breaks. Which reminds *me* to eat, walk, and take potty breaks.

But most of all, thank you to my husband. Thank you for eating leftovers as often as you do, for pretending not to care when the dust piles up, and for ignoring the strange grimaces on my face as I try to pick apart plot tangles. Without you I'd never be able to do this. I love you so, so much!

Made in the USA
Columbia, SC
01 September 2023